THE PERFECT NANNY

A Gripping Psychological Thriller That Will
Have You At The Edge Of Your Seat...

COLE BAXTER

Illustrated by NATASHA SNOW
Edited by VALORIE CLIFTON
Edited by ELIZABETH A LANCE

Cole Baxter

Contents

Preview of What Happened Last Night

Sign up for Cole's VIP Reader Club and find out about his latest releases, giveaways, and more. Click here!

Follow him on Facebook

Chapter 1

CYNTHIA

WHEN THE PHONE RANG AT NINE A.M., I WASN'T sure whether I wanted to answer it because of the name on the caller ID. *Dr. David Andrews* flashed across the screen with each ring, and I felt like my heart was going to explode in my chest. I had been simultaneously waiting for this call and dreading it.

Part of me was starting to second-guess why we had even done this in the first place. Maybe this wasn't meant to be. Maybe something horrible was going to happen and there was nothing I could do to avoid it. Maybe we were interfering with Mother Nature and this was all going to come back and bite us.

Or maybe it was going to be the answer to our

prayers. I wouldn't know until I answered the phone that was still ringing.

I hadn't really told anyone what we were doing, which made it harder. If I had told someone, then I could know that I would have support. But there was no one I wanted to tell in case it didn't work. What if they looked down upon me for doing it this way? What if they thought I was being greedy or selfish? What if I told them and then it didn't happen? There was nothing worse than saying something and then having nothing happen. I wasn't that person who got people's hopes up and allowed myself to fail.

I knew I wasn't a failure for making this choice, either. I knew it wasn't my fault and that I should be grateful for the science that was available to me. Instead, I was just a bundle of nerves. My two-year-old daughter was staring at me, and I knew she would pick up that something was wrong. We had taught her that phones needed to be answered, and here I was, just staring at it.

I had actually wondered last night if this call was going to come. I had lain awake, checking my phone many times during the night. I just had a feeling that today was going to be the day, and yet now, when it rang, I was scared of it.

I wished that Michael were here. I wasn't one of those women who needed their husbands for everything, but Michael was a big part of my life, and he was always able to stay calm in a high-pressure situation. He was good that way, which was why I suppose he went on to run a business and I went on to stay home with our daughter.

I told myself that wasn't the only reason. I had wanted to stay home with kids. We were financially able to have me stay home, and he said he would prefer to be at work. After all, he ran the company, so if he wasn't there, it would probably not function so well. He could take a day or two here or there, but there wasn't a time where he could disappear for six months.

Still, I wished that day he took was today so he could be here when the phone rang. It rang again, and I knew if I kept staring at it, there would just be a voicemail asking me to call them back.

At least, I hoped that's what the voicemail said. I hoped it didn't say something like they were going to drop me as a client.

"Mommy, are you going to answer the phone?" Anna asked, and I took a deep breath. For a two-year-old, she was smart.

"Yep," I said and picked it up. "Hello?"

"Hello, may I please speak to the Cynthia?"

"I, uh . . . this is she."

"Cynthia, this Nancy Cheng. I'm Dr. Andrew's nurse."

"Right," I said as I balanced the phone on my ear. Anna sneezed, and I handed her a clean Kleenex while I walked into the other room. I was terrified that she was going to tell me it wasn't going to work or they had another reason for a delay. I had been a nurse myself, and I knew that there were a million reasons to not succeed at what we were trying to do.

"We think we found a match for you," she said. "Her name is Olive, and she is such a lovely person. When would you and Michael like to come in and meet her?"

"Oh, my." I sat down. "Um . . . let me call Michael and then I'll call you back. His schedule is insane, so I just have to figure it out."

"Sure," she said. "I can send you some more details, but she is everything you asked for."

"Wow," I said. "You guys work fast."

"We try," she said. "Let me know when you've found a time that works."

"Does she have a schedule?" I asked.

Nancy chuckled. "She said she's willing to meet you whenever you want."

"Thank you."

I hung up the phone right away and dialed Michael's number. I knew there was a good chance that he wouldn't answer because he would be in the middle of a meeting or on a site. However, we had worked out long ago, when Anna was born and I was so sick, that if I called him three times in a row, he would know it was an emergency and pick up the phone right away.

"Hello?" Luckily, I didn't have to employ the emergency phone call method.

"Michael," I said. "Dr. Andrew's office called. They found someone for us to meet with."

"Already?" he said in surprise. "That was fast."

"Yeah," I said. "I expected our profile to sit there for months. But apparently, they've been searching for someone with all our requirements and this woman just popped up."

"Well," he said, and I heard him take a deep breath. "When do we meet with her?"

"Oh," I said. "Whenever you want? Apparently, her schedule is pretty open, so if you have a preference . . ."

"I can probably squeeze something in on Friday," he said. "The earlier, the better. Do you think Anna will be feeling better by then? To go to daycare."

"Yes," I said. "I think it's just a cold."

"Okay," he said. "Why don't you set something up for Friday, and I'll make it work?"

"Will do," I said and hung up. I knew Michael was busy and I didn't want to overwhelm him with my feelings. At least, not until he came home from work.

Michael was a successful architect and the CEO of his own multimillion-dollar firm. When he had first started the company, we'd been so young, and we really weren't sure how to run a company. But I knew Michael was a brilliant architect and I knew he was passionate and driven, and somehow, everything was going to work out. Ten years and one child later, everything worked out just fine. We were millionaires and we provided our one child, Anna, with a wonderful life. However, being parents to Anna had not been an easy feat. I almost died giving birth to her and she had almost died in the first little bit of her life. I gave up my career as a nurse in order to recover from the trauma and then to be a full-time mother to Anna. I loved being a nurse, but I loved being a mother more. I had been so traumatized by her birth that I was maybe a little bit overprotective of her.

Anna was my mini-me. Blonde with wide blue eyes and tall and thin, she was incredibly intelligent for a two-year-old, and I wasn't just saying that because I was biased. She was also shy and timid, and she preferred being surrounded by familiar faces rather than people she didn't know. She was a picky eater, but she made up for it with her beautiful smile and loving personality. At least, I told myself that every time she refused to eat a dinner I made and then gave me a hug. Currently, she was home from daycare with a cold, which I'm sure I was just being overprotective about.

I wanted badly to have another child, but I knew that wasn't possible. The birth trauma with Anna, combined with the uterine scarring her birth gave me, made another birth impossible. I didn't think I would be able to convince, and even if I were, I wasn't sure whether I'd be able to survive the birth.

So, after long talks with Michael, we had concluded that we were going to try surrogacy. We had thought about other options, but my medical brain knew that this was the best one if I wanted to be able to have a child that had both our genes. We had gone to Dr. Andrews because we heard he was the best. I had mixed feelings during the entire initial appointment, but it was just nerves. Now that I was supposed to meet someone who would carry my child, I was even more nervous.

It wasn't that I had always dreamed of being a mother. I mean, in one way, I had. When I studied science in school, I had been most focused on reproduction cells rather than diseases. I always knew that I wanted to be a nurse, and I had always known that I wanted to help people. When I was little, my parents could barely stop me from running around the neighborhood, playing nurse and doctor.

When I graduated from nursing school, I alternated between shifts in the emergency room and shifts on the maternity ward. My love of children had always been strong, and it was no surprise when I announced I was pregnant shortly after marrying Michael. Everyone knew that Michael had been the love of my life for as long as I could remember. I loved him for many reasons, and somewhere around our third date, I saw him hold the door open for a child and realized that he would also be a perfect father. That had sealed the deal for me.

When I became pregnant with Anna, I had been over the moon excited. After all, I was young and healthy, and I had always wanted a girl first. I spent hours decorating her room or trying to find the perfect clothes for her. I was even one of those mothers-to-be who wanted to find matching outfits for her. I thought that we would twin it up and go out for walks in the park together and everything would be perfect.

I hadn't expected pregnancy to be hell. I hadn't expected to be sick every minute of every day. When I gave birth to her, I went into labor knowing that I was in a high-risk situation, and there was a good chance one of us would die. In fact, the pain was so intense that I was sure one of us would die.

I begged God to let it be me. I pleaded with him that it should be me and that he should let my perfect little girl live.

In the end, we both almost died. I lost so much blood that I didn't get to hold my little girl until three days later, and even then, I was very out of it. When Michael brought us both home from the hospital, someone had to stay with me all the time because I could barely feed myself. All through it, he handled the stress perfectly.

Eventually, I recovered. Eventually, we forgot

the pain and the heartache and the tears. We forgot the trauma of hearing my heartbeat stop and all the blood that came gushing out. We forgot everything except how much we wanted another child until we realized that my uterus had been so scarred that it was impossible to do so. Then we had to look at other options.

We talked about adoption. We talked about fostering. We talked about surrogacy with only one of our biological contributions, which would have been cheaper. However, in the end, we decided we both wanted to be biologically related to this baby, so we just needed a surrogate with a viable womb to carry him or her.

Him or her. So many people had asked me what I wanted. At first, I told them I didn't care. However, the more I thought about it, the more I realized I wanted a boy in order to have one child of each gender. That was always the dream, and I just wanted to be part of it. It wasn't fair that I didn't have the ability to carry my child on my own. I felt so useless, and I was so glad that Michael was able to find this place.

I called the nurse back, and she answered with a perkiness that told me she maybe didn't realize she was changing people's lives.

"Is Friday okay?" I asked her. "Anytime. Knowing my husband, he probably prefers the early mornings."

"I'll set it up," she said. "And if you like our candidate, we will go right to setting up an appointment to have your eggs harvested."

"Right," I said. "And if I don't like her?"

"If you don't like her, then we'll find someone else," the nurse said.

"Okay," I replied. "Thank you."

I didn't want to sound cold, but I was really overwhelmed by all of it. I felt useless and broken, knowing that I couldn't carry another baby of my own. I felt like half a woman, and I felt like I was letting Michael down.

I wasn't sure how he felt on the issue. Despite being married to Michael for ten years and being mother to our daughter, it didn't seem like he ever shared his innermost thoughts with me. Michael was the strong, silent type, and although I had never caught him in a lie, I sometimes had questions.

"Mommy, who was that?" Anna asked.

"Just a doctor," I said.

"For me?" she asked.

"No, for Daddy and me," I said.

"Why, are you sick?" she asked, concerned.

"No," I said. "But we're hoping that maybe we can have a baby brother or sister for you," I said. "But you know Mommy can't do it on my own, so we need a little bit of help."

"Oh," she said. "What if I don't want a baby brother or sister?"

"You don't?" I asked.

She smiled. "No, I'm just fooling," she said. "I do."

"You are a trickster." I grinned. It was that bit of her personality that made me smile every time she was being difficult.

"When?" she asked.

"Friday, Daddy and I will go meet the woman who might help us," I replied. "While you're in school."

"What if I'm sick?" she asked.

"You won't be," I said. "Now, what would you like to do for the rest of the afternoon?"

Friday seemed to both not come soon enough and come too quickly. I was nervous, and I hadn't said too much to Michael, but he seemed like he was calm on the whole matter, and I didn't want to burst his calm bubble. Michael was my strength, and he held my arm tightly as we walked into the building where Dr. Andrew's practice was.

"Ah, Mr. and Mrs. Thompson," the nurse said. "Come right this way."

I clutched Michael's arm tighter as we walked through the clinic. This was far from the type of medical setting I had worked in. This was a boutique type of clinic that health insurance didn't touch. It was only for the elite, and yet there was something sad about it. All the money in the world couldn't fix my broken body.

Olive Grey was waiting in the room for us. The first thing that struck me was how long her hair was. It was dark and nearly came down to her waist. She struck me as a trusting person, with brown eyes and a nice smile. She was slightly chubby, but she dressed plainly and conservatively, which I liked. I was a fan of conversation and modern dress, wanting to focus on my husband and my family rather than showing off to the outside world. I preferred long skirts and blouses, and it seemed Olive was of a similar mindset.

"Hello!" Olive said and shook both of our hands. "It's so nice to meet you. I'm Olive."

"I'm Cynthia," I said. "And this is my husband, Michael. Thank you for coming in today."

"It's my pleasure," she said as the three of us sat down. "What questions can I answer for you?"

"Have you done this before?" Michael asked.

"Gosh, no," she said. "I've always wanted to, but I didn't get to until now. I suppose I wanted to make sure I was healthy and grounded."

"Were you not healthy?" I asked.

She shook her head. "I have always been healthy," she said. "I just wanted to make sure that I was going to give any potential mother the best experience she ever had."

"And you're twenty-seven?" I asked.

"Just turned twenty-seven," she replied. "So I'm hoping that this will be something that I can do again and again."

"This is very kind of you," I said. "To offer up your . . . womb to someone like me, who . . . can't."

"No, it's not," she said. "It's my duty."

"Your duty?" I asked.

"Yes," she said. "Because my womb is viable and strong. As they say, I want to help other women who have been through trauma."

"Do you want children of your own?" Michael asked.

Olive shook her head. "I don't think so," she said. "So this is the perfect middle ground. I want to help, and I can carry a child, but at the end of the day, it's yours."

I smiled at that. One of the fears I had was about the fact that our surrogate mother might want to lay claim to the child. After all, I knew first-hand how attached you could get to a child after nine months of carrying them.

Olive, however, didn't seem to have any misgivings about the situation. She was smiling and happy, upfront, and honest with all of our questions. You could always tell when someone was lying, especially about hard questions, but Olive struck me as kind and honest.

I knew that she was perfect. She ticked all of our boxes, and while she got up to go to the bathroom, I turned to Michael.

"What do you think?" I asked.

"I think it matters what you think," he said and glanced at the clock. "It's been an hour, so we have to make a decision one way or another because I have to get back to work."

"Yeah, I know," I said and squeezed his hand. "I think she's perfect."

"Then why do you seem apprehensive?" he asked. "I want you to be sure."

"It's not that." I took a deep breath. "It's just that I don't think I'll ever be sure of someone in this scenario. She's as close as we're going to get."

"Okay," he said. "Then let's make the appointment. I can't think of a reason to not go with her."

"Sometimes, you don't see trouble coming," I replied.

"Sometimes, trouble doesn't come," he said. "You ready to do this?"

"Yep," I replied with my heart pounding. I didn't want to keep him here any longer, especially given the fact that I couldn't think of a reason to not go with her.

When Olive came back, she was overjoyed, and I couldn't help but smile as well. We made the appointment, and Michael and I headed back out into the street.

"So, I'll see you at home?" he asked.

"Sure," I said and gave him a hug and a kiss.

"Baby, be happy," he said. "In a year, we could have another baby running around."

"I know," I said. "And that thrills me, really. Just give me a second to adjust."

He kissed the top of my head and then hailed a cab. I checked my phone and decided to walk. It was a nice day, and I needed a few minutes to myself. Maybe by the time I got home, I'd feel completely committed and excited.

Chapter 2

MICHAEL

"I'M SO EXCITED FOR THE PARTY TONIGHT! THIS is so kind of you! So, so kind!"

I smiled as I picked up my phone.

"You gave us a kid," I replied. "The least I could do is throw you a party."

It had been ten months since we met at the fertility clinic, and it had been a wild ride with Olive. Cynthia's egg had taken to her right away, and she had quickly conceived a baby boy whom we had named Grant. There had been absolutely no issue in handing Grant over to us, and now that Cynthia and I had gotten through the first week with having a newborn at home, we decided to throw Olive a party to celebrate everything. She was acting like we were giving her a million dollars, and I wondered if not many people had been kind to Olive in her life.

Over the past ten months, Olive and I had talked quite a bit. I knew Cynthia got overwhelmed quickly, and so I told her to text me if there were ever a problem. We were only supposed to communicate through the clinic, but Cynthia had wanted a more personal relationship. Olive had texted me about a few minor problems at first, and we had started talking more and more about everything. She was easy to talk to, and I felt an odd connection to her, knowing she was carrying my child. Now that she had delivered Grant, I wondered how things were going to go. She had basically become my confidant, and I hers. It was just nice to talk to someone who didn't judge you and who might not be in your life later on. We had so much conversation that I had assigned her a special ringtone on my phone in case she needed anything.

I didn't tell Cynthia how much we talked. It wasn't that I thought we were doing anything wrong, and I knew that Olive and Cynthia talked a lot too. I just felt like it was better if I didn't bring it up, with all we had going on in life.

I'm shopping for a new dress now, she said. *I'm at the best thrift store in town.*

I didn't think I had set foot in a thrift store in many years, and it bothered me that Olive needed to. We had paid her quite a bit for the surrogacy, but I knew that she had put it all in a savings account. She liked to save her money in case she needed something. She hadn't worked very much in the past few months because the pregnancy had overwhelmed her, so she had been living off what we gave her. I didn't mind that at all, as it meant she could make ultrasound appointments or something whenever we wanted.

I'm sure you'll find something nice, I said. *Talk soon.*

It was almost four o'clock, and I told Cynthia I'd be home early to give her a few minutes to change before the party started. She was exhausted staying home with Grant, and I had talked about the fact that we could hire a nanny if she wanted. We hadn't with Anna, but we had been in a different position then. Now, I was pretty sure she was more open to it, given that we were both older and a new baby was exhausting. The fact that we had a boy rather than a girl meant that Cynthia had gotten all new everything for Grant and then insisted on organizing everything herself.

I eventually turned off my computer and grabbed my bag. I was a workaholic, and I could work until midnight every night, so it was a struggle to leave early.

My BMW was waiting in the valet parking, and I got right in, hoping to beat the traffic. I turned on the Bluetooth as I drove, and Cynthia picked up right away. I could hear Grant crying in the background, and I felt slightly bad. I loved going to the office, partly because it was quieter than the house. Grant wasn't like Anna. He cried a lot and for seemingly no reason. I'm sure it was normal for some newborns, but it was also exhausting.

"Hi," I said. "I'm on my way home."

"Great," my wife said. "I feel like if I don't take a shower, I'm going to die."

I chuckled. "Hopefully not," I replied. "I'll take over so you can get in the bath and just chill out for half an hour."

"You're a lifesaver," she said. "Hey, I wanted to ask you something."

"Oh?" I asked as I got onto the highway.

"Olive was texting me today, and she said that she was buying a dress at the thrift store," she said. "And that just bothered me. I don't want her to feel like she's out of money now that we stopped paying her. I mean, she gave us a baby, and it's going to take a while to get back on her feet."

"So you want to keep paying her?"

"No," Cynthia said. "But maybe we could give her a bonus?"

"Sure," I said. "I can write a check for that when I get home."

"Thank you," she said. "See you soon."

"Bye," I said and ended the call. Mentally, I was trying to calculate how much of a bonus would be acceptable to give to Olive. Money was like water to us. It didn't matter at this point. However, I also knew that if I gave her too much, she might be insulted. Olive was a humble hard worker, and I didn't want to overwhelm her.

The decorator had come to the house today while Cynthia was taking care of Grant, and the house was all ready for the party. I held out my hands for my son, and Cynthia gladly ran upstairs to jump in the hot bath. It was one of her only guilty pleasures, and I was happy to give her the time to do it.

Grant had stopped crying by the time she handed him to me, and he gurgled happily as I bounced him. I rarely had a moment alone with him since Cynthia and Anna were always around. I smiled at my son and stroked the top of his bald head. He didn't have any hair yet, but it looked like he was going to have red hair.

"Where did you get your peach fuzz, buddy?" I asked him. "Where did you get that from? Not from me. Not from your mommy."

Grant gurgled and then his eyes looked to something past me. I turned around, but there was nothing there, of course. However, instead of going back to smiling, he suddenly shrieked and burst into tears.

That was confusing because I had no idea what went wrong. I was someone who liked to be in control, so the fact that Grant had started crying for no reason was baffling. I liked knowing why something happened and being able to fix it.

He eventually stopped crying, but like when he started crying, I had no idea why it happened. By the time Cynthia came back, I gladly handed Grant over. She was wearing a lacy white dress covered her knees and arms, and I thought she looked quite nice. Although I didn't tell her to dress conservatively or modestly, I did like the fact that she did so. She looked adorable and sweet, and I kissed her and told her so.

"Thank you," she said. "It's the first time I've felt pretty all week, if I'm honest."

"Well, it's not the first time that you've looked pretty all week," I replied.

Once Anna got home from daycare, delivered by the driver we paid for, we fed her dinner and then started to put the final touches on the party. We set everything out and finished just as the doorbell rang for the first time.

It wasn't long before our house was full of people. Each of them cooed and awed over Grant and congratulated us. We were quick, however, to give the credit to Olive. Olive was modest, as she always was, and she accepted people's congratulations with a shy smile.

I had thought about giving her the check in a big ceremony, but I knew she would be uncomfortable with the idea. So instead of letting everyone see, I slipped it to her quietly.

"What's this?" she asked in confusion.

"That's for you, and for all your help," I said. "Thank you for Grant."

"But you already paid me," she replied, confused.

"We know," I replied. "This is just a bonus. And if you ever need anything, please don't hesitate to ask."

"I don't think I could ask anything more of you and Cynthia," she said. "You've already been amazing to me."

"I mean it, though," I said to her. "Don't hesitate."

"I won't," Olive said. "But I know that everything is going to be just fine. I'm going to be just fine."

"Well, of course you are," I replied. "Now, go and enjoy the rest of the party. Everyone wants to meet you."

"If I'm honest," Olive said, "I think I'd rather slip out quietly. It's all . . . a bit much for me."

"Oh," I said. Despite the fact that I was slightly disappointed, I understood. I knew that Olive preferred to stick to the sidelines, so I walked her to the door. "That's okay."

"I'm sorry," she said.

I shook my head. "It's fine," I said to her. "Don't worry about it. Just text me tomorrow, okay?"

"Sure," she said. "Thank you again."

Once I closed the door behind her, I turned

back to the party. Now that she was gone, I didn't particularly want to keep hosting, but it was still early. We hadn't planned it to be a late-night affair, and it was still light out, so I knew we couldn't just kick people out yet. I went to find Cynthia to tell her that Olive had left and indicate that maybe we should get the party to end now that the guest of honor was gone. Cynthia was bouncing Grant, and she had that smile on her face that told me she was also done with the party.

"She left?" Cynthia said to me in surprise. "That's . . . oh. Without saying goodbye?"

"I think she just wanted to slip out quietly," I replied. "It's fine."

"Yeah," she said. "And she's probably lucky. I wish I could go to bed at the same time as Grant."

"Me too." I chuckled. "Me too."

Eventually, the party wrapped up and we headed to bed. I had sent Olive a text, but she didn't answer it, which I didn't mind. I assumed she was as exhausted as I was and wasn't even awake.

However, when I didn't hear from her over the next week, and then the week after that, I started to get worried. I texted and called her several times, but there was never any answer. I was starting to wonder if we had insulted her or made her run away. I didn't think a check would cause that many issues.

The check that I had given her had been cashed that night, which was even more confusing. If she was insulted by the check, she wouldn't have deposited it, would she?

I wasn't focusing on work and I wasn't focusing at home. When I came home three weeks later and found Cynthia in hysterical tears, it actually took a moment for my tired and confused brain to figure out what to do.

"Cynthia?" I asked, confused.

She threw herself on me, sobbing and shrieking, and I panicked.

"Is it Grant?" I asked her. "Has something happened to Grant?"

"No," she finally managed. "No, Grant is fine. But Olive . . . Olive . . ."

"Olive?" I asked. "Have you heard from her?"

"I just saw it on the news. They pulled her car from the river."

I felt all the color drain from my face.

"What?" I asked.

"She is . . . they think that's she's dead," she said and started sobbing all over again. I held onto her in shock, my brain swirling.

Olive was dead. My confidante, my friend and Grant's surrogate mother, gone from this Earth.

I couldn't believe it. She was just here. She was just here, and I couldn't believe that she was gone. She had changed our lives forever.

Chapter 3
CYNTHIA

"GRANT, PLEASE LISTEN TO ME," I BEGGED. "Please, please listen to me."

My seven-year-old child, of course, did nothing of the sort. He sat there for a moment and then grinned and carried on a conversation with nobody for a moment and then shrieked and ran out of the room.

I put my hands on my face and tried not to explode. I felt like today was one of those days that I just couldn't do it. I was a failure as a mother.

"I'm home," I heard Michael's voice call throughout the room, and I breathed a long sigh of relief. It wasn't that I wanted Michael to come home so I could dump everything on him, but I was so glad when he did. Sometimes, he was much better with Grant that I was.

"We're in here," I said, and Michael came into the large dining room. He raised his eyebrows as he looked around at the mess that surrounded it.

"Wow, it looks like a tornado came through here," he said with a soft smile that reminded me of when we were twenty and dating. He was still the same person, a little older and a little wearier, but he was still my Michael.

"Yeah, Grant is having one of his . . . episodes," I said. "And I haven't gotten him to take his three o'clock meds yet."

He looked at his watch and then raised his eyebrows.

"Okay," he said. "Let me see what I can do."

"You're a lifesaver," I said and sat in the dining room chair, exhausted.

Sometimes, Michael could just take the reins better because he hadn't been doing it all day. I hated just handing off responsibility like it was no big deal or like I couldn't handle it. Some days, I felt like I was going to explode.

My only reprieve was that Anna, who was nine, was a timid, shy child and didn't usually say a word during Grant's meltdowns. It was like she understood that I couldn't handle another thing and she just needed to be the perfect child. I often felt bad about that because she shouldn't feel like I couldn't give her any attention. Anna was a wonderful child, and I was blessed to have her.

I was blessed to have Grant too, of course. Sometimes, I just felt like I was being tested.

Michael came back into the room then, and he looked absolutely exhausted. It was interesting, because he had only been gone five minutes, but he at least looked accomplished.

"Hello," I said. "How was that?"

"He took it and he has settled down," he said. "I think he's playing with his toys. He seemed to be moving toward them when I left the room."

"Okay," I said. "Thank you."

"No problem," he replied. "Has he been like that all day?"

"Basically," I said.

"Why didn't you text me?" he asked.

I wanted to say something to him, but I knew it was futile. Michael said that because he wanted to feel like a good husband, but the truth was, if I had texted him during the day, he would say that he needed to work, and couldn't I handle it? I didn't blame him. He ran a multimillion-dollar company that gave us our lifestyle and all the benefits that we had. My job was to take care of the kids, and I didn't want to put that burden on him.

"I was just tired," I said. "Sorry."

"It's fine," he replied. "But maybe we should talk about a nanny."

"We can't just get a regular nanny," I said. "Grant has so many medications and special needs, and then there's . . ."

"Hey," he said and met my eyes. "This is not our fault. Neither of us knew that juvenile schizophrenia could run in our families. We still don't know that is the case. Grant could be an anomaly."

"I know," I said, even though I felt like it was my fault. "I wouldn't feel comfortable having someone here who wasn't medically trained, regardless. I mean, I'm a nurse and I'm overwhelmed, Michael. We need some sort of specialist."

"I mean, maybe I can look into them," he said. "See if there's anyone who comes recommended."

"Sure," I said. I swallowed the fact that I didn't believe him. Sometimes, Michael said that he was going to do something, and then he didn't follow through because he got busy at work, or worse. The fact that he offered was a good sign, but I really wasn't sure it was going to happen.

"Great," he said. "I'll see what I can do. In the meantime, what's for dinner?"

I didn't want to tell him that I was too exhausted to prepare something, so I just tried to smile.

"I thought we could order a pizza," I said. "After all of that."

"Sure," he replied and pulled out his phone.

If there was one thing I really admired about him, it was that he was extremely efficient. Michael always managed to make sure that something was done, no matter what situation we were in. He was productive and focused at times when my mind went everywhere. We were a good team, and we complemented each other. At the very least, I didn't think I could imagine ordering a pizza right now.

"Done."

"Great," I said and leaned back. Michael looked at me.

"Are you okay?" he asked.

I nodded. "I am. Now that you're home."

"This is why a nanny could be good for us," he said. "If we can find someone who matches what we're looking for."

"It's just . . . it's not like we're looking for a dog

walker, you know?" I asked. "This is our child, and our very special child. I can't trust just anyone."

"And I'm not going to hire someone on the spot," he replied. "I'm going to make sure you're happy with whoever it is. You can interview them, and you can make the final decision."

"I want you to be part of the decision too," I said. "I mean, it's your house and your son too."

"I'm aware," he replied. "I'm just trying to make life less stressful for you, darling."

I sighed. "I just . . . I wish I had known. Like, if we had done . . . I don't know. It wouldn't show up on genetic testing, I guess."

"But even if you had known . . ." He paused. "Would you really have done anything different?"

"No," I said quickly. "It's not as if I would have not gone forward with having him. I was going to say giving birth." I shook my head sadly. "But Olive gave birth to him. Dear Olive. I miss her."

"I miss her too," Michael said. "I can't believe it's been seven years."

"I can't believe that they never found her," I answered. "Like . . . you think they would have looked harder. A young woman who had just given birth, and then . . ."

"I know," Michael said. "And I think it's a little weird too. But there's not much that can be done."

"It's just . . ." I sighed. "I feel like if she were here, things would be easier."

"Why?" he asked. "I mean, aside from the fact that she was a wonderful person."

"I don't know. She just knew how to handle everything in life. She just seemed like a calm person who . . . got it."

"That makes sense," he said. "I know you two were close."

"We were. It was like I made a friend on top of everything else."

Michael reached across to take my hand and squeezed my arm. Anna came down the stairs then, carrying a book, and she smiled when she saw Michael.

"Hi, Daddy!" she said and gave him a big hug. "I didn't know you were home."

"Hi, baby," he said and put a smile on his face.

The other thing I admired about him was that he could always put a smile on his face and pretend like everything was fine. I wasn't so good at that. I was always highly suspicious of people and I didn't trust people easily.

"Are you okay?" he asked me as he hugged Anna.

"Sure," I said. "I'm going to get the table ready. I'm sure dinner will be here soon."

"What's for dinner?" Anna asked.

He smiled at her. "Pizza."

Anna shrieked with joy.

I got up and went to set the table, listening to Michael and Anna laughing. My shoulders started to lift as I heard them telling each other jokes. Maybe everything was going to be okay, after all.

The pizza eventually came, and we managed to have a decent family dinner. However, Grant had a meltdown shortly afterward, and Michael had to spend over an hour calming him down. It was late before we both went to bed, and I managed to get a few words out to Michael before we finally fell asleep.

"Maybe a nanny isn't a bad idea," I said. "Hopefully, you can find someone."

"I'll find someone," he said as he rolled over to snuggle me. It had been a few nights since he had done that, and I snuggled right into him. "Don't worry."

"Mmm," I said and closed my eyes. At this moment, I felt safe and completely comforted. I felt like Michael really was going to take care of his promise and find someone to take the weight off my shoulders.

If not, I supposed I would be no worse off than I was right now. I just needed sleep to process the rest of the day. The rest didn't matter, really. Tomorrow would be a new start, and hopefully, Grant would be better in the morning.

Chapter 4

MICHAEL

"HEY," I SAID TO CYNTHIA WHEN I GOT HOME one night. It had been a long day, but I needed to talk to her. "I've finally set up interviews."

"Interviews for what?" Cynthia asked. She was in the middle of making dinner and she looked a bit confused.

"Nannies," I said.

Cynthia gave me a surprised look. "Oh. I didn't think that was happening."

"Do you not want to do it anymore?"

"No, I do," she said. "Of course I do. I just didn't think it was still happening because I hadn't heard anything."

"You mean you didn't think I would do it," I said.

"Darling," she said, "I know that you're really busy."

"It's fine," I said, not wanting to get into a fight. "I know there've been some things that I didn't follow through on. It's fine."

She looked like she wanted to say something, but instead, she just tried to smile.

"Tell me about the candidates," she said. "Where did you find them?"

"I actually called our psychologist," I said, "because I knew that we needed someone special. I asked her for a list of qualified people, and she sent me over a bunch. There were a few who wouldn't work, just because of their availability, but I narrowed it down to a few. If you want, I could set up interviews for the weekend, when I'm home."

"Sure," she said. "That would be good. Thank you for doing that."

"Of course. But I want you to know that it's going to expensive. And I'm only telling you that because I want you to utilize them to their full potential. Whoever we hire is here to make your life easier, so you can't just go and do all the work by yourself."

"No, of course not," she said, but I knew she would have a hard time letting go.

"Cynthia," I said and gave her a look. "Promise me."

"I promise," she said and then pulled the dinner out of the oven.

After dinner, I sent emails to the candidates we had been sent and set up anyone who responded for the weekend. I thought I was feeling fine about it, but as the weekend grew closer, I realized that I was a bit nervous. After all, this was a complete stranger coming in to take care of my son.

In the end, we interviewed three candidates. We talked to each of them for over an hour, but it seemed that Cynthia and I managed to agree on the same person.

"Amanda?" I asked her when everyone had left.

"Amanda is perfect," she said to me. "I couldn't believe how perfect she was. And she was the one Grant seemed to like the most."

"Yes, I thought that too," I said. "He seemed to take to her the second she walked into the room."

"Yeah," she said. "Which I think is a much better sign than anything we think. If he likes her, we should go with that."

"So, you want me to hire her?"

"Just on a trial basis," she said. "We can give her like a three-week trial and then go from there."

"I suppose I can do that. I mean, if she's in high demand, we might lose her to someone else."

"So you just want to hire her?" she asked.

"Well, we could always fire her if it doesn't work out."

"That's true," she said, "but I would feel terrible doing that."

"Okay. I'll propose a trial and see how she responds."

"Thank you," she said. "I know this is a big change, but I also know that it's supposed to be better for everyone . . . and I want it to be better for everyone."

"Okay," I agreed. "I'll call her in the morning."

The longer the night went on, the more comfortable I felt with the decision to hire Amanda. When I called her in the morning and she didn't answer, I felt pretty disappointed. I was hoping that she would answer the phone right away.

However, she didn't return my call on Monday or on Tuesday. She also hadn't called back by Wednesday, and I was starting to get nervous. I called the psychologist, who said that she would try and get in touch with Amanda as well.

By Friday, though, Cynthia and I were starting to accept the truth.

"Maybe she's found another job," I said to Cynthia. "Maybe there was something about us that . . . she didn't think was right."

"Maybe," Cynthia said. "Or maybe something has happened to her."

"What would happen to her?" I asked.

Cynthia shook her head. "I don't know," she said. "I guess after Olive, I'm just paranoid."

"Darling," I replied, "you can't think like that. Olive was a freak situation. I know it bothers you that she was never found, but . . ."

"I know, I know," she said. "I just was thinking about her a lot today. Her birthday would have been this week."

"Yeah," I said. "I was thinking about that too. But we can't just assume that Amanda is dead because Olive is."

"Do you know what the worst part of that is?" she said. "Olive may not be dead. We have no idea."

I sighed. "Babe, she's gone."

"What if she isn't, though?" she asked. "What if she just . . . you know . . . what if she was so sad about giving us Grant that she just changed her name and ran away?"

I gave her a look.

"I know it's crazy," she said. "And I know it's not true. I'm just . . . I miss her."

"Yeah," I said. "I know. Look, maybe we need to comb through the candidates we have already interviewed and then just . . . I don't know . . . see if we want to give any of them another chance?"

"I don't really want any of them," she said. "Each of them had something that didn't quite mesh."

"So start from scratch, then?" I asked her, and she put her head in her hands.

"I don't know," she said. "I just wanted it to be sorted."

"Baby, I will sort it," I replied. "I just need to know what you want to do, and I'll take care of it."

"Okay," she said. "I just . . ."

She looked like she was going to have a panic attack, and I didn't want that. It wasn't that she necessarily had panic attacks, but Cynthia seemed to get overwhelmed so easily these days. I wanted to do anything I could to help out.

"Look, I'll take care of it," I said. "Just stop worrying."

"I wish it were that easy," she said through a half smile.

"I know. I know it's not that easy. It's like when

people tell me to take a break at work. The office isn't going to run itself."

"I know," she said. "I understand you. I understand that it's going to be difficult and that whoever it is will have to adapt to us as much as we have to adapt to her."

"Yeah," I said. "But you know what? Let's not deal with that right now. Why don't we take the kids out for ice cream or something?"

"Okay," she said. "I mean, we'd have to find somewhere Grant can eat. You know we're trying to follow a dairy-free diet."

"I know," I said. "I think the new place has dairy-free options. I'll call ahead and figure it out. You just worry about getting them dressed and out the door."

"Thanks," she said. "I appreciate it."

"Anytime," I said with a grin as I picked up the phone.

When Anna was young and Grant was just a baby, we used to go out for dinner all the time. It was easier then. Now, it seemed like an Olympic feat just to get Grant dressed and out the door.

In his lucid moments, he was lovely, smiling and laughing. However, it seemed like the lucid moments were fewer and farther between lately. We had him on a cocktail of medications, but they seemed to wear off quickly, and it didn't matter what we tried.

Anna used to be easier too. She was a happy child, but she didn't say much, and finding ice cream that she could eat was a whole different story. What she could and could not eat, based on her preferences, changed from day to day. She was such a picky eater that she was still as skinny as a rail. The doctor had determined that she didn't have any issues that could be categorized as an eating disorder, such as anorexia, but she certainly didn't eat very much.

"Are you okay?" I asked Cynthia when we finally got into the car.

"Yeah," she said. "We are excited for ice cream, aren't we, kids?"

"I don't want ice cream," Anna said.

"Oh?" I asked. "What do you want, baby?"

"I want French fries," she said.

I breathed a sigh of relief. "We could do that. Grant, do you want French fries?"

"Yes!" he called.

I sighed. At least for now, we could get them to agree.

I drove to our favorite fish and fries place, which

we indulged in often, especially when we were feeling lazy for dinner. They knew us well, and they always smiled widely when I came in because they knew that I also tipped well.

"This is nice," Cynthia said as we settled down. "We should do this more often."

"We should," I said as I passed around the fries that had just come out of the fryer. Grant dug into them greedily and even Anna looked pretty interested. "I think that if we got a nanny, we could do these things more often because we wouldn't spend our days so exhausted."

"Yeah," she said. "We just need to find the right one."

"We will," I said.

Anna looked interested. "We're getting a nanny?" she asked. "Why? Don't you want to take care of us anymore, Mommy?"

Cynthia's face fell and I knew that hit her hard.

"Mommy just needs a little bit of help," I said. "So that you can do all sorts of fun stuff together and she can enjoy it."

"Hmm," Anna said as she munched on a fry. I was worried that she was going to ask another question that would hurt Cynthia, but then she just stopped eating. "I don't want to eat these."

"What?" I asked her. "You wanted to come here."

"I know," Anna said. "But I'm full."

Cynthia went into full-blown parent mode, and I turned to Grant, who seemed completely engaged in his food.

"What do you think, buddy?" I asked him.

"I think it looks pretty good," Grant said. "I want more ketchup."

"I can get you more ketchup," I said. "Do you need anything else?"

"No," Grant said, and then he looked off into the distance. I saw his eyes change and I knew what was coming.

"Hey, Grant," I said. "Hey, buddy, stay with me."

It was too late, though. Once he started staring off into the distance and looking around like there were a million other people talking to him, I knew we were lost. I gave Cynthia a little nudge and then nodded toward Grant.

Cynthia gave me a look and my heart broke. I knew we needed to get a nanny because Cynthia was going to break long before Grant would.

I shot an apologetic look at the counter staff as I picked up Grant before he started to scream. I carried him outside, but half the street clearly knew what was happening by then. Grant was in full-blown hallucination mode, and it was clearly a scary one.

I felt like a failure of a father because I was supposed to keep my son safe, and I couldn't keep him safe from his own mind. I felt like I had been given one task in life, and I had failed. It didn't matter that I had my own multimillion-dollar business. All that mattered was that my son was not safe and I had failed.

Chapter 5

CYNTHIA

AFTER LAST NIGHT, I REALLY DIDN'T WANT TO get out of bed and get my day started. I was exhausted, and Grant hadn't slept through the night. He had woken up three more times with nightmares, and I knew that sending him to school today was not a possibility. Grant went to a special needs school, but even they had their limits when it came to meltdowns. So, I sent Anna off with the driver and then made Grant his breakfast, careful to pick his favorites. As far as I was concerned, there were some days when you picked your battles and some days when you didn't. If I was in a fighting mode, I would make sure Grant ate a completely healthy breakfast. Today, however, I poured him a big bowl of his favorite sugary cereal and added chocolate milk while I checked my phone.

I was surprised to find a text from Michael just an hour after he left. Normally, when he got into the office in the morning, it was chaos. However, the text message had an attachment.

I think I found someone perfect, said the message.

There was a resume and photo attached, and while I kept an eye on Grant, I opened up the attachment.

The picture that filled my screen was of a beautiful redhead with stunning eyes. I raised my eyebrows and briefly wondered if my husband was just being a horny loser.

I also knew that I was paranoid and that every woman who reached her forties worried about her husband having a wandering eye. I thought I was still fairly attractive, but this woman was completely out of my league. She was a few years younger than me, but she looked like she could have been a super model.

I opened her resume, expecting it to be lackluster. To my surprise, it was spot on. She had a degree in child psychology and she specialized in juvenile schizophrenia. This was not what I had expected at all.

The more I read her cover letter, the more I liked her. Her name was Helena, and she had twin boys. When I zoomed out on her photo, I realized the children were included in the picture. They were adorable boys, with red hair just like their mother.

The more I looked at the picture, the more I saw her to be a working mother with a beautiful smile rather than just some sexy woman I was going to be afraid to have in my house. Her resume was perfect, and I felt drawn to her.

Do you want to call her or shall I? Michael texted.

I can call her, I think it would be interesting to talk to her, one mother to another.

Good luck. Let me know how it goes.

I waited until Grant was lying on the couch, half napping and half watching TV, before I called the phone number listed on the resume.

It rang a couple of times, and then a beautiful melodic voice picked up.

"Hello?" asked the voice.

"Hi, is this Helena?"

"Speaking," she said.

"This is Cynthia Thompson. My husband I were forwarded your resume because we are looking for a nanny for our special needs son."

"Oh, hello!" she said. She sounded like we were the best thing to happen to her all day. "It's so lovely to hear from you."

"I just wanted to ask you a few questions," I said. "Is now a good time?"

"Sure, now is a perfect time," she said, and I heard her settling down. "When I saw your job posting, it seemed like it was written for me."

"Yes, it does seem like that," I said. "So, you specialized in juvenile schizophrenia. Why did you do that? Do you have a personal connection to it?"

"Yes," she said. "It ran in my husband's side of the family. So I got to see it firsthand when I was going to school for psychology, and I just . . . I wanted to specialize, to try and help."

"That's pretty noble," I said. "And you wanted to specialize in childcare because . . . ?"

"Because I love children," she said. "I don't know if you have the picture I sent, but I have twin boys. They are big boys, it seems like they're growing up so fast, and I just . . . I wanted to work with kids even more as my babies were growing up."

I connected with that right away.

"I know exactly what you mean," I said. "My

daughter is nine and it seems like just yesterday that she was a baby."

"Yeah," she said with a giggle. "So, tell me about your child. It's your daughter who has special needs?"

"No," I said. "It's my son."

"Right," she said. "And what is his name? How old is he?"

"His name is Grant, and he's seven," I said. "We had somebody lined up, but she just sort of . . . flaked on us."

"I know what you mean," she said. "I used to have a babysitter when the boys were young and I was going to school. And then she flaked, and I had to bring them to class."

"Could your husband not take them?" I asked.

"Oh, he, uh . . . he left," Helena said. "Sorry, I don't want to talk about it."

"Of course," I said. "I don't want to pry. I'm just trying to get as much information as possible, because . . . well, not to sound mistrusting, but because you're going to be in my home."

"Of course!" Helena agreed. "I want you to ask as many questions as you can."

"Sure," I said. "I used to be a nurse, so I have a pretty good understanding of things from a medical side. I know you went to school for this, but I don't want you to administer any medications to Grant or anything. I can handle all of that."

"Sure," she said. "I mean, I don't mind that, but I can do whatever you want. I am happy to work with Grant on his days off from school, or if he's homeschooled, I can deal with that too."

"Oh," I said. "Yeah, I suppose you hear him in the background. He's actually just home from school today because he's had a really rough night. He usually goes to a special needs school. My daughter Anna is gifted, and she goes to a different school."

"Heavens, that must be difficult," she said to me. "How do you manage it in the morning?"

"Oh, we have two different . . . uh . . ." I paused. "Two drivers. My husband makes quite a bit of money. He runs his own company."

"Oh, that's lovely," she said. "I would love to run my own company someday . . . but right now, it's just me and the boys."

"Well, I'd love to meet you," I said. There was something about her that made me feel comforted and familiar. I couldn't quite put my finger on it, but I felt like I had known her a very long time. "Maybe you could come for an interview?"

"Of course," she said. "You name the time and place and I'll make it happen."

"Thank you for being so flexible," I said. "So, you aren't working right now?"

"No," she said. "I'm doing my best to take care of my boys while I'm between jobs. I used to take care of another family, but they actually moved away, and I wasn't willing to move with them. You know, my boys are established here, and I didn't want to pull them away from their friends."

"Yeah," I said. "I know what you mean. I wouldn't want to pull my kids out of school, either."

"You get it," she said with a chuckle. "I'm always so glad when I talk to someone who understands me. A lot of my friends didn't understand why I wouldn't follow a well-paying job. My kids come first, you know?"

"Yes, that's exactly how I feel," I said. "And you have childcare for your kids while you work with my son?"

"I would," she said. "I would never bring them to work unless you said so. I'm there to work with your son, not take care of my own child."

"Thank you for saying that," I said. "Perhaps when we get to know you a bit better, that's something we could do?"

"Sure," she said. "I want to do whatever makes you happy. I'm so excited to meet you."

"I'm excited to meet you too," I said, and I actually meant it.

"Great!" she said. "I'll look forward to hearing from you regarding an interview time and place."

With that, she hung up. I went back to her resume, reading it over again. It really did seem too good to be true, and I couldn't believe my luck. I called Michael right away.

"Hey," he said when he answered. "Did you talk to her?"

"I did," I said. "And she actually seems pretty awesome. I said that we'd interview her . . . but truth be told, I'm kind of already sold."

"Really?" he said in surprise. "That's not like you at all. She must be awesome."

"Exactly," I replied. "So do you think that we could meet her this evening?"

He chuckled at that. "This evening is pretty quick," he said. "But if you want to move things ahead that quickly, sure. I won't be home late or anything."

"Perfect," I replied. "I'll call her back."

"Any reason for the rush?" he asked.

"I just . . . I guess I realized this morning how

much we really need someone," I replied. "I feel like a failure, but if Grant is continuously having meltdowns and missing school, that's not good for him."

"No," Michael agreed. "No, it's not. And I absolutely agree with you. I just wanted to hear it coming from you."

"Yeah," I said. "So I'll ask her for about seven p.m.?"

"Yep," he said. "I'm sorry, baby, I gotta go. Love you."

"No problem, love you," I said and hung up the phone. I went into the living room and rubbed Grant on the leg. "Hey, love, can we talk?"

"Okay," Grant said. "Am I in trouble?"

"No," I said. "Not at all. I just wonder if you remember last night at the restaurant, what Daddy and I were talking about? About a nanny?"

"Yes," he said. "You brought some other ladies here and said that Amanda would be my nanny."

I was surprised that he remembered her name. "I know I did," I said. "But it turns out that we needed to check out one more person."

"But I liked Amanda," he said.

"I know. I'm sorry, but she isn't available anymore."

"Why not?" he asked.

I decided not to answer that question.

"We are going to meet another lady tonight," I said. "Her name's Helena. And I want you to tell me whether you like her or not, okay?"

"Sure," he said and went back to staring at the TV.

I watched him for a few moments and then settled down beside him and hugged him. He was still my baby, and I wanted to soak up as much time with him as I possibly could.

Chapter 6

MICHAEL

When I heard the doorbell ring, I sprang up to answer it. Cynthia was busy in the kitchen and I didn't want her to overwhelmed by trying to get Grant to watch TV and trying to get Anna to do her homework.

I opened the door and was stunned by the beauty of the woman standing there. She had long red hair, sparkling eyes, and the most wonderful smile I had ever seen.

"Hello," she said. "I'm Helena. You must be Michael."

"Yes," I said and reached out to shake her hand. I was trying to be professional because there was something that I couldn't shake. There was something about her that I felt a connection to right away.

I told myself not to go down that route again. I had done that once, and it had ended badly. Besides, I didn't want to scare her away if she was really the best person for Grant.

"Come on in," I said. "Thank you for coming on such short notice."

"No problem," she said as I led her inside. "You have a lovely home."

'Thank you," I said. "It's a bit of a disaster right now, but we are doing our best. Sorry."

"No, not at all," she said as Cynthia came out of the kitchen. Helena extended her hand and Cynthia shook it.

"So nice to meet you," she said. "I think that we connected on the phone, and I was so excited to come and see you."

"Of course." Cynthia looked between me and Helena and then led her into the kitchen. "Can I get you something to drink?"

"Just water is great," Helena said as she settled on the stool like she had been there before. "So, do you both work?"

"I work," I said. "Cynthia was a nurse, but she mostly stays home with the kids now."

"Oh, how lovely," she said. "That is so wonderful that you're able to do that."

"Well, it is," Cynthia said. "But obviously, we need a bit more help."

"Of course," she said. "And there's nothing wrong with needing a little extra help now and again, especially when it comes to special needs children. They need so much love, and I'm happy to provide that extra love."

"I like that," Cynthia said.

I smiled at Helena. "That's a lovely way of putting it," I said. "We have been so careful with Grant, not to put him in a medical setting too often. We know that it's hard for him, and we want him to have as much of a normal childhood as possible."

"Absolutely," she said. "And I don't want it any other way. When Grant is working with me—if you hire me, of course—he will just feel like a normal little boy, going to school and coming home to hang out with someone who makes his life fun."

"I really like the way you put that. It's like you understand our mindset."

"I don't think it would be a good fit if I didn't," Helena said. "You want someone on the same page as you if they are going to be spending a significant amount of time with your child."

She took a sip of water and her eyes sparkled at me. I felt like I knew her, and I could see her working with Grant.

"Well," I said and turned to Cynthia. "What do you think?"

"I, uh . . ." Cynthia looked at me, and I could see she was being her usual indecisive self.

"I just have one question," Helena said. "Would this become a live-in position? I have two boys and I need to take care of them."

"What?" Cynthia asked, confused. "I thought that you said—"

"Of course, it could be," I said, talking over Cynthia, not wanting to lose someone so qualified over housing arrangements. "How about after your month's probationary period, we say that you can move in?"

"Where?" Cynthia asked me, clearly exasperated with me.

"Well, we have plenty of room, don't we, honey?" I said to her. "I mean, we have the guest bedroom up there and then the apartment downstairs and—"

"What?" she said to me, again.

She looked annoyed, but now that I had said it, I didn't want to take it back.

"Will that suit you?" I asked Helena, knowing that I would be having an argument with Cynthia later that night.

"Sure," Helena said. "I'm sure that you have some other questions for me. Please feel free to ask me anything you want."

"I have a few more questions," Cynthia said. Her attitude had changed, but I had a feeling it was because of me, not because of Helena.

However, by the end of the interview, Helena seemed to have turned Cynthia around from the bad mood I had no doubt put her in. The two seemed to be acting like old friends, and I felt like Helena could read our moods. She was completely on our wavelength, and I knew that she would be perfect for Grant.

"I think," I said to Helena, "you have the job."

"Really?" Her face lit up.

Cynthia didn't look entirely sure, but she reached out and shook her hand anyway.

"Congratulations," she said. "If my husband is onboard, then I'm onboard."

"Oh, this is fantastic," Helena said. "I won't let you down. Thank you. Thank you so much."

It really had been the best interview that she could have given us. When Grant had wandered into the kitchen, Helena had directed her full attention to him, and he had lit up like a Christmas tree. I knew she was the best person for the job, even if I had to argue with Cynthia. And sure enough, after the kids were put down and Helena was gone, Cynthia started in on me.

"Why were you looking at her the whole time like you wanted to bang her?" she asked me.

I was taken aback by her blunt attitude. "What?" I asked in surprise. "I wasn't!"

"But you were," Cynthia said. "It was so obvious."

"I wasn't," I said. "I swear. I just felt comfortable with her. Didn't you feel like you knew her?"

"I did," Cynthia said. "At least, I thought I did until you were looking at her that way. Then I felt like I knew her in a whole other way."

"Hey, that's not fair," I replied. "And I personally find it a little hurtful that you think I would be doing anything except thinking about Grant's wellbeing."

"I want to think that's what you're thinking about," she replied. "But at this point, I can't be sure about anything."

"Please," I said. "Cynthia, let's not go down this road again."

"Yes, I agree," she said. "Let's not do this again."

The two of us held each other's gazes in a stalemate, and then I sighed.

"You do have to agree that she's the best candidate, though," I said. "I mean, look at her resume. Look at her references."

"I know," she replied. "But that doesn't mean I won't be watching the two of you very closely."

"I know," I said. I was wrestling with both shame and resentment at the same time. I knew I had messed up once, but Cynthia said that she was over it last time, and she forgave me. I should have known that she was still hurt by my infidelity.

"Okay," Cynthia said. "I think you should sleep on the couch. I'm still upset with you, and I don't want to go to bed angry."

"Uh . . ." I wasn't sure how that would prevent her from going to bed angry, but I nodded. "Sure."

"Okay," she said again and left the room.

Once she was gone, I pulled out my phone, just to distract myself. I'd kept the same phone for years, despite the fact that I could have upgraded a long time ago. I had the money to upgrade. That wasn't the problem. It was just that I was often of the mindset that if something wasn't broke, there was no need to fix it. And my phone, somehow, still worked just fine.

One of the reasons I had kept the phone was because Olive's last text to me was on it. I knew that wasn't the only reason, but I couldn't shake the feeling that it was my last connection to her. I sometimes thought that if I texted her number, she might just text me back. However, I was also of the mindset that it would only work once, so I had to save it until I really needed it.

I knew that was a crazy theory. I knew it wasn't actually true. But that didn't mean I was going to get rid of my phone, either.

After lingering on Olive's last message for a while, I opened my emails and threw myself into work. Work was the thing that I tended to do when everything else was going wrong in my life. Or when everything was going right. In fact, work was just what I did all the time, which made me feel slightly guilty. That wasn't necessarily what I wanted for my family, but I didn't know how to remedy that.

"Daddy?" Anna popped her head into the kitchen, and I raised my eyebrows in surprise.

"Hey, baby, why are you awake?" I asked.

"I heard you and Mommy arguing," she said.

I silently cursed the fact that we had not been quiet enough.

"What were you fighting over?"

"Nothing," I said. "We weren't fighting. We were just having a discussion."

"Over what?" she asked.

She was such an inquisitive little child, and she was certainly her mother's daughter. Cynthia always needed to know all the facts and details.

"We were just talking about the new nanny," I said.

"New nanny?" Anna asked in confusion. "Did you get one already?"

"Yes," I said. "Her name is Helena and she starts tomorrow."

"But how do you know that she's a good person?" Anna asked.

I raised my eyebrows in surprise.

"Well, because she . . . she seems like a good person," I said. "Who taught you to ask such grown-up questions?"

"Mommy was talking to her friend on the phone right now," Anna said. "And she was asking how she knew Helena was a good person. That's her, right? The same Helena?"

"That's right," I said, wondering who Cynthia

was talking to. "But you don't need to worry about stuff like that."

"I know there are good people and bad people in the world," Anna said. "We read a book about it in school."

"Oh?" I said. "And how did the book tell you to tell the difference?"

"The book said that we should always ask someone who they are," she said. "And if they don't say the right things, we shouldn't go with them."

"Uh, you shouldn't go with anyone you don't know," I replied.

"Yes, but it's okay to go with a policeman or a fireman," Anna said, and I realized the book was perhaps a little bit simpler than I thought.

"That's true," I said. "It's okay to go with those people. But you should go to bed right now."

"I'm not tired," she said. "Can I stay up a little longer?"

"No, Anna. You need to go to bed."

"Okay, okay," she said with a sigh.

She looked exhausted, but she, like her brother, didn't sleep much. With Anna, I assumed it was because her mind was always active.

I got her a glass of water and she headed upstairs to bed. I turned my ear toward the stairs to see if Cynthia was still talking on the phone, but all was silent upstairs. I knew she had a lot of friends I didn't know, but it bothered me that I didn't know who she would turn to in her time of crisis.

Maybe things weren't as good as I thought they were.

Chapter 7

CYNTHIA

"I'm sorry, I don't think I love you anymore."

Those were words that I expected to hear my whole life, but when I heard them coming from Michael, they were like bullets to my chest. My whole world felt like it was ending. The world was crashing down, and I thought I was going to die.

I woke up with a start, absolutely terrified. My chest hurt and my mouth was dry.

It was a dream. It was just a dream.

And yet, it really hadn't been a dream. Michael had said those words to me once and then taken them back. It was as if his subconscious had come leaking out and he panicked. He had begged me to take him back after his affair and begged me to forgive him. I had taken him back, obviously, but on several very strict conditions.

I didn't expect him to actually adhere to those conditions. I didn't expect that he would make himself a much better person. I didn't expect to fall in love with him all over again and almost completely forgive him.

I think the key words were *almost completely forgive him*. I hadn't quite done so yet, and I often brought it up in our angry moments. I knew he was expecting me to drop it, but I couldn't. Now, the fact that he looked as if he was ready to bone our new nanny, and our only good prospect, was really bothersome to me.

Of course, I knew that it annoyed him that I hadn't forgiven him yet, and he was probably hoping that I would soon, but I couldn't do that.

Of course, I didn't know for certain that he wanted to bang her, but I could pretty much tell that he wanted to from the way he looked at her. I was hoping he'd be able to contain himself, but I didn't know for sure if he could.

I was supposed to be able to trust him, especially given that we hadn't had another option, but she was gorgeous, and I knew my husband's taste.

In any case, I still had no choice. She was going

to be here at any moment, and I really needed to make sure I was ready.

I checked my phone and was grateful to see that she wasn't on her way yet. She said she would text me when she was twenty minutes away, and there was nothing yet. I said I was flexible with my start time since we had given her such short notice. I knew I wanted to run some errands with Anna today, but I wasn't sure I was ready to leave Grant.

I showered and got both kids ready before Helena texted me that she was on her way. I asked Grant if he remembered the lady from the night before, and luckily, he said that he did, and he was excited to see her.

I breathed a sigh of relief and turned to Anna.

"I thought we could go shopping today," I said to her. "You need some new pants for school, and I need to make sure that we have some cleaning supplies."

"Okay," Anna said. "But can we stop at the leggings store?"

I sighed with a smile. Somehow, despite being only nine years old, my kid was addicted to *Lululemon*. I knew I shouldn't buy those things for her, but she wanted them, and I wanted to make her happy. I wanted to give her the childhood that I didn't have.

"Sure," I said. "Do you need new leggings?"

"Yes," she said.

I knew she was lying, but I didn't mind. I heard the doorbell ring, and I took a deep breath and checked my hair in the mirror. I was nowhere near as beautiful as she was, and I felt old and bloated today. I ran my hand through my hair and then took a deep breath and pulled open the door.

"Hello, hello!" Helena had a wide smile on her face, and she looked absolutely stunning. Her red hair fell into her face and she pushed it back. I hated how much she looked like a supermodel.

'Hi," I said. "Did you have any trouble getting here this morning?"

"Nope, everything was great," she said and held up a bag. "I brought some toys for Grant. I know they just came from my house, but kids like new toys, I find."

"They do," I said. "And Grant is a fan of anything new in the toy world. That's nice of you."

"I find that's easiest to work with on the first day," she said as she stepped inside.

Grant saw her, and to my surprise, he ran to her right away.

"Huh," I said. "I've never seen him do that."

"I have a way with children," she said with a smile, and then she gave Grant a hug. "Hello. We're going to have some fun today, aren't we?"

"Grant, honey," I said. "I need to show Helena around the house and show her where the important things are. Can you go play in your room for a few moments?"

"But I want to play with Helena," he said.

"I know," I said. "We won't be long."

"As soon as your mommy shows me the house, I promise we'll play," Helena said and handed over the bag. "Why don't you go through this bag and choose something fun? And then when we're done, we can play together?"

"Okay," Grant said. He took the bag and went up to his room as if she had magic powers over him.

I couldn't believe it. Maybe this really was the right choice.

"I'll show you where the emergency numbers are," I said. "And then I'll show you where we keep the first aid kit. As I said yesterday, don't worry about Grant's medication. I can take care of that myself."

"Of course," Helena said, and she took notes as

we walked. I wasn't sure what exactly she needed to take notes on, given that it wasn't a very extensive tour. As soon as the tour was over, I escorted her back to the front door.

"Okay," I said. "That's pretty much it. This is the coat closet, but the last thing I wanted to tell you is that Grant gets cold often, so we pretty much keep sweaters and coats everywhere."

"That makes sense," she said. "Thank you so much for taking the time to show me all of this."

"Well . . . of course," I said, confused. "I want you and Grant to have a successful relationship. As for pay, I can do direct deposit—"

"Would you mind cash?" Helena asked.

I raised an eyebrow. "Uh . . ."

"It's just I, uh . . . I don't have an account right now. Issues with my mother made me close my last one, and I haven't opened a new one because she's in banking and I don't want her to trace me through my account. She's not a very good person, so I try to stay away from her."

"Right," I said. "I suppose I can talk to my husband about that."

"Okay," she said. "I understand if things are a bit delayed. I'm just happy to work."

"Sure," I said and glanced at my watch. "So,

I'm going to take Anna out to run a few errands, if you think you can handle Grant?"

"Sure," she said. "Grant and I will be just fine."

"I'm sure you will be," I said to her and gave her a bit of a smile. I still felt uneasy, although I knew I was making the right choice.

Once she and Grant were settled down, I took Anna out to the stores. Michael texted me to ask how things were going, and I told him that all was well. At least, I thought all was well. However, while Anna was trying on leggings, I couldn't help but log onto the nanny cam I had installed. I turned on the sound just a tiny bit and then leaned forward, skipping through the monitors until I found them.

Helena and Grant were sitting in the playroom, and she was reading him a book. His red hair was mixed with hers as he sat in her lap, and she was reading out loud.

I wondered if he felt more comfortable with her because she had red hair. He had rarely met another redhead before, so I assumed that perhaps he was more comfortable due to that.

It took a moment for the sound to kick in, but I could hear her reading softly with her lilting voice.

"And sometimes," she said, "Mommy cuckoos

lay their eggs in another nest, and other birds take care of them."

"Why?" Grant asked.

"Because sometimes, they need a little extra help," she said.

"Do the Mommy cuckoos come to visit?" he asked.

"They do," she assured him.

That was an interesting choice of book to read to him, given that he was so young. It seemed like the more she read, the more it became scientific. I had also never read that cuckoos did that. Now I felt like I needed to look that up.

I didn't want to doubt her, because she was an expert in her field. Yes, I was a nurse, but she specialized in the conditions Grant had, so I wanted to at least let her try.

"Mommy, what do you think?" Anna said, and I looked up from the nanny cam.

"Oh," I said as I looked at her leggings. "Those look great."

"Good," she said. "Because I want to buy them."

"You want to buy them?" I said in surprise.

Anna had an allowance, of course, but she didn't normally want to spend it.

"Yes," she said. "I love them that much."

"That's great," I said. "You know how much you have in there, so if the leggings are in your budget, you're welcome to buy them."

"Yes," she said. "They are only fifty-two dollars."

I briefly wondered if my children were spoiled or whether I was giving them too much. However, Anna was spending her own money and budgeting, and that was important too.

Once we bought the leggings and the other new pants I knew she needed, we ran a few more errands before heading home. Helena looked almost disappointed when I finally walked through the door.

"I thought you'd be gone much longer," she said. "Grant and I had so many adventures prepared."

"Oh," I said. "Well, I didn't want to leave you too long on your first day. I wanted to make sure you were okay."

"Of course, we're okay," she said with a large smile. "I feel right at home here. And I feel like I've known Grant my whole life. He's such a wonderful child."

"Oh," I said. "Well . . . thank you?"

"No problem," she said. "Now, what can I help you with?"

"Help me?" I asked.

Helena smiled even wider. "Of course," she said. "I can't spend all my time with Grant or he'll get tired of me. Part of my job is helping you too."

"Oh, well . . ." I paused. "I was going to make dinner—"

"I can do it," she said and headed into the kitchen.

I followed her, a bit dumbfounded.

"You don't really have to," I said.

She shrugged. "I love cooking," she said, "so it's no trouble at all."

"If you're sure," I said. "And it's not something I expect you do every day."

"No, of course not," she said. "But I'm happy to do it today. What were you thinking of cooking?"

"Maybe some . . . burgers?" I said. "I have some bison burgers there."

"Oh, I love bison," she said, and I felt obligated to invite her for dinner. "Anna, do you like bison?"

"No," Anna said from behind me.

I turned around to her. "Yes, you do," I said to her. "You love bison."

"I don't," Anna said.

It seemed like she didn't take to Helena as much as Grant did.

"Anna, you can go play," I said, and she gratefully headed off into the playroom.

"Sorry," I said to Helena. "She can be really picky."

"That's fine," Helena said. "I'm sure that we can find something she enjoys."

"I hope so," I said as she took out the meat.

I wanted to just smile and accept her help, but something felt off. Hopefully, we would be able to find a middle ground where I was comfortable and Helena was happy. I didn't blame her for being beautiful, and I didn't blame her for my husband being attracted to her. I just hoped that this didn't end in heartbreak.

Chapter 8

MICHAEL

"CAN YOU MAKE SURE THAT IT'S DONE RIGHT?" I snapped at my employee before I even thought it through.

Josh's eyes widened, and he backed away. "Sorry, Boss," he said.

I retreated. "No, I'm sorry. That was my mistake. I shouldn't have yelled at you. I'm just frustrated with life."

"Oh," he said and stood there awkwardly.

"It's not your fault," I said to him. "And the sketch is fine. Just make sure you put the measurements in."

"Okay," he said and scampered off before I could bite his head off again.

I sighed and put my head in my hands. I hadn't

meant to snap at him, but I was just so annoyed at the moment.

Cynthia had said something to me that morning that had me upset. She'd told me not to come home until 5 p.m. so I wouldn't lust after Helena. I hadn't said anything to her, but I was so annoyed with the fact that she didn't trust me.

I knew I had given her a reason not to trust me. Things had not been good many years ago, but I had been better since then, and I hadn't given her a reason to distrust me in several years. I didn't think monogamy was an easy solution to life, and I wasn't the best at it, but I did it for her. I just wish that she would stop throwing my mistake in my face. I didn't want to live my life resenting my wife.

The fact that I was actually attracted to Helena probably didn't help matters, either. She was a very attractive woman, and she moved something inside me that felt like it had been asleep for many years. It was as if I knew her, and she awoke an old attraction in me, the old Michael.

I didn't want that to be the case. I didn't want to get caught in a mess again. I didn't want to be attracted to my nanny like some cliché.

I hoped I could get over it and just move on with life. After all, maybe the attraction would fade and then I could just focus on what was best for Cynthia and Grant.

I loved my wife. I loved my family, and ultimately, I was going to try and do whatever it took to create the best situation for them.

I think the keyword there was try. I wanted to try, and I wanted to succeed. Any man knew that trying was not that easy, though. Trying and failing was a common theme, but the wife didn't give points for failing, even when you tried.

After a few minutes alone in my office, I went out to walk the office floor. I sometimes did it, and I didn't startle the team too much. They mostly nodded to me, except for Josh, who looked terrified.

"I'm really sorry I snapped at you," I said to Josh. "Things at home are not the best."

We had the type of office that was pretty open with our employees. In addition, they knew that I had a child with special needs, and so they probably attributed it to that.

"No problem," Josh said. "It's cool. We all have days like that."

"The drawing looks much better," I said.

He smiled. "Thank you," he said and then headed off to photocopy it.

"What's going on?" my vice president, Terry,

asked me.

He had no doubt seen me walking around and apologizing to the minions.

"Nothing," I said. "Josh said something to me and I snapped at him, so I was just telling him that I was sorry."

"Oh," he said. "Because that's normal."

"No, it's not normal," I said with a sigh. "There's just some stuff going on at home."

"Oh," he said. "I'm sorry to hear that."

"No, it's nothing bad," I said. "It's just . . . different."

"Is there anything we can do?" Terry asked. "Is Grant okay?"

"Yeah, everything is fine. Don't worry. But I think I'm going to head home early, if that's okay. Do you have the fort?"

"Yep," he said and glanced at his watch. "It's only for another two hours, anyway."

"Indeed," I said. I couldn't actually go home because I knew that Cynthia would lose her mind, but I was hoping to just head to a coffee shop and clear my head. Maybe, if I took a little while before coming home, I wouldn't have an instant reaction to Helena.

I couldn't put my finger on the reason I felt like

I knew her. Once I got out of the office and went to a coffee shop, I spent some time *Googling* her. I was just trying to figure out if we had crossed paths in a past life, or maybe she was a friend of a friend or something.

To my surprise, Helena didn't exist at all on the internet. I checked *Facebook* and *Google*, a few business networking sites, but there was nothing about her.

I supposed it made sense, given the fact that she worked with children. I had read something about the fact that most people who worked with children preferred to be hidden from social media. Although I was glad that she took such precautions, it was a little bit annoying because it meant I had no chance of figuring out how I knew her or where we had crossed paths.

I ordered a cup of coffee and then another one and another one, so by the time I headed home for dinner, I was absolutely wired on coffee. When I let myself in the front door, I could tell right away that there was no one else in the house. Cynthia had a certain aura about her when she was relaxed and alone versus when other people were there.

"Hi," I said to her. She was reading on the couch.

"Hi," she said. "You're home early."

"Hopefully not too early," I said as I looked at my watch. "You said to come after five."

"No, that's fine," she said. "I just didn't expect you home right at five p.m. You usually work late."

"How was the first day?" I asked.

"It was good," she said. "I even took Anna out shopping, and Helena made dinner for us before she left."

"She made dinner?" I said in surprise. "That isn't part of her duties, is it?"

"I told her it wasn't, but she insisted," Cynthia said.

I sat down beside her and went to kiss her, but she pulled away.

"Sorry, I just ate some gross food."

"Helena's gross food?" I asked. "Is she a bad cook?"

She chuckled. "No, no," she said. "Just some leftovers. I was hungry but didn't want to wait for dinner."

"Right," I said and leaned back. I wondered if she didn't want to kiss me because she was mad at me. I didn't push it, however. "So, everything was good?"

"Yeah," she said. "There was just one thing."

"Uh oh," I said. "Was it bad?"

"No, it was just . . . weird," she said. "I was talking to Helena about how I was going to pay her, and she asked for cash."

"For cash?" I said. "Oh. That's a bit strange. Maybe there's someone she is hiding from?"

"She said her mother works in banking and she preferred that her mother not be able to trace her all, so she closed her account," Cynthia said. "That worries me. She said her mom wasn't a good person. I mean . . . what does that mean?"

"Babe, you don't know the situation," I said. "There could be a million personal reasons she doesn't want her mother to trace her, and she did say her mom wasn't a good person. Maybe she's a thief or something and Helena just wants to be sure she can't steal from her."

"I suppose," she said. "I said that I would talk to you."

"I don't have a problem with it if you don't."

She shrugged. "I suppose that's fine," she replied. "I just want to make sure that Grant is okay."

"I'm sure he's fine," I said. "I think her story makes sense, given that I was looking her up today and couldn't find anything."

"Why were you looking her up?" she asked suspiciously.

I sighed. I should have known better than to say something like that. "You know how you and I couldn't stop talking about the fact that we feel familiar with her? I was just trying to figure out if she was a friend of a friend or something."

"And?" she asked.

"Well, I couldn't find her anywhere online," I said. "So if she had a falling out with her mom, that makes sense."

"But what if it's something terrible?" Cynthia asked me.

"Go with your gut," I said. "Does it feel like something terrible?"

Cynthia sighed. "No," she said. "I don't think so. And as a mother, I would . . . I guess take my children and go if something was a problem."

"Well, if you ever run away, let me know and I'll go with you," I said.

Cynthia smiled. We talked for a bit more and then Grant came into the room.

"Hey, buddy," I said. "How was your day?"

"Good," he said as he came to snuggle with me on the couch.

"Did you like Helena?" I asked, and he nodded

into my chest. He seemed sleepy, and I assumed that she had played with him all day. "That's good. What did you do?"

"We read together," he said. "And then we made dinner."

"You helped her with dinner?" I asked in surprise. Grant rarely showed interest in helping his mother or me with dinner.

"Yes," he said. "It was fun. When is she coming back?"

"Tomorrow," I said. "Right, Cynthia?"

"Yeah," she said. "I guess so."

I gave my wife a look, but luckily, Grant didn't pick up on it.

The rest of the night was surprisingly peaceful. Usually, evenings with Grant were difficult, but it seemed like Helena had a magic touch. I commented on that and Cynthia shrugged.

"I mean, she does specialize in all of this," Cynthia said. "So I guess it makes sense."

"Why do you sound unimpressed?" I asked.

She shrugged with a smile. "I'm not trying to be difficult," she said. "I'm trying to be upbeat and positive, Michael. I just . . ."

"I know, baby," I said. "I know."

"Good," she said. "Because sometimes, I think

you don't notice when I try."

It was ironic that she said that, given that I was thinking that exact thing earlier in the day. I just smiled at her and patted the side of the bed.

"Come on," I said. "Let's go to bed and watch a movie or something."

"Really?" she said in surprise.

"Yes," I said. "We haven't done that in a long time. And I think we deserve a night off."

Cynthia's face lit up, and I could tell that we were making the right choice. Sometimes, I just needed to set life aside and snuggle up with my wife. I did love her, and I did want things to work out. I had spent most of my adult life with Cynthia, and I didn't know how to be without her.

I was going to work this out, no matter what. I would shake my attraction to Helena, and I would focus my attention on my family.

"What movie?" she asked.

I shrugged with a smile. "Whatever you want, baby." I handed her the remote.

She looked happier than I had seen her in a long time. I just hoped that I could keep her that way, for everyone's sake. I promised myself I was going to be different, and our family was going to be different. We were going to make it through.

Chapter 9

CYNTHIA

I heard Helena come in the front door, and I spent the extra moment to brush out my hair. Last week, I would have rushed down the steps to greet her, but today, I just waited patiently until I heard her get settled.

The truth was, she was turning out to be much better than I had anticipated. I had thought that even if she did really well, there would be some issues at the beginning. However, it seemed that Helena not only figured out exactly what we wanted right off the bat, but she also figured out exactly how to work out the problems we experienced. I had to admit that she was a bit magical, and I couldn't imagine life without her, even though it had only been a week.

I couldn't actually believe it had only been a week. I was sleeping better, I was eating better, and I had more time for things like actually brushing my hair or going to the gym. I was beginning to feel like a completely different person.

If this was the difference she made in a week, I couldn't wait to see the difference she made in a month.

Today, I was doing something that I hadn't felt comfortable doing in a long time. I was going out to lunch with a friend. Michael was on the golf course, as it was Saturday, and the kids were begging me all day for something fun to do. You'd think Helena was the bearer of all gifts and fun from the way they reacted when she was here.

Today, I heard both of them rush toward her with excitement. I was surprised that Anna did so, because she flipflopped on whether she liked Helena. Mostly, I noticed that Anna's issues with Helena circled around good. Whenever Helena served her food, Anna clammed up and didn't really eat. With Grant, though, it was like he was addicted to her cooking.

In any case, the kids were happy to stay with her today and I was happy to get a much-needed break away from the house.

"Hello," I said as I came down the stairs. She was just wearing jeans and a long tee shirt, but she somehow looked absolutely beautiful.

"Hello," she said. "How has your morning been?"

"It's been good," I replied. "Michael is at the golf course, and the kids have been dying to see you. You bring the magic here."

"Apparently," she said with a smile. She didn't know that I was going out to lunch yet, but I decided to tell her now, before the kids ran in.

"I'm just going out to a quick lunch with a girlfriend," I said. "Is that okay?"

"Of course," she said. "You go and take care of yourself."

"Is there anything that you need?" I asked. "I think the house is pretty well stocked, but—"

'No," she said. "I have everything I need. You go out."

"Okay. Thank you. I haven't been able to do this for so long."

"Of course," she said. "I'll call you if there's any issue, but I really don't think there's going to be a problem."

"No," I said as I grabbed my coat. "But I might just check in every once in a while, if that's okay."

"Of course," she said. "Video call me. The kids love it."

"I will," I said as I headed out the door.

I was meeting my friend Cally, and I hadn't seen her in a long time. When I stepped inside the restaurant, I almost didn't recognize her. She had dyed her hair and she looked like she had dropped several pounds.

"Hi!" I said and gave her a hug.

"Hi!" she said. "Oh, my God, it's been so long!"

'Yeah. I missed you. Sorry I haven't been able to get away. It's just been insane."

"That's okay," she said. "I know you have a difficult situation at home."

"It's not like we're starving or something," I said as the hostess came and took us to our seats. "It's just that we . . . you know, Grant takes a lot of our attention."

"Well, I'm so glad you were able to get out," she said with a grin as we sat.

"Well, that's the thing," I replied. "Remember I told you about the nanny we were looking at hiring?"

"Oh?" she asked with a smile. "Yes, you were worried about her around Michael. So you hired her?"

"Yes," I replied. "And she's pretty good. She specialized in juvenile schizophrenia, actually, so she's been a miracle worker."

"Wow," Cally said. "I didn't think that there was such a thing. I mean, I knew there were nannies who were good at certain things, but to specialize in that . . . you hit the jackpot."

"I know."

Cally raised an eyebrow at me. "So?"

"So?" I replied. I knew I wanted to tell her what was happening, but I was still wrapping my tongue around the actual words. It felt embarrassing to admit that Michael had cheated on me. I knew my friends didn't judge me, but it sometimes felt like I had failed.

"What's the problem? Still worried about Michael?" she asked.

I sighed. "She's really hot," I said. "Like, really, really hot. And just his type."

"Uh-oh," she said. "Let me see some pictures."

I pulled out my phone to show her Helena's resume and her eyebrows shot through the roof.

"Wow," she said. "You weren't kidding."

"I know, right?" I asked. "Like, I almost asked her if she'd been a model or something."

"I would believe it," she said. "Helena? What

kind of name is that? It sounds like a Greek goddess or a porn star."

I snorted and took my phone back. "Cally, don't be mean," I said.

She grinned at me. "I'm not being mean. I'm just telling the truth."

"Well, regardless," I replied, "as you know, I had misgivings about her. But aside from the fact that she looks like she stepped off a magazine cover, she's working out really well."

"Oh," she said. "But you're still worried about Michael."

"Yeah," I said as the waitress came to take our wine order.

"Well, has it been a problem yet?" she asked.

She ordered the most expensive bottle of wine on the menu, and I agreed with her choice. Cally was even richer than I was. She had a heart of gold, though, and was generous about it.

"Not yet," I replied.

"Not yet?" she asked. "Well, if it's going to become a problem, don't you think you should nip it in the bud?"

"That's not what I meant," I replied. "At least, I don't think it's what I meant. Look, when Helena first walked in the door, I was super worried. But she's not like that at all. She's kind and sweet and really good at her job. She has twin boys and she . . . I don't know. Grant just loves her."

"Well, isn't that what matters?" Cally asked. "At least . . . I mean, it's mostly what matters."

"No, it is," I said. "And Michael hasn't done anything wrong in years. I just . . ."

"I get it," she said. "You still can't trust him."

"I want to trust him," I said. "And most days, I do actually trust him. But when I look at Helena, I feel inadequate as a woman."

"Oh, honey," she said with a sigh. "That's no way to feel."

"I know," I said. "And I know that I should just . . . buck up and just keep an eye on my husband, like every other woman. But is it too much to just want him to love me like he used to?"

"Look," Cally said. "I'm not in your house every day, okay? So I don't know the ins and outs of your relationship. But from what I can see, Michael does love you. And he loves you more than he used to."

"You think?" I said. "How do you know?"

"Whenever you bring him around, he is so attentive to you. He gets your drink. He pulls out your chair. He's always smiling at you. I wish my husband were that attentive."

"That's because he's trying to make up for what he did wrong," I said. "He's sorry and he's trying to—"

"No, I know," she said. "But I don't think that you should view it that way. I think you should view it as the fact that he chose you and he loves you."

I sighed and looked down at my hands.

"She's so pretty, Cally."

"Not to play devil's advocate," she said. "But the woman can't help it if she's pretty. Does she come around with her boobs out or something?"

"No," I said. "She dresses quite conservatively."

"Well, that's good," she said. "Maybe she's making a real effort to play it cool. Maybe it's been a problem before and she's trying. Has she given you any reason to doubt her?"

"None," I said and then rethought it. "Well . . . no, that's not true. There are two things, actually. But I understand the reasons for both of them."

"Oh?" Cally asked.

"The first was that she asked me on the phone if she could have play dates with her own kids," I said. "Then she gets to the interview in person and asks if she could do a live-in position."

"And what did you say?" Cally replied.

"I didn't get a chance to say anything because I was confused that she was asking after pretending she wasn't going to. Michael, however, told her she could after her one-month probationary period."

"Ouch," Cally said. "So you were caught off guard."

"I was," I said. "And then there's the whole money issue."

"Money?" Cally asked with a raised eyebrow.

I could tell that she was absolutely feeding off my gossip and I didn't blame her. I would probably do the same in her situation.

"Yep," I said. "I asked her if being paid by check was okay, and she asked me for cash. She told me her mother was not a good person or in her life now and she didn't want her to be, so she closed her bank account so her mom couldn't trace her. Michael looked her up online and she doesn't seem to exist, so I suppose that made sense."

"Did she tell you why she was hiding from her own mother?" Cally asked.

I shook my head. "No, just that she's not a good person," I replied. "But I suppose if I had a falling out with my own mother . . . I would want to know that my children were safe. I'm trying to look at it from the perspective of one mother to another. Helena may just be protecting her children."

"Where is their father?" Cally asked.

"Gone," I said. "So she's on her own."

"Must be rough," Cally replied. "Again, not to defend her. It's just, normally, you'd tell me right away if you had any suspicions. It sounds to me like you are just describing a woman in a tough situation."

I sighed. "Yeah. I know. I just . . . I want to be sure."

"Of course you do," Cally said. "It's your house and your family. You have a right to be sure. Is she good at her job?"

"The best," I said.

She smiled. "Well, then that's your answer," Cally replied. "Don't worry about it."

I smiled and clinked wine glasses with her.

"I guess you're right," I said.

"Damn straight, I am," Cally said. "Now, should we order a feast?"

"Yes," I replied and opened my menu. I was able to have some me time because of Helena, so I needed to enjoy it. I could always call home in a bit or turn on the nanny cam and see what was happening. I needed to learn to trust her if this was going to work out at all.

If it didn't work out, I would probably go crazy because something really had to change in our lives. Neither Michael nor I could stay on edge and manage this many issues at once. We needed to heal and move forward, and this was without a doubt a good way to do it. I just hoped it lasted.

Chapter 10

MICHAEL

In all the years that I had been married to Cynthia, something that had never changed was the fact that I had found her very attractive. Yes, I'd had an affair, and yes, I had a wandering eye. But that didn't mean that I didn't find my wife attractive and that I didn't want to sleep with her every night.

Tonight, things seemed to really be going in my favor. We were both in good moods, and after some snuggling on the couch, we started kissing. One thing led to another, and soon, we were in the bedroom. I couldn't wait to undress her and make her feel amazing. This was going to be the first time that we'd had sex in a long time, and I was desperate for it.

At least, I was desperate for it until we heard a

cry on the monitor. Despite the fact that our children were grown, Cynthia kept a baby monitor in both of their rooms, just in case. Sure enough, Grant was having a nightmare, and he had the worst timing on the planet.

"I'll go," I said despite being incredibly frustrated. "It's my turn, anyway."

"Are you sure?" Cynthia asked.

I kissed her on the forehead. "I'm sure. Just stay here and relax."

I found my clothes and pulled them on before heading into Grant's room. He was sitting up in bed, and it seemed like the nightmare was gone. However, he was having a conversation with one of his imaginary friends, which I always found a little creepy.

"Hey, buddy," I said softly. The doctors said not to startle him when he got like this, and I didn't want to push him when he'd probably been asleep. "Hey, buddy, who are you talking to?"

"My friend," he said. I was surprised that he answered me right away, but I saw my chance to catch him in one of his half-lucid moments. I sat down on the bed beside him and gave him a hug. He seemed to relax in my arms, and when I pulled back to look him in the face, his eyes were even more blown than before.

"Tell me about your friend," I said. "What is his name?"

"Her name," he said. "Her name is Bella."

"Oh," I said. "That's a very nice name. What is Bella saying to you tonight?"

"She's saying to kill everyone."

I tried not to show how disturbing I thought that was. I knew we were crossing into dangerous territory, because the doctors all said to report to them whenever Grant talked about harming himself and others. I knew that it wasn't his fault, and mentally, he was quite ill, but I still felt like a failure of a father for not being able to protect him.

When they told me what Grant had, I broke down. I told myself we would find a way to protect him so he would never experience the terrors I knew befell many young schizophrenic patients. And yet here he was, starting to walk the same path. It broke my heart.

"Well, buddy," I said. "How do you feel when Bella says those things?"

"I feel like she shouldn't say those things," he responded. "I feel like they aren't very nice."

"That's right," I said. "And anyone who says

those things to you isn't a very good friend, are they?"

"No." He shook his head.

"So, what do you think you should do when you hear those things in your head?" I asked him.

"I think I should ignore them," he replied.

"I think you're right," I said. "But are you able to ignore them? Is it hard?"

"It's very hard," he said. "But I told my friend that you would come in and hug me and I would decide after that."

"And what do you think now?" I asked. "If I give you all the hugs, does it make your friend go away?"

"Yes," he said. "It makes it easier to tell her to shut up."

"That's good," I replied. "So all the hugs it is. Whenever you need."

"Okay," he said and hugged me again.

I wrapped an arm around him and put my chin on top of his head with a sigh. I wished that things could be better and easier for Grant. I felt bad for my son, and I often wondered whether I caused this. Did it run in my genes?

"Do you want to go back to sleep now?" I asked him.

He nodded.

"Okay," I said. "I'm going to be right next door, though, so you call me if you need me."

"I will," he said and then laid back down.

I sat with him for a while longer and then breathed a sigh of relief once his breaths became slow and even.

Part of me wondered if Cynthia would still be waiting for me and still in the mood when I got back, but she was reading on her phone, which told me the moment was over.

"Is he okay?" Cynthia asked.

I nodded. "He is," I said. "He just . . . you know. Life. Visions. Friends who tell him to kill people."

"Not again." Cynthia frowned, setting her phone aside. "He hasn't had one of those in a long time."

"I know. I was hoping that he wouldn't have them ever again, but it seems they're coming back."

"We should talk to the doctor," she said. "See if we can up his meds or change them. Sometimes, meds just wear off and people need a change. It's something to do with the chemical imbalance in their brains and the fact that their bodies adapt to the drugs."

"So, do we do that right away?" I asked.

"Yes," she said. "I can call in the morning."

I sat down at the end of the bed.

"Do you think that . . . maybe we should wait?" I asked.

"Why?" she replied, confused. "If he's having the visions again . . ."

"Well, I just don't really like having my son on drugs all the time," I explain. "And I know. I know he's sick. It's just . . ."

"You need to make sure you understand that he needs those meds," she said.

"It's not that I don't think he needs those drugs," I said. "I just . . . I hesitate to up them every time something goes wrong. He's only seven. I just worry about the effect on him. Maybe with Helena moving in, things will be better."

"Is Helena moving in?" she asked.

"Well, we did say that she could move in after a month, if things go right," I said. "And as far as I know, things have been going right."

"Yeah," she said. "But it's not just about Helena moving in. It would be her kids too."

"Is that a problem?" I asked.

She sighed and leaned back against her pillows. "What if her kids don't get along with ours? And we'll have to give them the guest suite in the basement."

"Yeah," I said. "So? Isn't that better than having them up here with us? I mean, it's kind of separate from us, right?"

"Yes, but . . . well, I like having guests," she said.

I gave her a look. "Honey, what's the problem?"

"The problem is that . . ." She shook her head. "Forget it. It's stupid."

"The problem is you don't trust me," I said wearily.

She sighed. "I don't want to get into this tonight. I'm really tired."

"Right, so we're just going to forget what happened earlier?" I asked.

"What happened earlier?" she asked.

I sighed. "You know what? Forget it," I said. "You look very tired. You should rest. I know life is hard right now. But it's not going to be this hard forever, baby."

"Thanks," she said. "You always know the right thing to say."

I wished it were that easy. It wasn't that I knew the right thing to say. It was that I knew her, and I knew what she wanted to hear.

As Cynthia rolled over and went to sleep, I got

up to take a shower. It was a cold shower, because I was frustrated, and the frustration didn't go away when I woke up the next morning.

All I'd wanted was to have a nice evening in and have sex with my wife. Apparently, despite the millions of dollars that I made, it wasn't enough for her.

"You're in a bad mood this morning," Cynthia said to me as I poured my third cup of coffee.

"I'm not in a bad mood," I said. "I'm tired. I got up with Grant three more times last night."

"You did?" she asked. "Why didn't you tell me?"

"Because I don't want you to lose out on sleep when I was already awake," I said.

"But . . ." she started.

I shook my head.

"Well, are you going to be okay for work?" she asked.

"I'll be fine," I assured her. "Don't worry."

"Michael, it's not that easy," she said. "You don't just tell me not to worry and assume I can turn it on and off again like a switch."

"I'm not implying that you can," I said. "I'm just trying to do the best I can here. The truth is, Cynthia, it's pretty common for one of us to be exhausted in the morning. We need Helena to move in."

"So she can be exhausted in the morning?" Cynthia asked. Her tone was harsh, and I wanted to beat my head against the wall.

"Her one job would be Grant," I said. "So her entire life would be focused on his wellbeing, and she'd sleep when he slept."

"Don't forget, she has two other children she needs to take care of," Cynthia said. "It's not as easy as you're making it sound."

"I'm sure it's not perfect," I replied. "But it's probably easier than getting up and heading to a job where you're in charge of everything and have had absolutely no sleep."

She gave me a look. "This is why I said that you should let me handle it."

I sighed and slurped back my coffee.

"Michael, I'm not sick anymore," she said.

I met her eyes. "I know that," I replied.

"I'm serious," she replied. "Yes, Anna's birth was nine years ago, and yes, I almost died. And yes, things like that can cripple a person for life. But I recovered, and I'm fine. I'm strong."

"I know you are," I said. "I'm not trying to doubt you. I'm not trying to——"

"So let me get up with him," she said.

"When are we going to discuss Helena moving in?" I asked at last.

"Tonight," she replied. "We can have the discussion tonight. I just need time to think."

Frankly, given the level of exhaustion I was carrying, tonight did not seem soon enough. However, I knew Cynthia and I knew that I couldn't push her on an issue. I knew that she had to be ready for a big decision or she would be completely shut down on the subject.

"I'm going to work," I said to her. "I'll see you later?"

"Bye," she said.

Normally, we kissed before I left for work, but today, she didn't seem up for it. I blew her a kiss anyway and then grabbed my briefcase and headed out the door. I briefly considered sending Helena a text that said that she should pack her things and move in, but I decided against it. Hopefully, when we discussed things tonight, Cynthia would be calmer and ready to move forward. I hoped that she saw it from the perspective of Grant needing help and not from a perspective of my wanting the hot nanny.

I would always find Helena attractive, as long as

she was working for us. However, I was pretty sure that I could ignore her. Otherwise, my family was going to be in big trouble. I could be stronger than that. I knew I could. For my family, and for Cynthia.

Chapter 11

CYNTHIA

MICHAEL CONVINCED ME, AND I WANTED TO SAY it was because I loved him and trusted him. But wasn't that what all loving wives were supposed to say when their husbands convinced them the hot nanny should really move in soon?

The truth was, he convinced me by listing a couple of reasons it was a good idea. Only one of them felt right. The first one, of course, was for Grant's wellbeing. I spent my day making sure that Grant was happy and that he was really making progress. I'd asked his teachers for their opinions and asked him directly. Each time I asked, I'd been rewarded with the opinion that he was making progress with Helena. He was happy and took well to her.

The other reasons Michael listed were not good ones. I wanted him to be happy and I wanted him to think that I trusted him. Of course, deep down, I didn't trust him yet, and I wasn't sure whether I ever would. I wasn't sure if I could bring myself to rest easy knowing that the hot nanny was living in my house, but I knew I had to try. If Michael and I were going to move forward, I knew it was the baby steps that were important. Every marriage counselor said that.

I just hated that it was me who had to take those baby steps and me who had to decide what to do when we were at an impasse.

I was cleaning the basement suite for Helena and her boys to move in the following week. Michael and I had decided that next week would be a good time, because the kids were off school and it would give them time to adjust each day, rather than coming home to strangers in their house. I wanted them to be happy, and so far, it seemed like they would be.

I supposed that I could have hired someone to clean the basement suite, but I wanted to do it myself. It was partly because I wanted to make sure that Helena couldn't complain about anything and partly because I wanted to know exactly what was down there before she moved in. I wanted to know what she had access to and what she was going to be using. I didn't often go down to the basement suite, which I knew seemed bad, but the house was just so big and we had no need to go down to the basement for any reason.

There was one more thing I was embarrassed about, and that was the fact that I had the nanny cam on while I cleaned. I just liked to keep an eye on what was going on upstairs, with Helena and the children, just in case Grant needed me. We hadn't had a chance to see his doctor about a change of medication, so I wanted to make sure Helena could handle it.

As I changed the sheets on the bed, I watched the nanny cam. I could see Grant and Anna being brought in by the driver, and they both went to Helena. I smiled as Grant hugged her because he very rarely comfortably hugged anyone. Anna looked up to Helena, and she was about to hug her too, but Helena shook her head.

"Anna, your hands are filthy," she said, and I didn't like her tone.

"Grant was playing in the dirt," Anna said in surprise. "I just stopped him."

"Grant has a reason," she said. "You don't. Go and wash your hands. Now."

That was not the first time I'd heard Helena say something like that. The other day, Anna had come back from a play date with friends, and Helena had snapped at her. I'd let it go then because I wanted to give her the benefit of the doubt. However, this time, I was slightly less forgiving. She needed to treat my children equally, even if she was hired to work with Grant.

I switched off the nanny cam for a moment and called Michael. I knew he was going out to lunch with some of his colleagues, but I was hoping to catch him before he left.

"Hey," I said when he answered.

"Hey," he said. "Is everything okay?"

"Yeah," I said. "I just wanted to talk to you. Have you ever noticed that Helena is a bit . . . short with Anna?"

"What do you mean?" he asked.

"Just . . . I mean, I know she was hired to work with Grant, but she's just . . . very short and dismissive with Anna, and that doesn't make me happy. I mean, don't you think she should treat both of the kids equally? And even if she doesn't treat them equally, she needs to be polite to Anna."

"Well, yes, of course," he said. "I've never noticed it, but you're home with her more than I am."

"Yeah," I said. "And I've noticed it more than once. Do you think we could talk to her about it?"

"Sure," he said. "If it's something that is bothering you, yes."

"Well, it's not just about it bothering me," I said. "It's about Anna."

"Of course," he said. "Should we ask Anna how she feels?"

"Sure," I said. "I'll ask her later when Helena leaves. I hope she isn't bothered. Otherwise, that's a big problem."

"Yeah," he said. "Cynthia, I have to go, but I'll see you at home?"

"Yep," I said and hung up the phone. I missed when Michael and I were twenty and all he had time for was me, but I knew that wasn't realistic anymore. He had an entire company to run and he'd be home in a few hours.

When Helena left, I managed a moment to get Anna alone.

"Honey," I said to her, not wanting to put ideas in her head. "Do you like Helena?"

Anna looked up at me, and I could see something flash behind her eyes.

"Grant really likes her," she said. "And Grant is so happy with her."

"I know that," I said. "But I asked if you like her."

"I mean . . . she's for Grant," she said.

"Do you think she is nice to you?" I asked.

Anna shrugged. "Sometimes," she said. "Sometimes, I feel like I'm doing something wrong."

"No," I said. "You are not doing anything wrong. Daddy and I wanted to talk to you before we talked to Helena, to see if you felt the same way we did."

"Is she mean to you too?" she asked.

"No," I said quickly. "But I noticed she's not too nice to you. I'm going to talk to her, okay?"

"Is she going to go away?" she asked.

"No," I said. "At least, not if she apologizes."

"But I don't want Grant to miss her," she said, and she looked worried.

"It's okay, honey," I said. "Daddy and I will take care of it. Don't worry."

"Okay," she said.

She seemed to accept that as an answer and went back to coloring. I wish it were that easy to just trust someone else when they told me not to worry. When Michael came home, we talked about it a little bit more and agreed to talk to Helena in the morning before she started work.

"I feel like I failed Anna," I said to him as we waited for Helena to come in. "Like I haven't been paying attention to her as much as Grant."

"Well, you caught this and hopefully nipped it in the bud," Michael said. "So I wouldn't worry too much."

"I hope so," I said as we waited for Helena to come.

I didn't deal with having hard conversations with people on a daily basis, so I was a bit nervous. Michael, however, hired and fired people occasionally, and he didn't seem too concerned.

"Hello?" Helena said when she came into the kitchen. When she saw Michael, she smiled widely "Why, hello. You aren't normally home. How are you?"

"I'm okay," Michael said. "Can you have a seat, Helena? We'd like to have a chat."

"Of course," Helena said and looked between the two of us. "Is everything okay?"

"We just wanted to have a chat with you,"

Michael said. "Cynthia has noticed some issues she'd like to bring up."

I gave him a look because I felt like he was throwing me under the bus. However, it did make sense that I was the one who noticed the issues since I was the one who was home with her all day.

"It's just . . ." I gathered up my courage and thought of Anna. "We've noticed that you are a bit short and dismissive with Anna some days, and that's concerning."

"With Anna?" she said. "Well, Anna doesn't listen to me and I'm just doing my best to keep her safe."

"I understand that you feel that way," I said. "But Anna doesn't have special needs and she is growing into quite an independent young woman."

"I'm sorry," Helena said. "I forget that some-times, I admit. I get so used to dealing with Grant, who's such an angel, that when Anna misbehaves, I forget that she is able-bodied."

"Uh . . ." I would call my son many things, but I wouldn't call him an angel. "Well, I think that you need to understand that Anna needs to be handled differently than Grant."

"Of course," Helena said. "And I will do my

best to make sure she doesn't feel like she's living in her brother's shadow."

"Uh . . . good," I said and glanced at Michael. I honestly hadn't expected this sort of attitude from her.

"Great," Helena said and looked between us. "So, we're all good?"

"Uh . . . sure," I said. "If that works for you, Michael?""

"I think it was a good chat," Michael said.

"Michael, can you come upstairs with me before you leave for work?" I asked him.

He looked confused, but he agreed. As soon as we were upstairs in our bedroom, I shut the door.

"Why did you throw me under the bus?"

"I didn't throw you under the bus," he said. "It makes sense that—"

"I know it makes sense," I said. "I'm the one home with her all day. But we could have presented like a team."

"I'm sorry," he said. "I didn't mean for it to come off that way."

"Okay," I said and dropped my shoulders. "To be honest, I don't think that went well."

"No?" he said, confused. "You don't think so?"

"She wasn't receptive to feedback," I said. "And it's clear that Grant is her favorite."

"Well, yeah," he said. "But isn't that a good thing?"

"I . . ." I paused. "I mean, she's supposed to be here for Grant. I just expected her to treat them a little more equally."

"But they aren't equal," Michael said. "And Grant needs Helena a lot more than Anna does. So of course she's going to play favorites."

"You think I have nothing to complain about?" I asked him.

He sighed. "I think you were right to bring it up," he said. "And now that we have, it's dealt with, and hopefully, we can move on."

"Yep," I said.

He looked me in the eye. "Is there anything else?" he asked.

I shook my head. "No, I guess that's it," I replied. "I know you have to get to work, so you should go."

"Okay," he said and then paused. "I love you, Cynthia. You know that, right?"

"I know," I said. "I love you too. I just want to make sure everything turns out okay."

"Well, my darling, you can't control the future,"

he said as he gave me a kiss on the head. "But I'm pretty sure everything will be okay as long as we just keep working together."

With that, he was gone. I wanted to point out that he didn't exactly work with me during that conversation, but I decided to leave it. I couldn't go into this situation with a sour attitude or it would be Grant who suffered most of all. We'd seen a situation, we'd dealt with it, and hopefully, Helena would change her ways. And hopefully, my husband wouldn't sleep with her because she had beautiful red hair and looked like a super model.

I glanced at a picture of us on the bedside table. It was many years ago, and we looked so young. His arms were wrapped around me from behind and he looked so happy. I hoped that we'd always be that happy.

Chapter 12
MICHAEL

I KNEW THAT GRANT WAS DUE TO HAVE ANOTHER episode very soon, since he was doing so well. At least, during the day. The fact was that at night, he was having nightmares nearly every night. That told me that the episode was coming with a vengeance. It was only a matter of time, and the fact that it hadn't happened yet was a surprise.

I came home early from work, and I'd planned to take the family out to dinner. I was just waiting until Helena finished her work hours and then we were going to get ready to go.

I heard Grant cry out and then I heard him shriek and start demanding something from an invisible presence in the room. I heard a crash from the living room, and I started to run over to him.

For a moment, I couldn't find him, and I was worried that he'd hurt himself or worse. I spun around the room, and then I saw Helena, already in the corner of the room. She was crouched down and talking to Grant slowly and calmly. She was rubbing his hand, and she was smiling.

He didn't normally break things when he had an episode, and the fact that he was surrounded by shattered glass worried me. Helena, however, remained completely calm and started to rock him once he looked like he'd returned to a more lucid state.

I stayed in the center of the room and just watched. I knew that too many people standing around him wouldn't help. It took a few minutes, but eventually, Grant returned to normal. He smiled at Helena and began to carry on a conversation as if nothing had happened.

It took a few more minutes before he was willing to play on his own, but he was soon back to his normal self. Cynthia had joined me in the room and both of us looked at Helena in awe.

"That was awesome," I said. "How did you do that?"

"Oh, practice," Helena said as she stood up. She still had a watchful eye on Grant, but she wasn't as tense as she had been a moment ago. "He'll be fine. Let me get a broom and clean this up."

"Okay," I said. "But I'd really like to know where you learned that."

When Helena came back into the room, she began to sweep up.

"So . . . where were you educated?" I asked as Cynthia went to sit by Grant and make sure he was really okay.

"A tiny little school," she said. "You wouldn't have heard of it, but they had one professor who was just a miracle in early childhood psychotic episodes and such. I think he had a personal connection."

"Oh," I said. "Where was that?"

"Midwest," she said. "You wouldn't have heard of it. Gosh, I hope this wasn't a family heirloom or something."

"Uh, no, it's fine," I said. "And why did you choose to specialize in childhood schizophrenia? It's so rare."

"My husband's family had some issues," she said. "Sorry, I don't like to talk about my past too much."

"Of course," I said. I felt like I was invading, even though I had every right to ask as her employer. "I just think that the program you must have been in was so good that I should give it a shout out to other parents with kids like mine."

"Oh, no," she said. "I'd be so embarrassed. Besides, sometimes, you just meet a kid you connect with."

"Well, it certainly seems that you connect with Grant," I said. "So I guess we got lucky. How many people were in your class?"

"It was just me," she said. "No one wanted to take the program, as I said. They didn't think it was worth it. They thought there would be no jobs."

"Oh, that's odd," I replied. "I didn't know that there were . . . so few people. I thought that people would be chomping at the bit to take a rare program."

"Turns out, they weren't," she said. "I think it's shut down now, to be honest."

"Oh," I said. "So I can't call the school and tell them what a great job you're doing?"

"I'm sure you could call them," she said. "But I doubt anyone would care. It was such a small program, and it was many years ago."

"How many years ago was it?" I asked, curious.

"A lady never reveals her age," she said with a smile. "There, everything is cleaned up."

"Thank you," I said and turned to Cynthia. "Do you think he'll be ready to go soon?"

"I think so," she said. "What do you think, Grant? Are you ready to go out for dinner?"

"I'm starving," Grant said.

Cynthia smiled and picked him up. "Let's go get you dressed, then," she replied. "Thanks for everything today, Helena."

"It's my pleasure," Helena replied. "You know that Grant is my favorite person in the whole world. Aren't you, Grant?"

Grant smiled and waved to Helena as Cynthia carried him upstairs. I let her out the front door and then went up to make sure Cynthia and Grant were okay. She was singing softly to him as she helped him get dressed. Cynthia had a beautiful voice, and I thought it was a shame that she didn't sing more often.

"What was that line of questioning?" she asked me as she helped Grant get a new shirt that'd be suitable for where we were going.

"What?" I asked. "I was just curious about her education. I wanted to know more because you have to admit, she's pretty awesome at her job."

"Yeah," Cynthia said. "But if there's one thing

I've learned about her, it's that she doesn't want to talk about her past."

"It must have been terrible," I replied. "But I mean . . . she must have gone to school somewhere, right? There's no way that you could be that good and not go to school?"

"That's true," Cynthia said. "It's the one thing I never questioned. You don't learn how to deal with children like Grant without being trained."

"I guess she really does want to keep things quiet," I said with a shrug. "It shouldn't matter to us. I just want to make sure she isn't in danger."

"Why would she be in danger?" Cynthia looked at me suspiciously.

"Well, because of the fact that she is hiding from her mother?" I reminded her. "And she wants to be paid in cash?"

"You know, I've toyed with the idea that it's not her mother," Cynthia said, "but her husband, the father of her boys."

"Oh," I said. "You think?"

"I don't know," she replied. "Because I could have sworn she said he was gone, and then said he was dead, and then she talked about him from time to time. So I just have a lot of questions that aren't appropriate to ask."

"Can't we ask her those things?" I replied. "As employers?"

"I don't know, Michael," she said. "I've never hired anyone before. Why don't you tell me?"

"I've never hired anyone in this sector before," I said. "And obviously, when they're living in your home, the rules are different from when you just see people at the office every day."

"Yeah . . ." she said. "You know, it's not too late."

"Not too late to what?" I asked.

"Have her not live here," Cynthia said.

I sighed. "It is too late," I replied as Grant ran off to play. "Besides, you see what good she's doing. It would have taken us an hour to stop that meltdown."

"Yeah, I know," Cynthia said with a sigh. She headed to our bedroom and I followed her up. "I wish we were better at it, though."

"Maybe Helena could teach us?" I replied. "To at least handle things a little bit better when she's not here?"

"Maybe," Cynthia said. "But if she's living here, then there's not much of a point, is there?"

"I don't view it like that," I said. "I think there's

a point. Besides, Helena isn't going to be with us forever, is she?"

"Well . . ." Cynthia said. "Some days, you make it sound like that."

I sighed.

"I'm going to go see if Anna is ready," I said. "Then I'll start the car."

"Okay," she said. "I'm sorry, Michael. I'm not trying to be difficult This is all really hard for me."

I paused by the door.

"I know," I said. "It's not easy for me, either."

"I just wonder if we're doing the wrong thing," she said. "I want to be the best parent I can be, and this feels like giving up."

"Cynthia, you're a nurse," I said. "You know that as good as any parent is, they can't replace a doctor. You would never say that if Grant needed surgery or something."

"No," she said. "But this is different."

"I don't think it's too much different," I said. "Your heart is just all tangled up in it."

"Of course," she said. "He's my son."

"Cynthia, my heart is right there with you," I said.

She smiled. "I know. Thank you for always keeping me on track and grounded."

"I'll see you downstairs," I said and headed down the stairs. Anna was sitting at the table, and she was dressed and ready to walk out the door. "Hi, baby."

"Hi, Daddy," she said. "Are we leaving right now?"

"Not yet," I said to her. "But soon. Mommy is just getting ready."

"What if I'm not hungry?" she asked.

I sighed. "Well, maybe you'll feel hungry when we get to the restaurant," I said.

I was worried about Anna because as she got older, this picky eating spell could turn dangerous. She was at the age now where the media could easily influence her, and I didn't want that. She was beautiful, and I wanted her to feel like she never needed to change.

"Can I just stay home?" she asked.

"No, you can't stay home alone," I said.

"That's probably okay," she said. "Because I don't want to run into any of Grant's imaginary friends. They're scary."

I paused and asked the next question very carefully.

"Anna," I said. "Have you ever talked to any of Grant's friends?"

She gave me a look. "No," she said like I was stupid.

"Okay," I said. "You're sure?"

"Yes, I'm sure," she said. "Grant's friends are scary."

"They are?" I asked her. "Why?"

"Because they tell him to do dangerous things," she said. "And I don't like that."

"Why don't you like it?" I asked.

"Because they tell him to hurt me," she said.

I felt my blood run cold. "Do you ever . . . feel afraid of Grant?" I asked.

She shook her head. "No," she said. "Because he says that he'll never hurt me."

"He will try his best to never hurt you," I said. "But sometimes, he isn't aware of what he is doing."

"I know," she said. "But somewhere deep down, in his heart, he would never hurt me, right?"

"He would never hurt you when he knows who you are," I said carefully. "But sometimes, he doesn't even know who I am."

"That's sad, Daddy," Anna replied.

I sighed. "I know. But we're doing our best to make sure that he is better."

"I know," she said. "I just don't think he's going to get better."

"Oh," I said. "I'm sure he will be."

"Right," she said, although she seemed like she didn't believe me. Frankly, I didn't even believe me, so I didn't know why she would.

"Anyway, let's get ready to go."

All we could do was just try to keep moving forward, even though I didn't know how we would in some moments.

Chapter 13

CYNTHIA

I WAS ABSOLUTELY EXHAUSTED. MY EYES WERE barely open, and I felt like I was dragging through the day. I felt embarrassed because I knew that Michael had to work full days and I couldn't even manage to handle the kids. However, I knew that I had a bit of an excuse with Grant, even though I felt like I shouldn't. As far as I was concerned, I didn't have any excuse over a normal parent.

I really wanted to know where this came from. Grant was sick, and it didn't make sense that it was just a random thing that had to happen. Childhood schizophrenia ran in families, and you didn't just get it on your own. It had to be somewhere, buried in our family lines.

"I think I'm going to email some people I

haven't talked to since our wedding," I said to Michael one day. "This doesn't make any sense. I want to know where it came from."

"Does it make a difference?" Michael asked. "The point is, he has it."

"I know," I said. "But if we find which family it's in, we can at least warn the future generations. I know I have at least three cousins getting married and you have at least two. They should know before they have kids."

"I suppose," Michael said. "If you had known . . . would you do something different?"

"I, uh . . ." I knew what he was asking. "Well, no. I love Grant."

"I know that," he said. "But at the time, you didn't know it was Grant. You would have just known that you had a baby with possible childhood schizophrenia."

"If you had known, would you do something different?" I asked him.

"Well, I don't have the medical knowledge that you do," he said.

I glared at him. "Michael, this isn't about medical knowledge," I said. "If you had known Grant would be like this, would you still have him?"

"Of course," he said, but I had a feeling he was lying. "Would you?"

"Of course," I said, and I wondered if he knew that I was lying. I wasn't saying that I didn't want Grant the way he was. But as a medical professional, I knew the dangers of childhood schizophrenia. I remembered reading about it during my studies, and it wasn't a good picture.

"Well, okay then," he said and looked down at his phone.

"Michael," I said to him, and he looked up, confused.

"What?" he asked.

"I'll need you to email your family, too," I replied. "Anyone who is blood related. I need you to ask them if it runs in your family."

"But if neither of us have heard of it . . ." he said.

I shrugged. "You never know how far back it could be," I said. "We need to ask. We need to know."

"Okay," he said.

I saw him open a new email. I reached for my phone, and for a few minutes, both of us were absorbed in our phones, sending emails out to anyone we knew whom we were related to. It gave me hope that we could get to the bottom of it, but also hope that perhaps we could reach out and connect with someone who had a similar struggle.

At least, I thought that we could figure it out, but as the emails started to come back, we realized that it wouldn't be as easy as we thought. The emails all said that we were basically alone. Our relatives were surprised, and each one said that they didn't have any idea what we were talking about. I grew more and more crestfallen, given what was coming in. No one was reporting any sort of even minor mental illness.

"This can't be right," I said to Michael. "This runs in families. None of the other factors that could lead to it were in play. Olive wasn't malnourished, she didn't do drugs, and she wasn't exposed to any toxins. Her pregnancy was perfect. It's got to be genetic. Someone has to be hiding something."

"I had a thought," he said. "And I hate it, but I think I need to mention it."

"What's your idea?" I asked. "Because this doesn't just happen on a fluke."

"No," he said. "But because Grant was a surrogate child . . ."

I paused. "You think that he got it from Olive's genes?"

"I don't know," he said. "I mean, is that even possible?"

I winced and tried to think.

"I don't think so," I replied. "I'm not a doctor and I don't specialize in genetics, but it was my egg and your sperm. Who the host was shouldn't matter unless they took drugs or were exposed to an autoimmune disease, and we know she didn't and wasn't."

"I know, he said. "They explained the concept to us. But what if it wasn't your egg? Or my sperm?"

"What do you mean?" I asked.

"What if . . . something went wrong and it was actually someone else's genes in there? And we didn't exactly look into Olive's family history— there was no need—maybe it was her genes?"

I took a deep breath.

"It can't be," I said. "Olive had dark hair."

"It's not like you have red hair," he said. "And neither do I. That's why I said maybe it's a completely different egg or sperm that they used."

"I . . ." I paused. "Mistakes like that are unlikely, Michael, aren't they? They have to be so unlikely."

"I know. But it would explain things."

"Perhaps we should call Doctor Andrews," I said. "Just for reassurance."

"I think that's a good idea," Michael said. "Even if he has nothing new to tell us."

"Well, that's something," I said. "If our relatives are telling the truth, then it has to come from a mistake at his clinic."

"Well, do you want me to call them?" he asked.

I shook my head. "You have a job to do," I said. "And I have nothing to do, especially while Helena is here. I think I should call them."

"Okay," he said. "If you don't mind."

"I don't mind," I said. "I promise, I'm going to get to the bottom of this."

It took me a few days to actually make the call because I was nervous. Then, when I finally got up the courage to get things done, Dr. Andrews wasn't available. However, after much phone tag, we figured it out.

"Cynthia," he said. "How is my favorite client?"

"I'm okay," I said. "But there is something I wanted to speak to you about."

"Oh?" he asked. "Do you want to add another beautiful child to your bunch?"

"No," I said. "Not right now. I was just

wondering if you still had the paperwork on Olive, our surrogate mother?"

"Olive?" he asked. "I may have. I'm sorry to tell you, Cynthia, but Olive passed away many years ago."

I felt a lump in my throat. Of course, I knew that, but hearing someone say it out loud brought back all the pain.

"Do you have confirmation of that?" I asked. "Because all I ever knew was that they pulled her car from the river and that was it. They said that they assumed she drowned, but they never found the body."

"I am reasonably certain she's dead," he replied. "I just have a feeling, and as a doctor, you have to trust your gut."

"Right, of course," I said. "But regardless of whether she is dead or alive, do you have the paper-work for her?"

"I do," he said, and it sounded like he was a bit nervous. "What can I look up for you?"

"Well, I was just wondering," I said, "whether childhood schizophrenia runs in her family."

Dr. Andrews paused for a moment and then burst out laughing. "What?" he asked "Why would that matter?"

"Because Grant has severe childhood schizo-phrenia," I said.

"So?" he said. "That is impossible. Your egg and Michael's sperm produced that child, so perhaps you should look within your own family."

"We did," I said. "We dug deeply and asked so many people. However, no one came back as even knowing what it was. I asked distant cousins who I am pretty sure aren't actually related to me. They didn't find anything, and it's the same with Michael."

"So . . . what?" he asked. "You think Olive switched the eggs or something?" He laughed out loud at that. "That's ridiculous."

"Is it, though?" I asked. "Because childhood schizophrenia is inherited ninety percent of the time. The other factors are drug use of the mother or exposure to an autoimmune disease, and we know Olive didn't do drugs and had a very healthy pregnancy. So this doesn't make any sense unless something like that happened."

There was a long pause on the other line before he spoke again. "Cynthia, are you completely sure that—"

"I'm completely sure," I replied. "I asked literally everyone in my family and Michael's. I'm telling you, something went wrong."

He paused and then took a deep breath.

"Well, I can look and get back to you," he said. "But don't expect it. It's so rare that anyone will laugh at me when I try to dig up data."

"Why don't you let me worry about being laughed at?" I said. "And you can worry about whether my son is really my son."

With that, I hung up the phone and stared at it. My hands were shaking, and I was terrified that Dr. Andrews would call back with what seemed like the truth. There was no other way Grant could have gotten this.

Just to satisfy myself, I sat down at my laptop while Helena was working with the kids and started to research. There was nothing on the internet about childhood schizophrenia being caused by anything except those few things we'd already looked at. No other possibility existed. It had to be genetics, like his red hair.

Maybe someone in my family was lying, and I had just accused a lovely doctor of a terrible thing. Or, if there were a mistake, maybe it was a very honest mistake and I had gone about it horribly wrong.

After all, Olive had dark hair and dark eyes and Grant had neither of those things. While it was true that it could be a recessive gene or something, I was pretty sure that there was a good chance he was genetically unrelated to one of us.

I briefly wondered whether we could test his DNA. Unless there was a court order, I had never heard of a DNA test happening. However, I wondered if they would consider our unique circumstances as a reason to perform a DNA test. I wondered if this was something I had to take to court in order to figure it out. I was pretty sure it wasn't. There were those Ancestry DNA testing sites. We could maybe use one of those?

I kept hoping for an easy answer, but the more I researched, the more I realized there wasn't going to be an easy answer.

"So, he sounded guilty?" Michael asked me when he came home.

"He didn't sound guilty, per se," I said. "But he did hang up the phone pretty quickly."

"Oh," he said. "So . . . then something probably happened."

"I don't want to think that way," I said. "But there is a pretty good chance that we . . . aren't

Grant's parents. At least, a pretty good chance that one of us isn't Grant's parent."

"Don't worry about it," he said. "It doesn't matter."

"But . . ." I said.

He shook his head. "Listen," he replied. "Does it matter who Grant's biological parents are? He's still our son."

"I know," I said. "But . . ."

"Cynthia." He took my face into his hands and looked right into my eyes. "It doesn't matter," he said after a few moments. "It doesn't matter."

I sighed. "I know it doesn't. I know it doesn't. But at the very least, getting to the bottom of it would make me feel less like a failure."

He smiled at me. "Cynthia, you have never failed anything in your life," he replied. "So don't think that you are going to start now."

I enjoyed Michael's faith in me, even if I didn't have faith in myself.

Chapter 14
MICHAEL

I HADN'T REMEMBERED THAT I HAD A CALL WITH Tom until I got into the office. As soon as I saw it on the schedule, though, I got excited.

Tom was one of my department heads, and although I wasn't supposed to be playing favorites, he was no doubt the one I was the most invested in. I'd hired Tom as an intern ten years ago, and now, he was the one I had the most faith in. Although I had VPs and people who assumed that they would take over the company, Tom was the one who I thought had the most know-how and the most creative mind. Currently, he was in Tokyo, over-seeing a project. He had been there for two months, and he was going to be there a little while longer.

He was a good guy with a family back home, and I was surprised when he agreed to go over to Tokyo to run the project. He said it was his lifelong dream, and I was happy to send him on the trip. Today was just a check-in, and I was happy to have a moment alone just to shoot the breeze with him.

"How are you?" I asked. "What time is it where you are?"

"It's almost nighttime, the next day," he replied. "How are you?"

"I'm okay," I said. "But you know how things are back home. Everything is boring here. I want to know how you are and how things are going on our biggest project to date?"

"Everything is going pretty well," he said. "I think the client will expand and keep us for another few months. He said he has some other projects he wants us to work on."

"Wow, that's great," I said. "When you get the details, pass it to the sales guys right away."

"I will," he said. "And I wouldn't mind staying out here. It's fascinating and beautiful."

"Really?" I quirked an eyebrow. "Don't you miss your wife?"

"Of course I do," he said. "But this is the experience of a lifetime."

"Well, maybe not if it's a regular contract," I said. "She must trust you an awful lot. And hey, must be difficult to stay faithful with all those beautiful Japanese women around."

"Oh," he said. "I mean, I love my wife."

"But how would she know?" I knew I was crossing the line, but I had questions.

"Well, I think she would know physically," he said. "I can't tell you how or why . . . I just . . . she would know, somehow."

"Oh?" I asked.

"Why are you bringing this up, dude?" he asked. "Something wrong?"

"No, nothing is wrong, exactly," I replied. "I just . . . there's a situation at home."

"Oh, no," he said with a groan. "What happened?"

"Nothing's happened yet," I replied. "It's just that . . . I don't know. Things are weird."

"Are you and Cynthia hitting a rough patch?"

"We weren't," I said. "At least, we weren't until the hot nanny came into the mix."

"The hot nanny?" he asked with a chuckle. "This sounds like a cliché waiting to happen."

"Yeah, I know," I replied. "And I don't want it to be that way. We needed some extra help with

Grant so we hired someone. And it's just our luck that she was the best person and specialized in childhood schizophrenia. Like, how do we find something like that?"

"I understand," he said. "And she just happens to be hot?"

"Super-hot," I replied. "Like red-headed super model hot."

"Ooh," he said. "That's tough."

"I know it is," I said. "And every day, she's around."

"What are you going to do?"

"Well, firing her is not an option," I said. "I don't have grounds to, and in addition, she's perfect for Grant, especially in the mess of everything that is happening."

"You mean the fact that she is super-hot?" he asked.

"Well, there's that fact and then there's the fact that she . . ." I paused. "She has pretty much shielded Grant from the fact that Cynthia and I aren't sure who his parents are."

"What?" Tom asked. "Back up."

"It's just, the sicker he gets, the more Cynthia and I look into this disease. And the truth is, for the most part, it runs in families. We couldn't find it in either of ours."

"Sure," he said. "But that doesn't mean it's not hidden somewhere."

"We're pretty sure it's not," I said. "We come from a pretty open family, and it's just . . . not there."

"Well, yikes," he replied. "So you think something happened when he was born?"

"Switched before birth," I said. "You know Grant was a surrogate baby. We think something went wrong there."

He let out a long breath. "Dude, I'm sorry," he said. "That must suck."

"We aren't entirely sure," I replied. "But something doesn't make sense. Cynthia is on the case."

"Well, is there anything I can do to help?" he asked.

I shook my head. "No, but thank you for asking."

"I mean, if I weren't a million miles away." He laughed. "I should go, Michael. Let me know if anything goes down, though."

"I will," I said and hung up the phone. It felt nice to talk to someone and at least get that burden off my shoulders, even if it didn't go anywhere. I wished I had someone who was in the same position as me, to at least share my feelings, but it wasn't like this was a common thing.

At least, I didn't think it was a common thing.

I was supposed to be working, but my mind kept drifting back to Grant and his genes. Before I knew it, I had opened up *Google* and was checking a few forums. I knew I was supposed to attend a meeting, but my mind was diving deeper and deeper into a rabbit hole. I wanted to know if this had ever happened before or if Cynthia and I were just being delusional.

I found a forum for a support network of those who had children through surrogacy. I clicked on a few threads, but it didn't seem like there was anything similar until I came across one.

She isn't actually my daughter.

I clicked on it right away. Sure enough, the forum spoke about exactly what we suspected. Someone who had a daughter through surrogacy had experienced all sorts of symptoms that didn't seem to run in the family. The more they dug into the case, the more they found that the daughter was actually born from the egg of the surrogate mother.

There were other cases of custody battles

between surrogate parents and birth parents, especially ones where the egg of a surrogate had been used with the father's sperm. It was complicated and confusing and not at all what I wanted for my little boy. Despite everything, Grant was still my son, and I wouldn't change that for the world.

At least, I thought I wouldn't change it for the world. I would change how sick he was, but until medical science game up with a cure, there wasn't much I could do on the matter.

I emailed the forum to Cynthia, knowing that she would want to know what was happening.

She emailed me back within the hour and then called my office phone.

"So it's happened to other people," she said.

"Well, these people say it's happened to other people," I replied. "They don't seem to have any medical proof."

"This makes me so mad," she said. "We signed so many papers. We paid so much money."

"Cynthia, you don't even know that's the case yet," I said to her.

"No, I don't know that's the case," she replied. "But the more I think about it, the more it makes sense. I mean, Grant doesn't look like us. Neither of us have it in the family."

"Have we thought about DNA testing?" I asked.

"I have," she said. "But how? Where?"

"There are places that will do it for a fee," I said. "They are private, so we just have to pay for them."

"Can we?" she asked.

I paused. "Do you really want to know?" I asked. "Does it make it any better?"

There was a long pause on the phone and then Cynthia sighed.

"No," she said. "I guess it doesn't."

"Exactly," I said. "So if it doesn't matter . . ."

"Right . . ." she said. "I guess I don't really want to know. I'd be terrified to find out the results."

"Good," I said. "Because honestly, darling, it doesn't make a difference to me either. It's not like it's going to make him better."

"No, I suppose not," she said and sighed. "Are you coming home soon?"

"No," I said as I looked at the clock. "But I'll text you later."

"Mmm," she replied. "You know, some days, I miss the days when it was just you and me, alone in a tiny apartment. No kids, no jobs . . ."

"No good," I pointed out.

She laughed. "Yes. But there were dreams."

"Oh yes, so many dreams," I answered. "And look, one of them panned out. Because despite all our problems, I'm happy with you."

I was trying to be sweet to her because I regretted the thoughts I had that morning. She seemed to understand, and she blew me a kiss through the phone.

"I'm happy with you too," she said. "I should go."

"Bye, love," I said and hung up. I was already late to my meeting, but I didn't care. I was the boss. No one was going to fire me.

I decided to check another forum to see if anyone had similar thoughts on the issue. There were a few cases here or there, but I noticed there was already someone arguing adamantly that it wasn't possible, that doctors didn't make mistakes, and whoever it was who felt that way should get off their high horse.

It was sad, and I knew I was wasting time. Eventually, I decided to get up and head to the meeting, which I was very late for. Everyone applauded when I came in, which made me feel a little more like a jerk.

"Sorry," I said. "Just had to deal with something at home. Let me catch up on what is happening."

I sat down at the head of the conference table and started going through the paperwork on the company. I realized quickly that this was our financial meeting and that I really should be paying attention. My mind, however, would not stop drifting back to the situation with Grant.

She didn't want to know, and I said I didn't want to know. Grant was safe, and he was happy. Helena was going to be moving in soon, and our lives would change, but hopefully for the better.

I was curious about Helena's two children, with her as a mother. All I knew about them were that they were twins, and they had red hair like hers. She hadn't said too much about them because she mentioned she wanted to keep her time at work focused on Grant. I wondered if they would get along with the kids or keep to themselves. I wondered how they would get to school.

Most of all, though, I wondered how I would keep my mind off Helena now that she was going to be under our roof twenty-four hours a day, knowing she was sleeping just underneath me.

I told myself that I had no indication she even liked me, so I had to move on. Thoughts plagued me, though, and I groaned inwardly when I realized the meeting was only half over. This way would never end.

And likely, if it did end, Cynthia was not going be there to relieve my frustration. I would have to take care of it myself.

Chapter 15

CYNTHIA

I COULDN'T BELIEVE THAT IT WAS FINALLY MOVE-in day. We had talked about it happening for so long with Helena that it didn't seem possible that we had at last reached that time. I wouldn't say I was excited because I wasn't. But I was relieved that Grant would have more help. I was relieved that I didn't have to worry about her coming in when we're going out or arranging things with her. We had made up a schedule that we thought was going to work well, and we had spoken to both the kids about work-life balance. I wasn't sure either of them understood, but it would be difficult at first with two families living under one roof.

I didn't know much about her boys, other than one was named Terrance and the other was named Roman and they were both around our kids' ages. It would be interesting, having other children in the house, but I didn't mind too much. We had separate spaces, and we weren't going to get in each other's way. The only difference would be when the children were playing together. I wasn't sure whether they were going to manage to be the best of friends, but it was worth a try.

"Now, you remember," I said to Grant that morning as I gave him his morning medications, "that once Helena comes in today, she isn't leaving?"

"Yes," Grant said. "She told me that she is going to move in and stay with us forever."

"Well, I don't know about forever," I said. "But she's certainly going to be around for a very long time. Do you feel like you're happier when she is around?"

"Yes," he said with a grin. "And all my friends are too."

"All your friends," I said cautiously. "Are they the ones who want you to kill people?"

"Yes," he said casually, like he was talking about dinner.

"What do they say these days?" I asked.

"They just say that they should listen to Helena," he said.

"Well, that's good," I replied. "Because they should listen to Helena."

"Yes," he said. "So they do."

"Good." I finished giving him his medication. It wasn't so much of a fight today, which made me sigh in relief. Some days, I couldn't get anything down his throat, and I could certainly see the difference. Of course, his medication also hadn't been working as well as it used to. He had more and more episodes, and he didn't seem to swallow them as often as he used to. "Now, go and play."

Just as he was getting off the bed, I heard Helena come in the front door. I took a deep breath and headed to the front entry hall in order to greet the roommate that I didn't really want.

"Hello, hello!" Helena said as she walked in. Her two boys were at her side, and they were adorable, I had to admit. One was lankier than the other, but they both had her eyes and coloring.

"Hi," I said. "These are your boys?"

"Yes, Terrance and Roman," she said. "Boys, say hello to Miss Cynthia."

"Hello," they both said. They didn't look terribly excited to be living here, but then, maybe I wouldn't be terribly excited to just uproot my house and home either.

"So," she said. "Shall we get settled in and then I can get to work?"

"This is normally your day off," I said. "So you don't have to work today if you don't want to."

"Oh." She looked a bit crestfallen. "If I'm honest with you, I was pretty excited to do some work today."

"Oh," I said. "Well, I mean . . . don't you want to get settled first?"

"Of course I do," she said. "But I want to see Grant first."

"You want to see Grant before you get settled?"

"I just want to introduce him to the boys," she said. "It's pretty important that we do that right away."

"Sure." I didn't see any harm in that, and I let her go and get Grant. Michael was outside in the garden, and I assumed he was working. My husband was a workaholic, and he was always working, it seemed, even on his days off. I wondered if he had somehow rubbed off on Helena.

"So, darling," I said to him as I sat down in a chair beside him. "We officially have roommates."

He smiled at me as he continued to type on his laptop.

"I don't know that we should look at it like that," he said. "After all, she is going to be living in her own apartment."

"That's true," I said. "But we are adding in room and board and we're not going to be changing her salary. Isn't there something about including room and board in a salary?"

"Well, technically," he said. "But honestly, does it matter? It doesn't really seem like we pay her very much, anyway, in the grand scheme of things."

"No," I agreed. "It doesn't. I just . . ."

"Besides, can you really tell her that there is going to be a cut in salary, with those two little boys?" he asked. "Twins, can you imagine?"

"Do you know, when I was pregnant with Anna, I started to wonder if I was having twins? I felt huge."

"Well, you looked beautiful," he assured me. "The whole time."

"You're just saying that." I blushed.

He leaned over and kissed me. "Nope," he replied. "I loved you the whole time."

"I hope you loved me the whole time," I replied.

"Because I carried that girl around for nine months."

I was joking and he knew it.

"Well, I think you did a fantastic job," he said. "Are they playing inside now?"

"They are," I said. "I thought I'd give them some time. Did you talk with Helena about her set hours?"

"Yeah," he said. "And I talked with her more about a work-life balance. Everything is going to be fine."

"I hope so," I said and sighed. "I mean, regardless, this is such a big adjustment."

"It kind of is," he agreed. "But at the same time, everyone on the forums says it's a good idea."

"Everyone on the forums?" I quirked an eyebrow at him. "What forums?"

"Oh, sorry," he replied. "The childhood schizophrenia forums. Wow, I sound like a freak with no life."

"No." I grinned. "You sound like a father who loves his child and wants to research more."

"Mmm," he said and nuzzled up to me.

We stayed like that for a few minutes and then he gently moved away. I knew that he had work to do, so I got up and headed into the house. I wanted to be as non-intrusive as possible, so I headed into the kitchen to cut up some veggie snacks for the kids' lunches. I was trying my hardest to be a better mom when it came to things like that, especially because there was no excuse to just not do it now that Helena was around. Yes, she could have done it for me, but I didn't want to completely lose touch with parenting. I still wanted to stay as the dominant female figure and not be one of those moms who just didn't do anything.

I was listening to the play date happen in the living room, and while Grant and the twins seemed to get on famously, it seemed like they weren't really including Anna. She was trying her hardest, and she was being polite, but it seemed like she was shut down at every opportunity. When she finally came into the kitchen, I made sure to make her a special shake and give her a hug.

"How are things going out there?" I asked her.

"Terrible," Anna said.

"Terrible?" I replied. "That's not good. Why are they terrible?"

"Because the twins are stupid," she said. "And Helena is mean."

I paused as I cleaned up the kitchen.

"What do you mean?" I asked her. "Have they done something to hurt you?"

"No," she said. "They just won't pay attention to me. And whenever I ask Helena for help, she doesn't help."

"Okay, thank you for telling me," I replied. "Do you think there's anything more you can do?"

"No," Anna said. "I think I'm being very polite."

"Well, I think you are too," I said. "Sometimes, especially when boys are that age, they don't get along with girls. However, that is no reason for Helena to be mean to you."

"Can you talk to her, Mommy?"

"Yes," I said and gave her a hug. "And you know that Daddy and I already talked to her once."

"I know," she said.

"Did it make a difference?" I asked.

She shook her head no.

"Okay," I said. "Don't worry, darling. Daddy and I will take care of it."

"Thank you," Anna said and wrapped her arms around me in a hug.

I hugged her back. "I want you to tell me if it ever happens again, though," I said. "No one should be mean to you, and no one should be rude to you. If they don't want to play with you or if they hurt you, you tell me, okay?"

"Okay," she promised. "Can I go to my room and read?"

"Yes, you can," I said and sent her off. I watched her go with sadness before turning back to what I was doing.

Had I made a mistake letting Helena move in? Had this all been a mistake?

The truth was, though, I had no specific proof that she had been mean or dismissive to Anna since we talked to her. It was true, Grant was her favorite, but that was technically what was supposed to happen. I couldn't force her to not play favorites. I could, however, ask her to make things a bit more equal.

In addition, I couldn't force her boys to play with Anna. I knew boys could be complicated at that age, so I didn't want to say anything right away. I wanted them to have a chance to get used to living in a house with two other kids, and then I might say something if things continued to go downhill.

There was only one other misgiving I had about Helena, and that was Michael's clear attraction to her. I thought it would fade with time, but he still made goo-goo eyes at her whenever she walked in the door.

I tried to tell myself that I couldn't blame him. He was a red-blooded male and she was quite attractive. As long as nothing happened, and that included inappropriate language, he was allowed to look.

That was the logical part of me. The illogical part of me wanted to put blinders on him and forbid him from doing anything. I knew that I couldn't, but I wished there were ones that came in human size.

"Everything okay?" Michael asked as he came in from the garden for lunch.

"Oh, yeah," I said. "Everything's fine. Why?"

"You just had that look on your face," he said. "That look that you only get when you're thinking really hard."

"I was just . . ." I shook my head. "Don't worry about it. I'm sure it's just moving day jitters."

"Sure," he said and took me into his arms. "Because if you're not too nervous later, maybe we could explore like it was our own moving day."

"What . . ." I started and then paused when he kissed me. "Oh. Oh, I see."

"Exactly," he replied. "What do you think?"

"Maybe," I said as I kissed him back. "Maybe."

I knew things with Michael weren't perfect, but I was going to make the best of things. My husband loved me, my kids were happy, mostly, and my house was beautiful. There were many who had much less, and I wasn't going to wallow in misery. I was going to enjoy being in my handsome husband's arms, and I was going to let him kiss me.

Chapter 16

MICHAEL

We had worked out what we thought was the perfect schedule. Helena would work with Grant and Anna in the mornings before school, helping them get ready, then in the afternoons from three p.m. to seven p.m., except on Grant's half days, when it would be from eleven a.m. to seven p.m. On weekends, she worked ten a.m. to seven p.m., and she had scheduled days off and room for emergencies. She seemed happy with the routine, although we were only a week in, so there wasn't much to complain about. It meant that we could still have weekend mornings and evenings together as a family, and Helena could spend time with her own two boys. The last thing I wanted was to take away her family time, knowing how precious mine was. She also seemed a lot happier and less tired, because her commute was simply up the basement steps. She got her kids off to school and then came up to see us. It was perfect.

Having her live here meant I could see her every day, and I didn't panic about not seeing her when she went home at the end of every day. I hadn't realized how attached I was to her, although I tried to remain professional. The truth was that Helena was a very comforting presence and I liked having her around. She was good with Grant and she fit perfectly into the family. There was nothing that she wouldn't do, it seemed, even when I told her she didn't have to do it. I knew that Cynthia had a few causes for concern, but I didn't really see it. I knew that Anna didn't really get along with the boys, but if I were truthful, I wouldn't have gotten along with girls at that age, either. I figured it was just an age thing, and they would eventually realize that girls were pretty cool.

When I headed out into the garden that morning with a late cup of coffee, I was surprised to find that Helena was already there.

"Well, hello," she said to me. "You found my secret spot."

"I'm sorry," I replied. "I can go inside if you'd like some private time."

"No, no, it's fine," she said. "I'm happy to sit and talk with you. We don't get to talk very often."

"No," I said with a smile. "We don't."

"So?" she asked me. She was wearing jeans and a tank top, and I couldn't believe that she was a mother. She looked gorgeous, slim and yet curvy in all the right places, with wide eyes and a perfect smile. "What's new in the world of Michael?"

"Nothing," I said. "When you run your own business, you devote every second to it."

"That's true," she said. "I understand that. For a while, I tried to run my own business."

"You did?" I responded in surprise.

She smiled. "I did," she said. "It wasn't very successful. It was just a cleaning business. But I thought, hey, why not?"

"Oh," I said. "That's awesome. And did you get tired of it?"

"Basically," she replied. "I was trying to do it and go to school and raise kids, and it just . . . wasn't working."

"Yeah, I know what you mean," I replied. "That would be too much. I thought starting an architect business was going to be easy, but instead, it damn near killed me."

"Oh, but you're so successful at it," she said with a smile. "And you charm everyone you meet."

I chuckled. "I don't know about that," I said. "But I try. The thing with running your own business is that there are people who rely on you. So you have to do everything you can to make sure that they are taken care of."

"Do you mean your family?" she asked.

I shrugged. "My family, my employees. It's scary."

"I understand," she replied. "Being on my own with two little boys hasn't been easy."

"It seems like you've done a fantastic job," I said. "They're well adjusted and pleasant."

"Well, that's a plus," she replied. "I know they aren't perfect, but children are never perfect. We just love them anyway, eh?"

"That's right," I said as I looked at her. In the morning sunlight, she looked like some sort of angel.

Frankly, I hated that she looked this way. Every time I felt like my attraction to her was cooling off, things kicked back up into high gear whenever I looked at her.

I needed to find a way to get rid of some of this frustration. What I could do was step up my sex life with Cynthia, and hopefully, that would help. We had sex often, but it wasn't often enough to kill my constant lust for Helena.

I needed to be better than this.

"I think I'll head inside," I said as I finished my coffee. "See you later."

"Bye," she said with a smile.

I let myself into the screen door and headed into the kitchen, where Anna was working on her homework. She was so focused that I hated to interrupt her, and I was prepared to tiptoe around her. However, just I was about to leave the room, she looked up with a smile.

"Hi, Daddy," she said.

"Hi, sweetheart," I replied. "What are you working on?"

"Just math," she said. "I actually really like math, but everyone hates it."

"Oh," I said as I sat down beside her. "Well, that's okay, isn't it? Who cares what everyone else thinks?"

"I do," she said softly.

"Sweetheart," I said. "Do you know what

people said to me when I wanted to start my own company?"

"No. What did they say?"

"Well, they said I was crazy," I replied. "And they said that I could never do it. They said that I should think about just working for someone else, and there were a million other architect firms out there."

"Oh," she said. "But you did it anyway."

"I did," I replied.

She smiled. "I wish I could be like you, Daddy," she said.

I touched her arm. "You can be, kiddo," I said. "Because you're my daughter."

She grinned at that and leaned down to work on her homework again. I sat with her for a little bit, checking my phone and contemplating making another cup of coffee, when I heard the boys, Terrance and Roman, coming upstairs to head out the door for school. Even though they didn't say anything to her, Anna's face fell as she worked.

"Hey," I said. "What's the matter?"

"Nothing," she said. "They're jerks."

"Why are they jerks?" I asked.

She shrugged her tiny shoulders. "They are just jerks," she replied. "And I don't like them."

"Oh," I said. I knew this had been her complaint before, but I wanted to make sure it wasn't getting worse. "Have they said anything to you?"

"No," she said. "They haven't. They just ignore me."

"Well, who wants to play with boys, anyway?" I asked.

She smiled. "That's true. Boys are icky."

"Yeah, they are," I said.

She giggled. "But Daddy, you're a boy."

"Oh, yeah," I said. "I forgot. Do I count?"

"Hmm," she said. "No."

"Good," I said and kissed the top of her head. "Because I don't want to count."

"I guess I should get ready to go to school too," she said. "Is my driver taking me today or is Helena?"

"Yes, your driver will still be taking you and picking you up," I said. "Helena will need to get her kids to school in the mornings. She'll go to get Grant on his half days and her boys will ride the bus home, but you still get to go with your driver."

"Okay," Anna said and then got up. She was easy to please, and just as she was about to leave the kitchen, something clicked in my head.

"Hey," I said to her. "Don't you want to eat?"

"No," she replied. "I'm not hungry."

"Anna," I said. "You need to eat."

I often worried about her, and I knew Cynthia did too. It seemed like she never had an appetite, and when she did, she wanted one specific thing and wouldn't settle for anything else. Feeding her was pretty complicated sometimes. When she said she was hungry, it was an Olympic event to feed her before the window closed.

"Well . . ." She looked torn. "Do we have apples?"

"We do have apples," I said and practically dove for the fridge. I found several different kinds of apples, including her favorite, the juicy red ones, and handed them over. "Boom."

"Wow," she said. "You're magic, Daddy."

"That's what I try for," I said with a grin.

She took the apple and went up to her room, and I hoped that she ate it.

"Why is Anna juggling an apple?" Cynthia asked as she came in.

"Was she juggling it?" I asked. "I was trying to feed her, and I guess . . . she took matters into her own hands."

"Well, at least she has an apple near her," Cynthia said and yawned.

"Did you not sleep well?" I asked her.

"No," she said. "I haven't been sleeping well for a while."

"I feel guilty," I said, nuzzling her neck. "Like I should at least be contributing to that."

She chuckled. "Well, I mean, if you are so inclined . . ."

"Baby, I am always inclined," I replied. "I just don't know when you want it."

"Always try," she said and leaned into me for a kiss.

"Oops, I'm so sorry," Helena said as she came into the kitchen.

Even though Cynthia and I weren't doing anything wrong, we pulled apart.

"I was just going to check the schedule to make sure that Grant was on a half day today."

"He is," Cynthia said. "I told you that yesterday."

"I know, but my memory is terrible," Helena said with a chuckle. She went over to the schedule on the fridge and took a look. "Yep, half day today. Sorry to interrupt."

"It's not a problem," I said to her as she left, but Cynthia glared at me. "What?" I asked her.

"You could tell her to be more cautious before just barging in," Cynthia said.

I raised an eyebrow. "I mean, I could," I said. "But it's not like the kitchen has a door. And she has a real reason for coming in."

"I know," Cynthia said. "It seems like she has a real reason for coming in a lot."

I sighed. "Babe, is everything okay?" I asked. "I thought we were past this?"

Cynthia met my eyes. "Sure," she said. "Sure, we're past it." With that, she left the room.

I sighed and went to get my own apple out of the fridge. She said we were past it, but we clearly weren't. Whatever was going to happen, it would have to be when we weren't going to be interrupted by Helena.

I saw the clock on the fridge and realized the kids had to get to school, and soon.

"Anna!" I called up the stairs. "Grant!"

I really should go to work, but I wanted to make sure they were off before I did, to relieve some of the pressure off Cynthia.

"I'm not ready!" Anna called down the stairs.

"Well, you're going to have to be ready soon," I said. "You'll be late!"

"I'm not ready either!" Grant said.

I sighed. "I'm coming up," I said after a few moments, when neither of them said they were coming down. If they were going to be late, it was going to be because something unexpected happened. Being slow to get dressed was not unexpected, and I wanted them to know that. "You'd better be ready."

"I don't want a cherry!" Grant screamed suddenly.

I sighed. He was clearly having a hallucination and I needed to step in before it got worse. It wasn't even close to the time Helena was going to take over, but I wished I could call to her now. I knew Cynthia had misgivings, but we needed her around.

Chapter 17

CYNTHIA

I couldn't believe that I just had sex with Michael for the third night in a row. This hadn't happened since we'd gotten married. When we were dating, we were horny all the time for each other, but as we got older, with children, it went from twice a week to once a week to once a month, and then for a few months, nothing. Sometimes, I initiated and he didn't want it, and sometimes, he initiated and I didn't want it. This week, however, it was like we were perfectly in sync. Everything was right. Everything was perfect, except for Grant.

I wasn't angry at Grant. I loved Grant. But Grant was starting to have more and more melt-downs. He was refusing his meds in the morning and refusing his meds more at night. Everything was a fight, and the meds that I did get into him weren't working. I was exhausted, and staying up late or waking up early to Michael loving me was wonderful, but I also wondered where that motivation came from.

I was starting to wonder if it was because Helena was in the house. She was beautiful, of course, and I knew that Michael was watching her. I had already told him in no uncertain terms that I would be watching him, but I knew that wouldn't matter. He had done it once before, so I worried he would do it again. I worried that he would find a way, if he really wanted to, to cheat on me.

I wanted to trust him. I wanted to make sure that he was mine and only mine. I also didn't want to start a pointless argument because I had absolutely no proof that there was even an issue. Michael had not been gone for unaccounted for periods of time. He had not found a way to sneak off, and he was completely attentive to me all the time. I should be over the moon, and I knew that I shouldn't be looking for small inconsistencies wherever I went. I knew I should be happy, but instead, as I told my fears to Cally over lunch one day, she told me why I was afraid.

"You're afraid of things being perfect," she commented.

I quirked my eyebrow. "What?" I asked. "No, I'm not. That's silly. Who's afraid of things being perfect?"

"You, apparently," she said. "Cynthia, listen to me. Think of all the times that things have gone right in your life. Think of your wedding. Think of graduating nursing school. What did you do?"

I forgot that I had told her about those times.

"I freaked out and said that there was something wrong," I replied. I felt like I was a dog and should hang my head in shame.

"Exactly," she said. "And then what happened?"

"Something became wrong," I answered. "But Cally, this isn't like those times. Michael is acting like we're dating."

"You know, maybe he's just fallen back in love with you," she said. "There's nothing with that."

"Does Steve do that to you?"

She shrugged. "I mean, we go through periods, but so does everyone. Sometimes, he's loving and attentive, and sometimes, he's terrible. But it's the same with me. Sometimes, he's the sexiest man on Earth, and sometimes, I can't stand him."

"Yeah, but it's never been like that with Michael

and me," I said. "Sometimes, I love him and some-times, I'm in love with him. I have never been anything but a wife to him."

"No," Cally said. "You are far more than that. You're the mother of his children. You're his rock. You can't just decide that he doesn't want you."

"I know he wants me," I replied. "But I think when he closes his eyes, it's actually Helena he wants."

"And you never fantasize about the sexy man on TV?" She quirked her eyebrow at me.

"I mean . . . sometimes," I said. "But never when I'm having sex with him. Always when I'm . . . you know, alone."

"Ha," she said. "You're missing out. Fantasizing is part of a healthy relationship. Didn't they teach you any of this in nursing school?"

"Apparently not," I replied. "In any case, it doesn't matter."

'Yes, it does matter," she said. "And you're not going to sit there and act like it doesn't. You're going to march home and have sex with your husband."

I blushed at that. "Can I at least finish my lunch first?"

"I guess," she said, and we dug into our salads and giggled.

This was why Cally was my best friend. She got me in more ways than I ever got myself.

"How are things with you and Steve?"

She nodded. "Good," she said. "They're good. He says he's going to whisk the kids and me away for a weekend in the Alps, and frankly, I'm not going to complain."

"Wow, that's so lucky," I said. "I wish I could do that."

"Why don't you?" she asked. "I mean, you guys have the money and all."

"I know we have the money," I said. "But it's not exactly money that's the problem."

"What is it?" she started and then realized what it was. "Ah, Grant."

"Yeah, he doesn't take well to changes of scenery," I replied. "It's best to keep him in his routine and in his environment."

"Surely, now that you have a nanny, things could be different?" she asked me.

"Like Helena could come with us?" I asked.

"Or she could stay home with the kids?" Cally asked. "It sounds like you and Michael really need a weekend away."

"We do really need a weekend away," I said. "But I don't think we could do that."

"Pfft, what is the point of having a nanny then?" she asked.

"Cally, it's not that easy when you have a child with special needs," I said. "You can't just leave them with someone else."

"So you don't trust her?" Cally asked.

"It's not that I don't trust her," I said. "She's great with Grant. It's just, she's got kids of her own . . ."

"She lives in the same house," Cally pointed out. "And no doubt you are paying her a ridiculous amount of money. You can do this!"

"I don't know," I said. "Where would we go?"

"What do you mean, where would you go?" Cally asked. "You could go a million different places!"

"I don't want to be gone very long," I said. "Listen to me, already planning an imaginary trip. Anyway, I don't think I can do it."

"You can," Cally said. "I know you can."

I sighed and smiled at her. "You, Cally, are an inspiration. You're always pushing me out of my comfort zone."

"I'm pushing you into wedded bless," Cally

said, "which is where you belong. Michael is a catch."

"I know that, and you know that," I said. "And half the women who see him think that. More like seventy-five percent, if I'm being generous."

She snorted. "Come on, Cynthia. Not even a weekend away to a country home?"

"I don't know," I said. "Maybe. I'll ask Michael. This weekend, I think we were just thinking of taking a joint family outing to the zoo or something."

"Joint family outing?" Cally raised her eyebrows. "You sound like one of those chicks who is accepting that her husband has a mistress."

"I'm not," I said. "And I meant with the nanny's family."

"I know," Cally said. "I'm teasing you. Don't listen to me. I'm sure it'll be fun."

"Yeah," I said and yawned. "That is, if I can get more sleep. Between Grant's nightmares and Michael's . . . you know . . . I can't sleep much."

"I mean, there are worse reasons to not sleep," Cally said with a shrug. "I hope we get our own chalet or something when Steve takes me away. I want to have hot vacation sex. Although any kind of sex right now would be okay with me."

"How long has it been since you two had sex?" I asked.

Cally snorted. "I dunno," she said. "I stopped counting. A long time. Too long."

"I know what that feels like," I said as the waiter came around with our desserts They were giant bowls full of decant chocolate ice cream, and I dug into mine with a vengeance. "This is great. We don't have ice cream at home."

"You don't have ice cream at home?" Cally looked at me like I was crazy. "Why? Diets?"

"Sort of," I said. "Helena suggested that Grant go on a gluten-free and sugar-free diet. She said it helps a lot of kids with his condition."

"So what, you just blindly listened to her and chucked everything out?" Cally asked. "Why?"

"Because . . . she's the expert?" I said. "And who needs ice cream and chocolate anyway?"

"Kids?" Cally suggested. "Grown women who need a break now and again? Hungry husbands?"

"No," I said. "None of those things are true. Helena explained it to me and . . ."

"For heaven's sake, Cynthia," Cally said. "I didn't say it was good for you. I just said it was good to have at home for a treat. Unless you don't do treats anymore."

"Apparently not," I realized. "God, what has my life become?"

"It's okay. It's not too late to fix it," Cally replied. "Just go home, have sex with your husband, and buy loads of chocolate."

I chuckled at that. "See, you always know the right thing to say," I replied as the waiter came with the bill.

Cally picked it up, and I protested, but she shook her head. "Nope," she said. "You paid last time. Besides, you're the one going through a rough time right now."

"I'm not going through a rough time," I protested, even though this was probably the roughest time of my life.

"Let me pay," she said. "Go home."

"Thank you," I said and gave her a hug. "Do you know that this is probably the most we've seen each other in a year?"

"Yes," Cally replied. "That nanny is good for something."

"I guess she is," I said as I checked my watch. "I really should get going."

"Bye, girl," she said, and I gave her a light air kiss. I headed out the door, but her voice echoed in my ear long after her face left my vision. Maybe she was right. Maybe I really did need a weekend away.

I called Michael before I got home, and he answered the phone quickly.

"Hello, lovely wife," he said.

"Michael, can you take me somewhere this weekend?" I said. "Even if it's just the zoo?"

"Haha," he said. "You want to jump in a cage with me?"

"I'll jump anywhere with you," I said. "But I was just talking to Cally and she was talking about going away with her husband. I know we can't go away, but I want to go somewhere."

"Sure," he said. "We're planning that outing anyway. It'll be an official date. Wish I could take you on a better one right now."

"Our time will come," I assured him. "For now, I'm just happy that we're going to spend the weekend together. I'll see you at home?"

"See you then," he said.

I hung up the phone. I felt like we were dating again. Maybe I really did need to get thoughts of Helena out of my mind and just focus on Michael and my family. Just because she was around didn't mean he wanted her more than me. Maybe he was thinking of me when he closed his eyes and maybe I was the sexiest woman he ever saw. Maybe he was thinking of someone we didn't even know. Or maybe he was thinking of Helena. Who cared, as long as he loved me and we were together? The rest could wait.

Chapter 18

MICHAEL

"HEY, EVERYONE," I SAID ON THE CHAOTIC Saturday morning after Helena had first moved in. All the kids were upstairs playing together, and it was a lot noisier than it usually was. However, no one was fighting, which the adults counted as a bonus. "Let's go to the zoo today."

That seemed to get their attention instantly. Everyone stopped and looked at me. Grant reacted first.

"The zoo?" he asked. "Daddy? The zoo?"

"Yes," I said. "Mommy and I can take you to the zoo!"

"Wheeeee!" He got up and flung himself into my arms.

I was glad that at least Grant was happy about

it. Anna looked slightly apprehensive, but she was at least willing to go.

"That should be a fun outing," Helena said.

I realized I hadn't been clear. "Oh, I'm taking everyone," I said, and her eyes widened.

"That's far too generous," she said. "Really, it's—"

"It's fine," I replied. "As long as you and the boys want to go."

"Of course we do," she said and turned to the twins. "Boys, go and get ready."

Both of the boys went to get their coats. I turned to Cynthia, who was on her third cup of coffee.

"You okay to go?" I asked, worrying about her.

She yawned but nodded. "Yep," she said. "Just let me chug this and I'll be ready."

"Just like the old days," I said. "Only that was . . ."

"Thanks," she said with a grin. "I'm aware." With that, she finished the coffee and went to get ready as well.

I was excited to go to the zoo, even though we went frequently. Helena and her boys had never been, and I was even delighted to see Terrance talking to Anna when we walked in. Neither one of them looked like they were fighting, which was a victory in my book.

"Well," I said to Cynthia as I looked at the map, "you want to make a deal? I'll navigate and you just keep an eye on the kids?"

"Sounds good to me," she said, and we started to walk. The zoo was huge, and navigation really did require most of my energy. I noticed Helena talking sternly to Terrance as we walked, but I didn't say anything about it. It wasn't my business if she decided to discipline her children, even if I didn't know what it was for.

We were just passing the bear cage when all of a sudden, I heard a shriek. I spun around, and to my horror, Grant had that glazed-over look in his eyes. He was climbing the wall to the bear cage, clearly in a full-blown hallucination. I wasn't sure who had shrieked, but I raced to the wall and grabbed him before he could tumble over the other side.

"Grant!" I said. "Grant, buddy, what are you doing?"

He looked at me, but it was pretty clear that he wasn't seeing me at all. He started to look right past me and headed right for the cage again.

"Grant." I picked him up so he would stop

trying to run there. "What's the matter? You can't go there, buddy. There are bears there."

"What happened?" Cynthia rushed over.

I raised an eyebrow. "I thought our deal was that you watch the kids," I said, feeling exasperated with her, "while I get us through the zoo."

"I was," she said. "I just—"

"No," I said. As the adrenaline wore off and thoughts of what could have happened flooded my mind, I got angry. "You clearly weren't watching them! Grant was nearly bear food just now!"

"I didn't think—"

"Well, that's the thing, Cynthia," I snapped. "You probably didn't think! Were you looking at your phone? Were you texting? Were you—"

"I was watching," she pleaded with me. "I closed my eyes for half a second. You have to believe me, Michael."

"You just closed your eyes for half a second?" I looked at her in shock. "Why would you think that was a good idea?"

My voice was raised, and I knew people were staring, but I didn't care. Cynthia wasn't watching him, and if I hadn't heard that shriek, Grant might be gone by now.

"I'm just exhausted," she said. "But it won't happen again. It's just—"

"No, it won't happen again," I snapped at her in frustration. "How could you be so irresponsible?"

She looked like she was going to cry. Normally, I would feel bad for yelling, but at this point, I didn't feel bad at all. Cynthia had nearly gotten our son killed because she wasn't paying attention. As far as I was concerned, this was her fault. It was the type of parenting we read about in the news and made fun of or said a prayer for because there was a tragic accident. We didn't take our eyes off our kids, especially Grant. She *knew* that!

"I wasn't being irresponsible," she protested. "I'm just tired."

"No, you don't get to just be tired! Not when something like this could happen!" I said. "I clearly can't trust you today."

"Why don't you give me Grant?" Helena swooped into our loud conversation. "I'll keep an eye on him. It's clear that you two need some time."

"Fine," I said and put Grant down. Helena took his hand right away. "I know that you'll watch him."

Helena and Grant wandered off to look at an animal and I turned back to Cynthia.

"You know she'll watch him?" she mocked me. "Because she's his mother?"

"At the moment, she's more responsible than his mother," I said. "I swear, Cynthia. We get a nanny so you barely have to do anything at all, and this happens!"

"You think that's why we got a nanny?" She looked at me in shock. "Because you think I want to be lazy?"

"Well, sometimes, it seems like that," I said, my tone harsh.

Cynthia shook her head. "I can't believe how condescending you are," she said. "There are other skills in life besides running a business, Michael."

"I know there are," I said. "And it seems that you don't possess them."

I walked away, leaving her standing there gaping at me. I didn't mean to be so mean to her, but I was so angry. What if I hadn't heard that shriek? What if something tragic had happened?

The rest of the day, Helena and I kept a close eye on Grant and the rest of the children. We didn't say anything to each other besides the usual small talk, but I couldn't stop making eye contact and smiling at her. I knew that when Helena was watching my son, I could actually look away to look at the animals for half a second.

When we got home, I managed to find a private moment to thank Helena.

"You don't have to thank me for anything," she said with a shrug. "Couples fight sometimes. It's normal."

"I know it's normal," I said. "But Cynthia . . . she just doesn't get it. She's a good mother most of the time, but sometimes, she just spaces out a little. I don't want to say anything mean about her—she's my wife and all. But sometimes . . . it's nice to have someone around who is responsible all the time."

"I understand your frustration," Helena said. "And Cynthia was sick for quite some time, wasn't she? Maybe she never recovered properly?"

I briefly wondered whether Cynthia had told her that. Maybe there was hope for their friendship, after all.

"Yes," I said. "Yes, she was. She almost died when Anna was born, and Anna almost died too."

"Oh, I'm so sorry," she said. "So you took a risk with having Grant?"

"Oh, we used a surrogate for Grant," I said.

She reacted in surprise. "Really?" she said.

"With a surrogate egg? Sorry, I'm just very interested in this."

"No, that's okay," I said. "We used our own . . . er . . . DNA, and the surrogate was just the host."

"Well, that's very forward thinking of you," she said with a smile. "And where is the surrogate now? Do you keep in touch?"

I could feel the sadness settle over my body. "We don't," I said. "You see, she uh . . . she passed away."

"Oh, I'm sorry to hear that," Helena said. "In childbirth?"

"No," I said. "She actually had an accident after Grant was born. They pulled her car out the river. They never found her body, but they assume . . ."

"Oh, my God." She put her hand to her mouth. "That must be terrible."

"Yeah, it was pretty hard on all of us," I replied. "Olive was basically family to us."

"Olive?" she said with a smile. "What an interesting name."

"She was an interesting person," I said. "She just . . . clicked with us."

I didn't want to mention that she particularly clicked with me, but luckily, Helena had more questions.

"Well, that was also very forward of you to let her be involved in your lives," she said. "How long did Grant have her in his life?"

"Well, he was just a baby," I said. "Barely a month old."

"Poor thing," she said. "To go through all of that."

I wasn't sure whether she was talking about Olive or Grant, so I just nodded.

"And she was happy with the arrangement?" Helena said. "Giving up her baby?"

"Well, it wasn't her baby," I said to her. "It was ours."

Helena's eyes darkened slightly. "Of course, genetically," she said. "But Olive must have felt a link with Grant?"

"I don't know," I said. "I suppose, since she was around so often after he was born, that she must have felt some sort of link. It doesn't matter now, of course. She's been gone seven years. Wow, I can't even believe that."

"Well," Helena said, "I believe in a higher power, and maybe they'll meet again someday."

"Maybe they will," I said. "Anyway, it doesn't matter now. It's late and I just wanted to say thanks again."

"Anytime," Helena said.

I headed back up the stairs. I wasn't ready to talk to Cynthia yet, so when I found Anna in the living room, I went over to her.

"Hey," I said. "Did you have a fun day at the zoo today?"

She nodded and I sat down beside her.

"What was your favorite animal?" I asked her, and it took her awhile to answer.

"Hmm," she said. "I think I liked the raccoons."

"The raccoons?" I said in surprise. "Anna, you can see raccoons anywhere."

"I know," she said. "But there's something about them. They are sneaky."

"And you like sneaky?" I asked.

She giggled. "Yes," she replied.

"Hey, I saw Terrance talking to you," I said. "I guess it was the first time he was nice to you, because you looked so surprised when he came up to you."

"I thought it was really weird," she said. "He's never talked to me like that before."

"Well, maybe the zoo brings out the best in everyone," I replied. "It's getting late. Don't you think you should go to bed?"

Ever since Anna turned nine, we were trying to

get her to be more responsible. That meant setting her own bedtime, for one, even if she ended up not getting enough sleep. Some nights, it worked and some nights, I felt like she needed some gentle prompting.

"I should," she said. "Good night, Daddy. Thank you for taking me to the zoo."

"Good night," I said and gave her a hug before she headed upstairs. I took over the spot in the armchair where she had been setting and leaned back. I briefly considered sleeping down here instead of going upstairs to reconcile with Cynthia.

All the marriage books taught you to never go to bed angry. It wasn't that I was angry anymore. It was just that I couldn't believe she had done something like that. I wasn't sure if she would do it again. What if next time, he made it over the bear enclosure just because she was tired?

Cynthia had always been responsible, but sometimes, her attention wandered. I worried about her being distracted and losing track of one of the kids. I was glad that we at least had Helena as backup.

Chapter 19

CYNTHIA

WAS I BAD MOTHER? WHAT THE HECK HAD happened at the zoo? Normally, I had my priorities in order. I paid attention to everyone. I saw everything coming my way. I had no idea what had happened at the zoo. I felt incredibly guilty, and I questioned my own ability to do anything. Maybe I shouldn't have been a mother. Maybe I was bad at it. Some women were just bad at it. Maybe I shouldn't be a mother. Maybe I should just walk away.

I knew that there was no way to just do that easily, but I felt completely depressed about the whole situation. I had no idea how to fix the situation. Michael didn't normally fight with me like that, but then, I didn't normally let my children down like that. He normally took all the pressure in stride and always smiled through everything. He'd never behaved like that before, especially in public. I didn't know what to do. I didn't know how to climb out of this hole.

"Mamma?" Anna asked.

I looked up. She hadn't called me that in a long time, and I was almost honored. She was standing in my doorway, and she looked quite sad.

"Are you okay?"

She smiled. "I'm okay," she said. "But you're not."

"Oh," I said. "I'm fine. I'm just a little bit sad."

"Because of Grant?"

I nodded. "Sort of," I said. "It's very complicated, and you shouldn't have to worry about it. This is something an adult worries about."

"I know, Mommy," she said. "But I want to help you."

"I'll take a hug," I said and opened my arms.

She gave me a hug and I wrapped my arms around her.

"How are you?" I asked. Making sure my children were okay was my top priority. At least, I thought it was my top priority, and that made what happened today even worst.

"I'm good," she said. "I'm just confused. I wanted to ask you something."

"Sure," I said. "What can I do for you?"

"It's Terrance," she said.

I knew exactly what she was talking about. "Is he being mean to you again?" I asked.

"No," Anna said. "That's what the confusing part is. It's not that he's mean to me . . . he wants to be friends with me."

"Oh?" I asked. "Well, do you not want to be friends with him?"

"I do," she said. "But his mother said no."

"His mother said no?" I quirked my eyebrow. "Why would she say no?"

"I don't know," she said with a shrug. "All I know is that he told me he wants to be friends, but Helena said not to."

I paused, trying to think that through. I couldn't possibly understand why Helena would say that, unless she didn't want my family to be bothered because she was living with us and working for us. Maybe she didn't want to bother us with a friendship that would no doubt make things complicated if we had to let her go.

I considered this for a moment longer and then decided it didn't matter. It was probably a quote that was taken out of context. I knew how children were, and I didn't want to pry.

"I'm sorry," I said. "That's strange, but I'm sure if you wanted to be friends with Terrance, you could make it work."

"So . . . we should just ignore what his mother says?" Anna asked.

I bit my lip. "It's not that I want you to ignore it," I said. "It's more that I want you to do what you feel in your heart. You know that I always tell you to follow your heart."

Anna smiled. "You do," she said. "And I love it. You aren't like other moms."

She gave me another hug and I decided to accept it as a compliment. I wasn't sure what else she could have meant, and I knew Anna was not a mean-spirited person.

"I'm going to go play," she said and disappeared out of the room.

I took a look in my mirror and ran my hands through my hair. I looked old and haggard. I felt like I had aged fourteen years instead of seven since Grant was born. I felt like no man could find me attractive and I might as well just give up.

This wasn't the first time that I'd had an identity crisis. When I was a nurse, I'd felt like I knew who I was. I had a career, I worked hard, and I knew exactly what I was going to do with my life.

At least, I thought I knew what I was going to do with my life. I had found Michael, and I had a child, and then I'd gotten so sick with Anna that I knew there was no way I could ever work again. I used to judge the women who did that until I got sick with Anna. Then, I knew there was no way, even though I wanted to. I missed my career very much, and I still remembered a lot of it. But I'd been so sick, and life was short.

But then, maybe it would be better for my kids if I went back to work and Helena took care of them all the time. Maybe I wouldn't bother them so much. Maybe I wouldn't fail them so much. Maybe I would be able to actually have them survive until adulthood.

"Penny for your thoughts." I was surprised Helena was upstairs until I noticed that she was standing there with several towels. She was bringing the laundry upstairs, which was sweet of her.

"Oh," I said. "It's nothing. I just needed to . . . have a few moments alone."

"Well, let me know if there's anything I can do," Helena said with a smile. "They say I'm pretty good at talking to people."

"Just really tired," I answered as she put the towels away in the linen closet.

"Maybe I could help," she said. "Maybe I could extend my hours?"

"Oh?" I said. "I don't—"

"I wouldn't want more money," she said quickly. "I just want to help more. You only have me working until seven, but I don't think it would hurt to do another hour or two."

"I mean, not much happens here after seven," I said. "We just give Grant his medicine and then put him to bed."

"Maybe he would be happy for me to put him to bed?" she said. "I would be happy to help. No increase in salary."

"Well, I . . ." I paused.

"I just want to help," Helena said. "So you could have a little more free time."

"I don't know," I said. "I'll talk to Michael and see what he thinks."

"Sure," she said with a smile. "But I think he would be okay with it."

"Oh?" I asked her. "How do you know?"

"Michael and I have discussed it a few times," she said. "And he's onboard."

"Oh," I said, confused. "Well, this is the first

I've heard of it."

"We didn't want to overwhelm you," she said.

I raised an eyebrow. "You didn't want to overwhelm me?" I asked. "The two of you?"

"Sorry, I don't want to overstep my bounds," she said. "I just think that you would benefit from something like that. At least promise me you'll think about it? For your own sake?"

I paused and then I sighed. "I'll think about it," I said at last. "For my own sake."

"Great," she said and headed back downstairs.

I paused and stared into the mirror again, fluffing up my hair and wiping away the makeup under my eyes.

I didn't walk around looking that overwhelmed, did I? I didn't really feel like I was that bad of a mother, did I?

I knew that mental illness was real, obviously. I knew that mental illness could absolutely sweep you away and prevent you from doing anything. Obviously, since my son suffered from mental illness, I knew that it could hurt you if you weren't careful.

But I liked to think I was stronger than that. I liked to think I was a superstar when it came to energy and juggling many different balls in one go.

However, this did not seem the case. It seemed

like I was going to be absolutely overwhelmed if I didn't do something.

Even though I knew it was the best option, I couldn't help but resist. I didn't want Helena in my life more. I didn't want Helena to find out what was happening after seven. I didn't want her to put Grant to bed.

But if I didn't let her, what was going to happen? Was she going to take over my life because Grant would get taken away from me? Was she going to overwhelm me with her kindness? Was I going to fail as a mother?

I didn't know what to do and I didn't want to put Michael in a position where he had to choose if he had already told her yes. Normally, I would be absolutely appalled if Michael talked to the nanny without me, but the truth was, I knew he was thinking about the children. He was going to make sure that the children were taken care, and I knew he would stop at nothing to achieve that goal.

That worried me. What if he wanted me out of the picture? What if I somehow wasn't part of this plan any longer?

What if I was going to have be the one to make the hard choices?

What would happen to my children? What

would happen to my house and my marriage if I couldn't keep them safe?

I was useless.

I tried to shake the thoughts out of my head because they were overwhelming. I knew this wasn't me—it was some chemical imbalance in my brain talking. I knew that if I didn't snap out of it, things would get worse and fast.

Maybe what I needed to do was get away for a bit with Michael. Maybe Cally wasn't completely crazy. Maybe Michael and I needed to reset.

I took another deep breath and then headed out the door and downstairs. I was going to talk to Grant, or Michael or Helena, whoever happened to be around. I wanted to make sure this was a good idea and get all the details. However, no one was around.

I listened and heard laughter coming from the playroom. I went to the playroom and saw Michael and Helena standing there with Grant. Grant was wearing his gorilla head mask and he was running between them, pretending to scare them. Both of them were laughing, and because Helena shared the same coloring as Grant, she looked like his mother.

They looked like a happy family, and something

remained deeply unsettled in my soul. I hated it. I hated how happy they looked. I hated that I couldn't smile right now.

"Hey," Michael said as he looked up. "Everything okay?"

"Yep," I said.

"Did you want to talk?" he asked.

I shook my head. "No," I said. "No, I'm going to bed."

"Oh," he said and glanced at his watch. "It's only eight."

"I know," I said. "I'm just really tired."

I didn't want to talk. I didn't want to smile. I didn't want to play. I needed to sleep, and hopefully, things would look much clearer in the morning. If they weren't, I was going to have to make some major changes, for both my health and my family's health. I cared about them more than I cared about myself, and something had to change.

Chapter 20

MICHAEL

"MICHAEL, CAN I TALK TO YOU?"

I had learned long ago that when you were a husband, those are words that you never wanted to hear. A wife generally didn't say them unless they were angry, and I could tell today that Cynthia was angry. It had been two days since we'd been at the zoo, and she'd barely spoken to me. She had the anger bubbling over the surface, and now, she couldn't resist bringing it out.

I frankly didn't want to talk to her because I knew that she was just going to yell. However, I knew that we had to deal with it sometime. Today, the kids were in the back yard playing with Helena, so this was technically the best time.

"Sure," I said. "What's up?"

Maybe I would get lucky and I'd be happy to just kiss and make up with her. From the look on her face, though, it was clear that was not the case.

"About the zoo," she said. "Were you just going to wander around not apologizing to me?"

"Excuse me?" I said. "Why should I be the one to apologize? You're the one who nearly got our son killed."

"This is ridiculous," she said. "You are constantly second-guessing my judgment and moving in favor of Helena."

"You think this is about Helena?"

I sighed. I knew that we were going to get into a big fight one of these days. I just wished she had waited a few more days until she calmed down.

Neither of us said anything for a few moments. We continued to glare at each other and then we took a deep breath at the same time.

"If it's about Helena, I'm a monkey's uncle." It probably wasn't the most mature thing to say, but it was all I could manage.

"What are you talking about?" she asked. "Why are you acting like an idiot?"

"Is that what you think?" I said. "See, this is classic, Cynthia. Anytime I joke around, you say that I'm acting like an idiot. It's not about Helena.

It's about the fact that you literally walk around judging others, but you can't get your own act together."

Her mouth hung open. "Are you serious right now?" she asked. "You think I can't get my act together? You can't pick your jaw off the floor whenever the nanny walks into the room."

"I wasn't the one who nearly got our kid killed by letting him climb into a wild animal cage!" I protested.

She looked like she wanted to slap me. "You have to stop blaming me for that," she cried. "I took my eyes off him for a second. I would have gone after him!"

"Would you, though?" I asked. "Would you really? Or did you just not care? I know that you wouldn't mind having a little more free time!"

"Did you seriously just accuse me of wanting to *get rid* of Grant?" I asked. "Our son?"

"Yes, but—" I started.

She shook her head. "No," she said. "No, I'm not dealing with this. Just like I'm not dealing with the fact that you walk around lusting for the nanny and then have sex with me while thinking of her."

"I don't—" I started, but that wasn't enough for

Cynthia. She knew it was true, and she held my gaze.

"I swear," she said, tears in her eyes. "If you ever touch me again, I'll divorce you."

"Because I yelled at you for nearly getting our kid killed?" I asked. "Yeah, that's real mature, Cynthia!"

"That's not the reason and you know it!" she cried. "You're so stupid that you can't even understand why I'm angry."

"You don't have a right to be angry!" I said. "I'm the one who has a right to be angry! I'm the one who has a right to second-guess your opinion! You are acting neurotic and more sleep-deprived by the minute!"

"I'm sleep-deprived because our son keeps having nightmares!" she shouted. "And you're the one who doesn't get up."

'What?" I asked, taken aback. "I get up in the middle of the night with him all the time."

"Maybe in your head you do, Michael," she said, tears streaking down her cheeks. "Or maybe you get up once. But Grant doesn't get up just *once*. Grant screams all night long, and you just don't hear it!"

"So now you are accusing me of not—"

"Stop," she said. "You know what I'm accusing you of."

"I sleep through nightmares," I said in exasperation. "I don't let the kid fall into a bear cage and die!"

"But he didn't die, did he?" she screamed at me. "He was just fine, and he would have been just fine! I was momentarily distracted, Michael, because I was exhausted! But I would have seen him! I would have saved him!"

"Would you?" I asked.

She looked around for something to throw at me. "I'm his mother," she screamed.

I could have said so many hurtful things in that moment. But instead, I kept my mouth shut.

"I'm sleeping in the guest room," she said at last. "Tonight and possibly every night for the rest of our marriage, however long that may be! Don't try and follow me!"

"I wouldn't dream of it!" I responded. "Not even for half a second! You're vile and rude, and you can't accept that you possibly made a mistake!"

"And you're a horny cheat!" she said. "Who's horrible at monogamy and can't even pay attention to the wife who gave him a child and loves the other one so dearly that she would give her own life up! I nearly died for Anna, Michael, and I would have died for Grant if that were the case! Both of them have my heart, my whole life!"

"Then why don't you act like it?" I asked. "Why do you insist on acting like a zombie mother who just wants to lunch all day with her friends?"

"I hate you," she said and stormed out of the room.

I resisted the urge to look for something to throw at her too. Instead, I gripped the counter and took several deep breaths.

I couldn't believe that she couldn't see her own mistakes. I couldn't believe that she didn't see what had happened. If that had been me, I would have been begging her a thousand times over to forgive me. I would have been asking her to give me something to do to prove that I wasn't a bad father. I would have been on my knees, begging God to make sure my son was safe in the moments that I'd failed.

Cynthia, however, just seemed to care that I was lusting over the nanny. I didn't know why she was jealous. It wasn't like she initiated sex. I was the one who had to instigate everything. I was the one who had to ask her to love me in the middle of the night, or anytime during the day. She just lay there like a limp rag doll. I was sulking and I knew it.

I didn't want to compare what Cynthia was with my thoughts of what Helena could be. First of all, that wasn't fair, and second of all, that was a road to disaster. Helena was not going to be my wife or the mother of my children. She probably wasn't even interested in me.

But at the same time, Helena was so lovely. Not only was she beautiful, she was kind and intelligent and smart. She was a creature who I couldn't stop staring at. Every time I looked at her, I discovered a new way that she was beautiful. Every time I looked at her, she smiled at me and I felt like my soul lit up.

I really did not want to go down the route with Helena that I was in danger of going. I didn't know that she didn't react that way to every man she met. I just assumed that she was kind to everyone . . . but maybe I was special.

"Penny for your thoughts?"

"Speak of the devil." I tried to smile as Helena came into the kitchen.

"Is everything okay?" she asked. "I heard raised voices and left the children in the back yard for a moment."

"Everything's fine," I said. "Cynthia and I just had a . . . disagreement."

"Ah, yes," she said. "Well, every couple fights."

She smiled at me, and I felt that familiar warming in my soul.

"What was it about?" she asked.

I paused. It wasn't that I was hesitant to tell her. I realized it was more that I didn't want Cynthia to overhear that I was telling her.

"It just . . . it was about the zoo," I said. "And how she sometimes doesn't pay enough attention in the real world."

"I'm sorry," she said. "I saw the incident at the zoo, of course. I wasn't going to say anything . . . but I really did feel like she wasn't paying enough attention."

"Thank you," I said. "I'm glad somebody backs me up."

"I'll always back you up, Michael," she said with a smile. "You and I, we're alike. We think alike and we move alike in life."

"Do we?" I asked. "How so?"

"Well," she said. "For example, we both decided that we wanted two kids at the same time in life."

I raised my eyebrow.

"Did I tell you when I decided that?" I asked.

She nodded. "You don't remember telling me that?" she asked. "It was late one night, the night we stayed up until two a.m. talking. You said you wanted two kids, and you knew you wanted that from the time you were sixteen."

I didn't remember telling her that, but it was true. "You decided at sixteen too, eh?"

She nodded. "I did," she said. "And life had a few other plans for me . . . but I got two kids."

"Yeah, but you got them in one go," I teased her. "You're lucky."

"Yes," she said. "You know, I was thinking the other day. I really am lucky."

"Well, yes," I said. "Your boys are beautiful."

"It's more than that," she said. "Yes, the boys are lovely. But I have a great job, a dream job that I've always wanted, and I have employer who is kind and sweet."

Our eyes met and I paused. I was about to say goodnight and go upstairs, but I knew I couldn't leave just yet. When our gazes connected, I felt like there was lightning coursing through my veins.

"Well, I'm glad that we found you," I said. "You've been a godsend, and you just popped up out of nowhere."

She smiled at that. "I guess it was a coincidence," she said, "or maybe it's fate."

"Either way, I'm glad you're here," I said. I waited another moment or two and then finally found the strength I was looking for. "I should go upstairs. I know it's early, but I have to get up at four a.m. tomorrow. You should bring the kids in. Would you mind putting them to bed after I give Grant his medicine?"

"Not at all," she said. "That's what I'm here for."

We both lingered for another moment or two, and eventually, she took a step back.

"Goodnight, Michael," she said and then headed out into the back yard and the setting sun.

It was quite late in the evening, and the sun seemed to last forever these days. It was early to go to bed, and I knew that I shouldn't. I was sort of a failure of a parent for not putting my kids to bed when I could. But I was just so soul-weary, and I couldn't take being around people anymore . . . not even my own kids.

What I needed to do was sleep. Hopefully, with a good night's sleep in a bed that was all my own, things would look better in the morning.

Once I'd given Grant his meds, I found myself

wishing that someone was joining me in bed, but I didn't think of whom. I didn't dare think of whom, just in case the world was about to change. There was no point in tempting fate when fate was seemingly coming to you.

Chapter 21

CYNTHIA

I had only lingered in the guest room for a few minutes before I decided that there were better choices than sleeping there alone. If I couldn't sleep with my husband, then I would stay in Grant's room to make sure that he was okay. After all, I had been pretty much spending half of my nights there anyway, so I didn't think that sleeping there would let me get any less sleep. Grant woke up once and was thrilled to have me there, so I assumed that it would be fine. At the very least, I could get to him very quickly when there was a nightmare. I hoped that the arrangement would mean that we got more sleep as a unit.

There were a few times where he woke up and had nightmares and was able to go back to sleep

because I was right there for him. I had never realized how unrestful his nightmares were until I
witnessed them from the very start. They started
with thrashing and then there was some whim-
pering and then he would usually start to cry out,
which was the part that I usually heard. He seemed
very frightened the whole time, and it broke my
heart because I couldn't imagine what he was
dreaming about. I had nightmares too, but I didn't
think they were ever that violent. They were usually
pretty sad and depressing, and I woke up crying.
However, I never woke up screaming. Screaming
was not something that I usually did. I held all my
pain inside, and if we were in another circum-
stance, I would commend Grant for letting it
all out.

Once in the night, I awoke to hear what I
thought were voices. They were whispering, and
when I cocked my head, I saw that they were
coming from the baby monitor.

The voices didn't sound like anyone I recognized, and they didn't even sound like they were
coherent. They sounded broken and they sounded
like they were giving orders.

It creeped me out at first, but I then remembered that sometimes, baby monitors pick up other

channels, so it wasn't that scary. What had more than likely happened was that we had some cross signals.

I reached up and turned off the monitor because we didn't need it when I was sleeping right in Grant's room. While I was awake, I stood up and looked over at my sleeping child, just to make sure all was well. For the most part, he was more peaceful when I was here. It was like he could sense my presence. I reached up and touched his little face and then lay back down.

A million thoughts were circling through my mind as I lay there. Was I ever going to make up with Michael? Was I ever going to have a good marriage again?

It wasn't that I strove for a perfect marriage. I knew that perfect marriages didn't exist and the people who pretended that they did were probably lying about what their favorite food was as well. I was always suspicious of my girlfriends who never complained about their husbands.

Mind you, I didn't complain about Michael very much. Up until recently, we had been doing quite well, and I thought that we were happy and content. Yes, he had been not entirely faithful to me, but that didn't mean that I was unhappy. It meant he was unhappy with me. Frankly, I also thought that it meant he was unhappy with himself, because if he could do that, he probably wasn't thinking very much about the repercussions.

I tried to not think about Michael's actions very much because I knew that I would never sleep if I did that. I needed to think about myself and my sleep and about Grant. Those were the only things that mattered.

I had managed to lure myself back to sleep when I heard another noise. I opened my eyes, and to my surprise, it wasn't the baby monitor or Grant. It was Helena standing there, with her eyes on me.

"What the . . ." I stood up. "Helena, what are you doing here?"

"Sorry," she said. "Sorry, I was just checking on Grant."

"Why were you checking on Grant?" I asked. "I'm up here."

"I didn't know you were up here," she said. "Sorry, apologies again."

I gave her a strange look.

"Well . . . even if you didn't know I was up here, I have the monitor," I whispered. "So this shouldn't be a problem."

"Sorry," she said.

"Helena, you need to go back to your quarters," I replied. "I will be sleeping in Grant's room for a few nights, so you don't need to worry about anything."

"Oh," she said. "Okay. Sorry."

She slinked away, and I felt like my privacy had been violated.

Why was she up here? What was the issue? Why did she think that my son needed to be checked on in the middle of the night? Why did she think she could walk into the upper floor of the house, which was traditionally private?

I shook my head and lay back down. My eyes were burning from being so tired, and I thought I might pass out if I didn't get some sleep. Still, my mind raced.

She was so good with Grant, but she was causing so many other problems. What was the issue?

Why did she not understand that she wasn't part of our family?

Was she really worth it?

These were the thoughts I went to sleep with, and they weren't good ones. When I woke up, I felt like I hadn't slept at all. I rolled over to glance at

Grant, who was completely cuddled up on his blanket.

He looked like a sleeping angel, but I knew that he wouldn't be when he awoke. He had such a restless night that I hoped he would at least manage to take his meds and have a good day at school.

I hauled myself out of bed and left the room, heading toward the bathroom. I just wanted to shower and have a fresh start to the day and try to smile.

Michael happened to be in the bathroom, shaving, and he scooted over to let me in.

"I'll be done in a second," he said.

This was always how it was when we had fights. In the morning, we would be civil to each other because at the end of the day, we were still parents and we still ran a household together. We needed to have a time to fight and a time to just be responsible people.

"It's fine," I said as I grabbed my towel. "Hey, I want to ask you something. Did you notice Helena coming upstairs last night?"

"What?" he asked, confused. "Why would Helena come upstairs?"

"Because she was checking on Grant?" I said.

"She said that she was just checking, but I felt like she was staring."

"Well, then she was just checking on Grant," he said. "What's the big deal?"

I looked at him like he had three heads.

"The big deal," I said, "is that this is the upstairs of the house and she had no reason to be up here in the middle of the night. I mean, even if I wasn't sleeping in Grant's room, I had the monitor on. She knows that. We've talked about it."

"Yeah," he said with a shrug. "But she's just doing her job."

"But that isn't part of her job!" I protested. "She doesn't need to do that."

"Cynthia," he said. "When someone goes above and beyond in my workplace, I don't yell at them for it."

"I don't feel like this is above and beyond," I said. "I feel like this is an invasion of privacy."

"So you want to talk to her about it?" he asked. "Or do you want me to talk to her about it?"

"Could you?"

He shrugged. "I mean, I could," he said. "But if I'm honest with you, I don't see your point of view."

"Yeah." I rolled my eyes. "I know. All you see is beautiful, lovely Helena, who could do no wrong."

"I don't think that's the case," he said. "The fact that you think my vision is clouded and I wouldn't want what is best for my children is a serious problem."

I sighed. I really didn't want to get into another fight, especially this early in the morning. I had to choose a different route.

"Okay," I said. "Fine. Whatever. I'll talk to her."

I practically slammed the shower door, which made him jump. I could hear him sigh and then go back to shaving. I turned the water on full blast and then put my head under it. I wished I could wash away all the stress and all the bullshit of the morning, but I couldn't. The worst part was that it was six a.m. and I had a whole day ahead of me.

When I finally got out of the shower, I toweled off and then headed downstairs. To my surprise, Helena was already up and singing as she made breakfast. She had her own kitchenette downstairs and didn't need to be upstairs making breakfast for me or my kids. It was supposed to be my private time, and here I was, expected to praise her for doing something nice for me.

"Hi!" Helena said when she saw me. "Eggs?"

"I'm okay," I said. "I'm just going to have some coffee this morning."

"Suit yourself," she said with a shrug. "I can make you something else?"

"Actually, Helena," I said, and she turned to me. She looked so earnest and so innocent that I actually felt bad about what I wanted to say.

"Yes?" she asked.

"Nothing," I said.

She looked so happy in that moment that I couldn't say anything. "Nothing?" she asked, humming. "It doesn't sound like nothing."

"It's fine," I said. "Maybe I will have eggs after all."

I could have kicked myself for being a chicken. Why wouldn't I tell her how I really felt? Why couldn't I tell her that I felt like she was infringing on my family?

I wasn't hungry, but I sat there and ate her eggs. I shoveled them into my mouth and then I gulped down my coffee. She seemed satisfied with that and offered me another round, but I shook my head.

"I'm full," I said. "It's fine."

"Okay," she replied. "But anytime you want more, you let me know."

"Thanks." I stood up and poured myself

another cup of coffee before returning to the bedroom. Now that Helena was there, I technically could spend all day in bed and not worry about a thing. She would take care of the kids, and I could just be myself.

Except I didn't really know who myself was anymore, nor did I know what I was supposed to do with myself for the rest of the day.

I took my cup of coffee and crawled back into bed. I was exhausted and I briefly considered going back to sleep. Instead, I turned on my phone and started to scroll through the social media feeds for the day. Maybe this was going to be my fate. I was just going to be a useless housewife who read her phone and drank all day while her nanny took care of the kids.

I didn't want that. I didn't want to even think that was a possibility, but I saw myself doing that and it worried me.

I didn't know how to get better, either. Maybe I needed help, or maybe I just needed to buck up and tell myself that I needed to be better. Before I lost my family to Helena.

I took a deep breath and downed my coffee. Maybe I would do that, but today was not the day. Today, I was broken and I was done.

Chapter 22

MICHAEL

I was managing to cope. I was managing to spend time with both kids and go to work and somehow deal with the escalation in tension between my wife and my nanny. I bet many people didn't have to say that. Grant seemed to be sleeping a lot more peacefully with his mother there, which solved a lot of our problems. Helena, on the other hand, seemed to dislike the fact that Cynthia was there, which did not make sense to me. Why would it matter to Helena what she did or how she did it?

I didn't want to ask, because frankly, I didn't want to rock the boat. If Cynthia and Helena were at slight odds, I could live with that, as long as they were civil to each other and had the children's best interests in mind. As long as they made sure to not argue in front of the children, I was also fine.

I realized that made them sound like a married couple, and I grinned. It was kind of like we were all one big family, which I approved of. I was happy to have her here and I was happy to have her work with Grant on some of his worst days. I had no idea why Cynthia was so upset.

I had no idea why everyone was upset, frankly, and I just didn't want to get in the middle of it.

"You're staying late," John, one of my employees, said as he stopped by the office.

I was still typing away and it was almost seven at night. "Yep," I said. "Just finishing up a few things."

"So dedicated," he said.

I shook my head. "No," I said. "It's just more peaceful here."

"Ah," he said. "Well, that I understand."

I snorted. "So . . ." I said. "What are you doing here so late?"

"Actually, just working," he said. "And my wife is out of town, so I have no reason to go home."

"Ah," I said. "For me, it's the opposite." I was honest with my employees because I felt like it made them honest with me.

John shrugged. "Well, that sucks."

"Eh," I said and gestured to my computer. "Lots of work gets done."

"Makes sense," he said. "Hey, how is your little boy?"

I briefly remembered that John had a son with learning disabilities, and we had discussed it on a few occasions. Of course, Grant was much different from a kid with learning disabilities, but we did find some similarities from time to time.

"He's okay," I said. "I don't think he had a very good day today, from what the nanny said, but he's fine."

"Hmm," he replied. "Do you think he would benefit from a play date? My little guy will be home all next week because his EA is out of town. Maybe we could get them together?"

"Uh, sure," I said. "Let me text the nanny and see what we can arrange."

"Text the nanny," he said with a smile. "You sound very fancy."

"Just trying to keep my life a little more organized," I answered. "And I have to admit, the nanny has been great in most areas."

"In most areas?" he asked. "So there are some where she's lacking?"

"Well . . ." I replied. "The part where she gets along with my wife."

"So the most important part," he said.

I sighed. "I mean, I guess," I said. "It's just a bit hard. Hence my being here."

"Yeah," he said. "I know what you mean."

"Eh." I shrugged. "It's fine. Get on home."

"See you tomorrow," John said and headed out the door. He was clearly exhausted, and I wanted to tell him something about the fact that I admired his work ethic or I admired his ideas. But I was too tired to do any of those things. I'd been here since seven a.m. and I didn't feel like I had accomplished much. I was managing, but I knew that I could be far more productive if I just didn't spend so much time thinking about the problems at home.

Eventually, I knew I had to go home or I would be completely overwhelmed. I was exhausted and exhaustion was usually the reason I broke down. I shut down my computer and was about to put on my coat when Helena texted me.

Hey, you, she said. *When are you coming home? I made a fantastic dinner.*

I smiled at that. Something like that brought me more joy than I realized.

I'll be home very soon, I texted back.

She made me smile in a way my wife had never done. Cynthia would never text me something like that. She would tell me to come home for dinner or I'd starve. And it wasn't necessarily done maliciously. It was done with the intent that we did things productively. She didn't want to waste time on dinner if I wasn't going to be home. I didn't want to waste time coming home starving if she wasn't ready for dinner.

She was tired, I was tired, and we were raising kids. I got it. But something about the way Helena did it made me smile.

I eventually got home and managed to hang up my coat before heading into the kitchen. Helena was there with an apron around her waist and a smile on her face.

"Just in time," she said as she pulled a pot roast out of the oven.

"Daddy!" Grant ran through the living room and hugged me.

I picked him up and put him on my hip before smiling at Helena. "That smells fantastic," I said.

She grinned. "Thanks," she said. "I mean, I didn't work too hard on it. But I tried."

"You didn't work too hard on it? It's awesome.

It looks like something a restaurant would have made."

"Oh, Michael," she said. "You're too kind."

"Nah, I'm just telling you the truth," I said. "And I wasn't hungry when I came home, but I'm hungry now."

"Great," she said. "Everything is almost ready."

"Where's Cynthia?"

She glanced upstairs. "She's been mostly upstairs until now," Helena said, which concerned me.

"I'll just go and see her," I replied and then put Grant down. "I'm just going to see Mommy, okay?"

"Can I come?"

I patted him on the head. "Nope," I said. "Not right now. Stay with Helena and I'll be right back."

If there was something wrong with Cynthia, I wanted to make sure she had everything she needed. We may be angry at each other, but that didn't mean I didn't care about her.

When I got into the bedroom, I was surprised to find her fully dressed and just sitting on the bed. She looked up at me in surprise.

"Hi," I said. "Everything okay?"

"Yep," she said and went back to reading the magazine she was reading.

"Uh . . ." I paused. "Helena says you haven't been downstairs all day."

"Is my presence required?" she asked. "Or am I allowed to live my own life?"

"Cynthia, don't be like that," I replied. "She was just worried about you."

"She has no right to be worried about me," Cynthia said. "I went downstairs, I ate her eggs, I let her talk to me about the day, and then I said I would be upstairs. What's wrong with that?"

"Well, nothing," I said. "It's just not like you to just sit up here and ignore the children."

"It's not like me to give up and get a nanny either," she replied.

I sighed. "Okay," I said. "What can I do to help? What's the problem today?"

"Nothing's the problem," she said. "I'm just tired and I felt a little sick. Am I not allowed to feel that way, Michael? Or do I have to sit here and just pretend like everything is okay?"

"Of course you don't—" I said.

"Or do I have to sit here and pretend like I'm a superhero, like you are?" she asked me.

"What are you talking about?"

"Well, frankly," she said, "you always make it out to be that anyone who isn't perfect and calls in sick even a day in their life sucks. And you never do that. You built this business from the ground up. You must be superhuman, and anyone who is anything less is a terrible person."

"That's not what I . . ." I paused. "I don't sound like that, do I?"

"Yes," she said. "You sound exactly like that, and so anyone who does less is a total asshole."

"Cynthia," I said. "If you need a sick day, you can have a sick day. It's not a big deal."

"With you, it's a huge deal," she said.

I rolled my eyes. "Okay," I said. "What else happened today?"

I didn't want to fight any longer, so I let her take control of the conversation.

"I had to take down the baby monitor," she said. "And the nanny cam."

"What?" I asked. "Why?"

"Because I kept getting crossed signals in the middle of the night. I kept getting signals that were like . . . weird voices."

"What?" I asked. "What are you talking about?"

"I would wake up in the middle of the night and hear weird voices, or I would think I heard something that wasn't there. I thought I was hearing things until I eventually realized it was coming through the monitors. I think that our signals are crossed with someone else's or something. And who knows how long that's been going on?"

"Oh, that's interesting," I said. "I'm glad you took them down."

"Oh?" she asked.

"Yeah. These things can be hacked."

"Hacked?" she looked worried. "By whom?"

"It depends," I replied. "This is a nice house and all. People might think we have a lot to steal."

"But we do have a lot to steal," she responded.

"Well, now we do," I said. "Once upon a time, the house was basically all we could afford."

She smiled. "I do remember that," she said. "I remember the fact that we used to have paper plates because we had those from the old house, and we couldn't afford real ones."

"Yep," I said. "And I remember having to borrow chairs from my parents' house whenever we wanted to have guests."

Both of us smiled at each other, remembering the past. Then, Cynthia got up from the bed.

"I guess I am feeling a lot better," she said. "I could come downstairs with you for dinner?"

"That'd be great," I said. "I'm going to order

new equipment. I don't want to take the risk that those have been hacked."

"Sure." She shrugged. "I especially want the new nanny cam first."

"Yeah, I'll see what I can do," I said. I pulled out my phone and started looking on Amazon for options. There were plenty of options, but I wanted the most expensive and the most secure. I could deal with things inside the house going haywire, but I could not deal with things outside the house going haywire. There was enough drama at home without any of that.

I ordered one and then I ordered a second one for backup. I was still a bit annoyed at Cynthia, but she was truly trying to bury the hatchet, and I had to try. I had to try because it would be easy for the family to fall apart if I didn't.

I ended up going downstairs after a few minutes, and when I went into the kitchen, I saw Helena first, rather than Cynthia. My smile was wide and it took a second before I even looked for my wife. When I did, Cynthia was glaring at me.

Five minutes. We couldn't even go five minutes without fighting. This was a problem.

"Sit down," Helena said to both of us. "Dinner is served."

Chapter 23

CYNTHIA

I KNEW I NEEDED TO CHECK IN WITH HELENA. I just needed to sit down with her and have a good chat, but for some reason, that bothered me. I didn't know why, so I continued to avoid it for nearly a week. When I told Cally I was procrastinating on it, she laughed at me.

"Are you afraid of your nanny?" she asked.

I shook my head. "No," I said. "I'm not afraid. I'm just . . ."

"Because that sure sounds like you are afraid," she said. "It sounds like you don't want to talk to her, and you don't want to deal with anything she touches. And that you can't even correct her when she's doing something wrong."

"I can do all of those things," I said. "It's just so

much stress, and you know what they say about stress and health. I've been feeling so off lately."

"Maybe you're pregnant," Cally said with a grin before she realized what she said. Her grin faded. "Oh, my God, I'm sorry."

"No, it's fine," I said. "It's fine. I know I'm not pregnant, so there isn't an easy reason for why I feel like crap."

"Maybe you're coming down with something?" Cally suggested. "You're the nurse. You should know these things."

"No, I think it really is just stress," I said. "I mean, these things happen when you're in a new situation."

"How's Michael doing?"

I sighed. "Fine. Great. He's over the moon. He loves Helena."

"Ah, but does he love her for the wrong reasons?"

I closed my eyes. "I don't know," I said as I took a sip of wine. "Someone once told me that if my husband was going to cheat, there was nothing I could do about it. I couldn't be nicer to him. I couldn't dress sexier. I couldn't make him look my way when his brain was tuned into someone else."

That was so frustrating because I liked being in

control. At least, I thought I liked being in control. Lately, it seemed like control was slipping through my fingertips.

"So . . ." Cally said. "What you're saying is it's not your fault he cheated, and you might as well just relax and not do anything about it?"

"It's *not* my fault he cheated," I said.

"No, I'm not saying it is," she assured me. "But what I am saying is that maybe you should consider doing something to make sure he doesn't have someone else to look at, at the very least."

"I can't lock him in the house," I cried.

"Maybe the house is the problem," she said.

I sighed. "I can't get rid of the nanny without looking like a jealous bitch. There's no reason to."

"Maybe there's no reason to," she said. "But it doesn't mean you can't do it."

"Oh, my God." I put my face into my hands. "You know, Cally, Michael and I started out with nothing. We weren't elite, we weren't upper class. We were just downright poor. And as we started to climb the social ladder, I told myself that I would never be the type of wife who did something like that. And yet . . ."

"And now you see why we do that type of

thing," she said with a grin. "Because they are actually justified."

"Yeah, I see that now," I said and then sighed. "But I can't just do that to her."

"Well, you have to talk to her," she said. "At the very least, you have to talk to her."

"I will," I said. "Let's finish lunch and then I'll go home and figure it out."

"Okay," she replied. "But you'd better text me to tell me all the details."

"Ha," I said. "Maybe."

I didn't know why it bothered me so much. It shouldn't have bothered me at all. But by the time I got home, I felt like there was a lump of fear building in my throat that hadn't been there before. Maybe it was because I was intimated by her. She was so pretty, and she always knew the answer for everything. Maybe I was afraid that if I said the wrong thing, she would just take my husband and run off.

Or maybe it was just because I had been a coward lately, and I didn't know what to do with anything anymore.

"Helena, could we chat?" I said when I got in. She was sitting at the kitchen table, knitting, and she seemed perfectly innocent and wide-eyed.

"Of course," she said. "Have a seat. What can I do for you?"

I felt like she was the mistress and I was the servant, and it bothered me.

"Actually, I just wanted to check in with you," I said, "and see how you were doing?"

"I'm doing okay," she said. "I think the boys are settling in great, and they're getting along with your kids."

"Really?" I asked. "Because I felt like Anna and Terrance—"

"Oh, there's no tension there," she quickly dismissed it. "Children will be children, after all."

"Of course," I said to her with a smile. "So you don't think there's going to be any sort of problem going forward?"

"No," she said. "I think that they will settle into a routine and all will be well."

"Well, that's good," I said. "Because I was starting to feel like things were a little bumpy."

"No," she said with a wide smile. "No bumps. Not anymore."

"Okay," I replied and sorted through my thoughts in my mind. "So, I think we've sorted the schedule for the next two weeks and—"

"I was actually wondering," she said. "Do you think that we could talk about Grant's medication?"

"Uh, what?" I said. "Why?"

"Well, just because I want to help you out more," she said. "And I can't help you out if it's all hidden. What if you're busy or not feeling well and his medication gets lost in the shuffle?"

I was horrified about that.

"What?" I said. "That has never happened. Literally never happened. I told you from the start that Michael or I will be handling all of Grant's medications."

"That's completely fine," Helena said. "It's just that, since I will be picking him up from school, do you not think I should know what the schedule is for his medication? In case the school asks? Or in case something goes wrong? I am not asking to give it to him, Cynthia. I would never take that away from you. I just want to make sure I know it, especially if something happens."

I paused. That did seem like a reasonable request, and she was around my child every day. If I trusted her enough to be around my child, then I should trust her enough to at least know the medications schedule.

"I can write it out for you," I said. "So you have a copy to carry around, just in case."

"Just in case," Helena said. "Thank you, Cynthia. I knew you would understand what's best for your children."

"Of course," I said. "And I understand that you would never use the list unless something happened."

"Never," she promised me. "I was going to ask you one more thing, though."

"Oh?" I couldn't imagine what she wanted to hear after the medication list. It seemed Helena thought that everything was fair game, and it made my blood boil when she asked the next question.

"Do you think I could hook up the monitors?" she asked. "They arrived today. Michael ordered them, and I thought that they could be useful."

"For Grant's room?" I asked. "Why? I'm sleeping in there every night."

"Surely, you won't be sleeping there every night, though?" she asked.

I bit my lip. "I mean . . . not every night, but for the foreseeable future."

"Just in case something happens," she said. "You know he's been so much worse lately."

"I know that," I said. "I've been thinking of taking him back to his doctor."

"No need to do that," Helena said. "I honestly think he just needs to settle into his new routine. I'll work with him a bit more."

That didn't seem possible, but I trusted her judgment on that. "Thank you," I said, and she gave me a wide smile.

"Thank *you*," she said, "for this amazing opportunity."

I really didn't think it was that amazing of an opportunity, but I let her think that. If she was happy, then I was supposed to be happy as well. The truth was, I had never been in charge of anyone except the kids before. The gardener, the drivers, everyone else was left up to Michael. I was on my own with Helena, or at least, I felt like it.

"Glad we had this chat," I said and retreated up to my room. I meant to text Cally right away and tell her how it went, but something made me pause. I went into Grant's room, and just for a test, plugged in the new nanny cam that had been placed there.

Nothing happened, aside from its usual startup noises. It was perfect and there was nothing that alarmed me. Maybe the old one really had been hacked, or maybe we had just gotten crossed signals for a moment. In any case, it was great, which put my mind at ease. However, we didn't really need it set up if I was with Grant every night.

I left it unplugged and headed to my bedroom, which I hadn't been in for a few nights. Michael had kept it clean and tidy, which was important. What caught my attention, though, was a single pair of lacy black underwear, just tucked under the bed.

I stared at them for a long moment before I went to pick them up. You could barely see them, so I understood how they got missed while we were cleaning.

What got me, however, was the fact that they were so generic that I had no idea whose they could be. They could be mine, but they could be any woman's.

They could be Helena's. They could be mine. They could be some other woman's that Michael had brought home.

I felt cold shivers up and down my spine as I stared at them. There was no way to figure it out.

I told myself that I couldn't assume they were someone else's. I was here all the time, and when I wasn't here, Michael wasn't here either. I didn't know what else to believe. We hadn't had sex in like a week. I hadn't been in here for days. Could I possibly have missed it in the cleaning?

I knew I couldn't play these mind games. Either he was screwing someone else or he wasn't. That was it.

I put them in the laundry bin. They were mine. They had to be mine. There was no way around it.

I sank down on the bed and I started to text Cally.

Hey, I said. *It went well. I think. But she has some weird requests.*

Like what? Cally asked.

Like she . . . I don't know. I shouldn't judge. She's being responsible. She's being a good nanny. She's just not . . . I don't know. I can't put my finger on it.

You know, if you're not comfortable in your home . . .

I'm not uncomfortable, I said. *It's just an eerie feeling. I feel like I know her, and then I relax, but then I realize that I don't know her at all.*

That is eerie, she said. *You sure that you haven't come across her before?*

I'm sure, I said. *I think she's just one of those people with one of those faces.*

Makes sense, Cally said. *Keep me posted.*

Will do, I said and signed off for the day. Cally

would get back to her family and I needed to get back to mine.

Hopefully, Michael would be home soon so I wouldn't have to awkwardly stand here and pretend that I liked Helena and that she was my best friend. I wanted the best for my children, that was all, and she was the best. That was what mattered.

Chapter 24

MICHAEL

WHEN I WOKE UP IN THE BED, I WAS COMPLETELY alone. I had been completely alone for over a week, of course, and it seemed to activate my dreams. Every night, I had dreams of having sex with someone. It wasn't always Cynthia, but it was always sex, and it always ended with me waking up with a raging hard on. I usually had to do something about it before anyone walked in. The kids liked to pound on the door early, and I didn't want to be in an awkward situation. When Cynthia was in bed with me, she would sometimes take care of it, of course, but that was not the case today.

Today, I had been dreaming about one of my exes, and I wasn't sure what woke me. At least, I wasn't sure what woke me until I saw Helena standing at my doorway.

I couldn't believe my eyes. She was dressed in a lace black negligee that came down to her knees. Her long red hair swept down her back and her milky white skin was reflected in the moonlight.

At first, I couldn't believe my luck. If I had thought my dreams were good, real life was better. But then, as I lay there and sleep left my mind, I realized exactly what was happening. She looked worried.

"Michael, I'm sorry to wake you," she said. "It's just that Roman is sick. Can I borrow some aspirin?"

"Aspirin?" I answered sleepily. "Uh . . . yeah . . . sure . . . of course."

She breathed out a long sigh of relief.

"Thank you," she said. "You're a lifesaver."

"I don't know about that," I said as I got up. I froze halfway though moving, as I realized that I had a raging hard on. I couldn't approach her like that.

I frantically looked around for my hoodie that I had been wearing before bed and pulled it on. It was quite long, and I tugged it down, hoping that it would be long enough to cover my hard on. Helena seemed oblivious, but I wondered if she was just being polite as I headed toward the master bathroom.

"Here you go," I said after digging through the cupboard. "I think that is what you need."

"Thank you," she breathed.

"Do you need anything else?" I asked her "If he's very sick, I could take him to the hospital?"

"Oh, no," she said. "He'll be okay. Especially now that I have this. Thank you, Michael. I could hug you."

"That's, uh . . . that's okay," I said. As much as I wanted a hug from Helena, it would not be a good idea right now. "Just let me know if you need anything else."

"Oh," I will," she said and disappeared.

I blushed and went back to the bedroom. It took a lot to make me blush like a schoolgirl, but here I was, embarrassed and yet so passionate. What was this woman doing to me?

If I ignored her, it seemed the thoughts only got worse. For days following the encounter, I started to have sex dreams about her. I dreamed that she was doing all sorts of X-rated things to me, and I was doing nothing to stop it. When I saw her during the day, it made it even worse. I was obsessed with her, and I needed to do something. I knew if I didn't deal with this soon, it would become more than just an obsession.

I wished that there were some manual that told me how to do this, or someone in my life that I could speak to without judgment. Yes, there were the boys at work, but they seemed to fall into two categories. There was either the cheat on your wife category or the category that never would. There didn't seem to be the middle ground of guys who were really struggling to heal themselves from infidelity. There were only the people who didn't understand me.

I had briefly considered going to a therapist about it. I knew there was no shame in doing so, but I couldn't bring myself to go. I didn't want to admit what I had done when I thought that I could heal myself and my family without drastic measures.

Of course, that was silly to assume. I had hurt Cynthia drastically, and I had hurt everyone else around me. Even the children knew that something was wrong when their mother and I would fight every night and she would cry.

Frankly, I don't know why we were even fighting. I deserved every insult that Cynthia had hurled at me when I had cheated. I should have just hung my head and let her yell at me. I was the one who was in the wrong. I was the one who had messed up. It was in no way her fault. She hadn't driven me to it. She was still perfectly desirable and sexy, and I had screwed up.

I hated myself for it. And I had never done it again. I knew there were times when she suspected that I had done it again. There were times when she had been certain I had been having another affair, and she didn't believe me when I said I hadn't.

Yes, I had been tempted. Yes, I had looked. Yes, I had gone so far as to even get someone's number. But I had never done it again and I couldn't get her to believe me. Every time I was working late, every time I didn't call exactly when I said I was going to, all the old pain came back.

Of course, I couldn't blame her. I was the one who had created that situation. I just wished that somehow, a little more trust could have been built up. I wasn't going to do it again. I was going to be strong.

I loved my wife. I loved my family. I loved my kids. I loved my house. I needed to do something.

"Cynthia," I said one night when I got home. She was standing in the living room, barefoot and in sweatpants. I thought she looked beautiful. "Let's go out for dinner."

"What?" she looked at me in surprise. "But what about the kids? What about dinner?"

"The kids can stay with Helena," I said. "And she can feed them dinner."

"But I've just made a spaghetti dinner." Helena appeared in the living room, looking half hurt and half betrayed.

Normally, that would have worked and I would do whatever Helena said. However, I had made a vow when I was at work to work on my marriage more, so I was going to stick to that.

"Well, I'm sure the kids will love it," I said and went to kiss Cynthia. "Let me take you out for dinner."

Both women looked a little bit shocked, and I didn't care. At least, I told myself I didn't care. But the entire time Cynthia was getting ready, I found myself hanging around the kitchen talking to Helena.

"You could have told me," she said. "I would have made you two a nice romantic dinner."

"That's kind of you," I said. "But, uh . . ." I paused. I felt so open with Helena, even though I knew that I shouldn't share everything. "You know that Cynthia and I have been arguing a little bit, so I want to give us a fresh start."

"That's very nice of you," she said. "But sometimes . . . sorry, I shouldn't say anything."

"Sometimes?" I prompted her.

"Well, I don't know you," she said. "And I don't know anything about your marriage, of course. It's just sometimes, it's better to let it go, for the kids' sake, than to hold onto something that isn't working anymore. Not that I think that's the route you're going. It's just . . . yeah . . . I had friends who held together long after they should have let go."

"Well, hopefully, I never get to that point," I said. "Because I really want to make it work."

"Sure, of course," she said. "I don't want to intrude."

"Hard not to intrude when you live in the same house," I said.

She smiled. "Well, I like living with you," she said as Cynthia came down.

Cynthia smiled at me and then turned to Helena. It looked like she hadn't overheard a single thing, which was good. Whenever I talked to Helena, I felt like I had done something wrong. It was just because Helena made me feel comfortable. I could discuss everything with her, and then I felt guilty afterward, despite feeling awesome in the moment.

"You ready to go?" I asked Cynthia.

She nodded. "Do I look okay?" she asked.

"I think you look beautiful," I said to her. "I feel like I'm not dressed up enough."

"You're always dressed up," she said with a smile. "Because you go to work dressing well."

"I guess that's a perk," I said and turned to Helena. "Is everything okay?" I asked her. "You don't need anything?"

"Nope, I'll call you if I do," she said.

I took Cynthia's arm and led her out the door. "What happened?" she asked me as soon as we got into the car.

"What?" I asked. "Why would you assume that something happened?"

"Well, because . . ." Cynthia chose her words carefully as I started the engine. "Because you have never walked into the house and just wanted to take me out for dinner."

"Oh," I said. "I just wanted to take my wife out for dinner."

"Yeah, but . . . because you were hungry, and you didn't want to eat Helena's cooking?"

"No," I said. "Because I was thinking at work

that I really wanted to be with you and the kids. And I know that we've had a lot going on and we've not been connecting in the right ways, so I wanted to show you that I choose you, no matter what."

That seemed to shock Cynthia, and she looked at me with tears in her eyes.

"Really?" she said.

"Yes," I said and reached over to take her hand. I squeezed it and she smiled at me.

"So, where are we going for dinner?" she asked me.

"Uh . . . well, I thought we could just drive around until we find a place?"

She looked at me in shock. "You didn't make reservations?" she asked.

I raised my eyebrows. "No, I had five minutes to plan this," I said. "So I couldn't call anyone. Come on, baby. It's fun, like when we were in college."

She smiled. "Yes, we'd just wander and go to random restaurants," she said. "But back then, we were going to fast food places."

"We'll find a good restaurant," I said. "And we're frequent patrons of a few places, so if they have any space, they'll let us in."

"Of course," she said and then squeezed my hand. "This is really nice."

"It is, isn't it?" I asked. "It is nice, because we are taking time just for ourselves."

"I agree," she said. "Why don't we do this more often?"

"Because we're terrible at making time for ourselves," I said. "All we do is focus on the kids. And while there's nothing wrong with that . . . we have to do it once in a while, or we'll lose touch."

"I agree," she said and leaned over to kiss me.

We drove around for a little while, but we eventually found a place that we both enjoyed. I felt proud, escorting my beautiful wife and the mother of my children into the restaurant.

"So," I said once we had both gotten a glass of wine. "What do you think about coming back?"

"Coming back where?" she asked.

"To the bedroom," I said. "I've missed you so much."

She took a deep breath and looked at me over her wine glass.

"Things will have to be different, Michael. We said some terrible things to each other."

"I know we did," I replied. "I know we fought, and I know we are both sorry. I know we're not perfect, and I know that we'll probably fight again.

But I think we need to try, Cynthia, and soon, or we'll never make up."

She took a deep breath.

"Okay," she said. "But as long as you promise me that there is nothing going on."

I knew that I must have looked confused. "There's nothing going on?" I said.

"You know what I mean," she said, looking down at the glass of wine in her hand. "With . . . someone else."

"Cynthia," I said. "I promise you that there is nothing going on. There is nothing going on with anyone but you."

"Okay," she said and then raised her glass. "To us."

"To us," I said and clinked glasses with her.

We ended up having a perfect dinner, and when I drove us home, I felt completely overtaken with love.

"We should do this more often," I said to her. "Maybe once a week, if we can."

"Yeah," she said. "But maybe we should make a reservation first?"

I chuckled. "Sure," I said. "I'll plan out everything. Once a week for the rest of the year?"

"Sounds like a plan," she said.

When we got home, I took her arm and escorted her up the stairs like the princess she was.

"I . . ." she paused at Grant's bedroom. "I'm just going to check on him."

"Okay," I said. "Don't be long, my love."

"I won't be," she promised me.

I headed into the bedroom to change and wait for her. I knew that if I had sex with her tonight, I would likely be thinking of someone else. However, I was going to do my best to push her out of my mind and think of my wife. My beautiful wife, with blonde hair, rather than the other woman living in my house, with her red hair that ignited lust in me.

This wasn't going to be an easy journey, but I was excited to walk it with Cynthia.

When she came back to the room, I smiled at her.

"You want to get into bed with me?" I asked. "And cuddle?"

"And just cuddle?"

I shrugged. "I guess we'll see where it goes," I teased her.

She smiled. "Okay," she said. I couldn't wait to see where the rest of the night led.

Chapter 25

CYNTHIA

When I woke up in the middle of the night, it was to the most terrifying scream that I had ever heard in my life. I thought that I was about to be murdered until I realized that it was Grant screaming.

"I got it, I got it," I said to a dozy Michael. I rushed out of bed and into Grant's room. He was sitting up and was as white as a sheet, screaming and yelling at someone who wasn't there. "Hey, baby, hey," I said as I wrapped him in my arms. "Hey, baby, it's okay!"

"Kill!" Grant was yelling. "Blood!"

It was the most distributing thing I had ever seen or heard. My heart sank into my chest and I pulled him closer.

"Shh," I said to him. "It's okay. It's okay."

"Die!" he said and then seemed to half recognize me. "Mommy . . . die!"

That was certainly not what I wanted to hear. I pulled him closer and started to hum a soothing tune that my mother had taught me. It took a long time, but he eventually began to calm down.

It seemed to take the longest to calm him down when I was there. With Helena, it seemed like it was just seconds. With Michael, all he had to do was give him a hug and all was well. Even Anna seemed to be able to talk her brother down faster than I could.

I finally managed to calm him down enough to lay him down in bed again.

"It's okay," I said to Grant as he whimpered. "It's okay."

"Mommy," he said. "Why do the people keeping showing me blood?"

"What people?" I asked him.

"The people," he said. "The people in the room."

"There are no other people here, Grant," I tried to assure him. "There's just us."

"Yeah, but . . ." he started.

I shook my head. "There's no one else here," I

said. "You have to trust Mommy. You trust Mommy, don't you?"

"Yes," he said.

I kissed him on top of the head. "Good," I said. "There's no one else here."

I lay there with him for a while longer before I started singing to him. He eventually fell back asleep and I tiptoed out of his room. Michael, to my surprise, had not fallen asleep. He was sitting up in bed reading, and I crawled in beside him.

"Nightmare?" he asked.

I nodded. "I thought they were getting better," I said. "I don't understand."

"Maybe they are getting better," he said, "but this is just a rough period."

"I don't know," I said. "It doesn't seem like a rough period. It sounds like a terrible time that is only going to get worse."

"Well, you are a medical person," he said with a small smile. "You tell me."

"I don't know," I said. "It's normal with mental illness to have dips and such . . . but this is just . . . you know, different. It seems like he's getting worse and not getting better. I really think we should take him to the doctor."

"I agree," he said. "So, what's stopping us?"

"Well, Helena said she is going to work with him a bit harder," I said, "and research some new techniques."

"Okay," he said. "But clearly, that isn't working."

"I know," I said. "So we'll have to make an appointment in the morning."

"Do you think he's asleep now?" Michael cocked his ear. "He sounds asleep."

"Here," I said and turned the monitor on with my phone. It took a second to load, but there was soon an image of Grant lying there. He seemed to be sleeping peacefully, and we were about to turn it off when I suddenly heard the voices again.

"There," I said to Michael. "There, did you hear that?"

"I think so," he said and cocked his ear downward, toward the phone. We heard it again and his eyes widened. "This is the new one?"

"Yeah," I said. "Do you think it's crossed wires?"

"I don't know," he said. "Maybe we've been hacked again."

"I don't think we've been hacked," I said. "Who would want to hack us?"

"This isn't about how important we are," he said. "These hackers will hack anyone and take whatever they can get."

"But . . ." I listened again. "See, I can never make out what they want. I can never figure out if they are whispering or talking or what is happening."

"I think you should unplug that," he said. "I don't know what's going on, but there's something in this house that's picking up that signal. We have to do something, a signal blocker or something. But until then, go and unplug it."

"What?" I asked. "Right now?"

"Yes," he said.

I headed to Grant's room and unplugged the monitor. He was still sleeping peacefully, and I carefully crept out again. When I got back into the master bedroom, Michael was Googling solutions for the supposed hacker.

"Okay, everything is done," I said. "But what are we going to do?"

"About Grant?" he asked. "I don't know. He clearly needs some sort of monitor or . . . a person in there."

"Maybe we could take turns sleeping in the

bed?" I asked. "With him? Would that make it better?"

"It would probably make it better, but then we wouldn't have any time together," Michael said. "And I don't like that solution when there's another solution."

"What is the other solution?" I asked him.

"Well, that's easy," he said. "We have Helena stay with him."

"No," I said right away.

Michael raised an eyebrow. "No?" he asked. "Why not?"

"Because there is no reason to do that when we are two very capable parents," I said. "Besides, I don't want her doing that."

"She mentioned the other day how she was thrilled to spend more time with him," Michael said. "What do we pay her for? That way, we get more time together and everything is okay."

"I'd really rather not," I said.

"You can't not trust her," he said. "After all this time?"

"I do trust her," I lied through my teeth. "It's just . . . that seems a bit much. Then we're not doing any parenting at all."

"We are," he said. "We still are. It would just mean that we sleep at night."

"Let me think about it," I said.

He sighed. "I guess I can agree to that," he replied. "But sleeping on it means you have to promise to discuss it with me first thing in the morning."

"Fine," I agreed and then leaned over and kissed him. "I'm glad that you're worried about us having time together. A few months ago, that would not have been at the top of your mind."

"I'm glad that it is now," he said. "I forgot how good you could be."

Michael and I had a fantastic night, and I was in an amazing mood in the morning when I woke up. I was tired, but I was tired in a good way. As soon as I got up, I knew the answer.

"Yes," I said to him. "Yes, she can stay with him."

"Perfect, baby," he said. "That's great."

"I still don't like it," I said. "But I do value our time together, and this seems like the best solution."

"Good," he replied. "I'll tell her."

"No . . ." I paused. "I'll tell her."

"Excellent," he said and kissed me on the cheek. "I have to get ready for work. See you soon."

As soon as he was gone, I headed downstairs to find Helena. She was making coffee, and when she saw me, she smiled.

"Hello, Cynthia," she said. "How did you sleep?"

"I slept okay," I said. "But actually, there's something that Michael and I wanted to talk to you about."

"Oh?" she asked. "I hope I haven't done anything wrong."

"On the contrary," I said. "We were thinking about how you said you wanted to spend more time with Grant . . . and we think we've come up with solution. You know the monitor system I've installed? It appears to have been hacked again."

"Oh, no!" she said. "Are the children in danger?"

"They aren't, don't worry," I replied. "But . . . there is some danger in the sense that we don't want to leave it on, and we don't want Grant to be alone. So we were wondering . . . if you would mind staying with him from time to time?"

"Of course!" Her face lit up. "I would be thrilled. I could do it every night, if you'd like."

"That would be great."

"Every time I think that we are out of new adventures, you come up with a new one."

"Oh," I said. "I wouldn't really consider this a new adventure. I would just consider this . . . you know. Life."

"Well, I try to look at everything like it's a new adventure," she said. "So consider it done."

"Your boys won't mind?" I asked.

"No, of course not," she said. "They're old enough to understand. Plus, I'm sure they'd like a little privacy to get up to mischief with me not right on top of them."

"Right," I said. "Well, then . . . let's, uh . . . let's make it happen. Michael can start moving your stuff upstairs . . . or if Grant wants, he can move his stuff downstairs. Whatever he thinks will make him more comfortable."

"Yes," she said. "I think that would be a good idea. And I think that Grant would like to do either, as long as I'm with him."

That was an odd thing to say, but I let it go. I decided to be a good employer.

"Thanks, Helena," I said.

"No problem," she replied. "Is there anything else I can help you with?"

"No, that's all," I said, even though I didn't

want it to be all. I wanted to tell her that I couldn't choose between my husband and my child and that was why we were doing this. I wanted to tell her that I was a good mother. I wanted to tell her everything to put her in her place, but I couldn't.

"No, that's all," I said. "Do you think that we should do it tonight? We could wait a few days to get Grant used to the idea, and then—"

"No, I think we should do it as soon as possible," she said. "Tonight would be best. We don't want to delay."

"Why don't we want to delay?"

She smiled. "Because it will help Grant, won't it?"

"Right," I said. "It will help Grant."

"Exactly," she said. "I'll talk to him when I get him from school."

"Okay," I replied, even though I wasn't sure she should. However, if she was the one spending the night with him, maybe she was the best person to approach the subject.

"Thank you so much, Cynthia," she said and went back to what she was doing.

I pulled out my phone and went to text Cally. I felt like she was the only person I could truly talk to these days. Everyone else, I had to put on a front for.

So it's totally a good idea to have the nanny stay with my son overnight, right? I asked.

Better than having the nanny stay with your husband overnight, she pointed out.

That's true, I answered.

Chapter 26

MICHAEL

"So, how are things with Cynthia?" Tom asked me on the phone. He was due to come home from Tokyo soon and we were discussing all sorts of things. One of our topics was how much his wife missed him, which led to our discussing Cynthia.

"Things are actually much better," I said. "She's moved back into the bedroom and things are much better . . . in that department too."

"Good." He chuckled. "So things with the nanny are . . ."

"Oh, she's still hot," I said. "But she's not my wife, you know?"

"Yeah," he said. "I know exactly what you mean. So, it didn't happen?"

"It almost happened," I admitted. "But I

stopped it because I really didn't want to tear my family apart. Family is important."

"I know," he said. "I miss mine so much. Thank you for swapping out who's out here."

"I get it," I said. "And I'm sure you'll go back someday."

"I'm sure I will be," he said. "So, is there anything else you'd like to discuss?"

"No, I think that's it," I said. "See you soon, Tom."

I hung up the phone and tried to get back to work. However, I was distracted by instant messages on my computer from Cynthia.

I really think we should follow up with that fertility specialist, she said. *I have been digging deeper into our families and there's nothing suspicious. Something went wrong during the surrogacy, I'm sure of it.*

If you like, I said. *We can. Do you want me to do it?*

I'll do it, she said. *You're working hard. I'll keep you posted.*

Thanks, I typed back. *I guess we never did anything about it when we brought it up a few months ago, did we?*

Nope, she replied. *But I'm really going to follow through this time. See you soon.*

I was glad that she was going to handle it. I was just useless when it came to anything medical. I didn't even know that childhood schizophrenia mostly ran in families until Cynthia made us search through our family trees.

When I got home, Helena was sitting at the kitchen table with the children, doing homework, and Cynthia was on the phone.

"Yes," she was saying. "But there was nothing in our families, absolutely nothing. I really think we should look into this more. Please." She paused and then nodded. "That will be fine. Thank you."

She hung up the phone and then turned to me.

"They're going to look into it," she said with air quotes.

"Oh," I said. "Well, hopefully, they actually mean it."

"What's going on?" Helena asked.

"Oh, just drama," Cynthia said as the children finished their homework and went to play.

"I'm sure I can help," Helena said with a friendly smile.

I always trusted her, even with our darkest secrets, so I told her our story.

"We had Grant via surrogacy, as you know," I said. "But childhood schizophrenia doesn't run in either family, and as far as we're aware, Olive had a perfect pregnancy, nothing unusual, and we know she didn't take drugs . . . so we are a bit concerned that something happened during the procedure."

"Something like what?" Helena asked.

"That the egg wasn't her egg," I said. "Or the sperm wasn't mine, or something."

"Oh," Helena said. "I'm sure that isn't true. These fertility doctors are very careful, you know."

"But it just doesn't make sense." Cynthia was apparently frustrated enough with the subject to let her emotions out. "It has to be inherited. We don't have it."

"I'm sure there's an easy explanation for this," Helena said. "Didn't you tell me your surrogate mother, Olive, was patient and kind and loving?"

"Well, yes," Cynthia said.

"So, surely, she can't be behind it?" Helena asked. "There has to be some other reason."

"Oh," Cynthia said. "I don't think it was Olive at all. I think there was some mistake made during the procedure, a nurse or something who misla-beled things."

"Cynthia," Helena said with a smile, "you worked with doctors, didn't you?"

"I did," she said. "For most of my career."

"How many times did they make a mistake?" Helena asked.

"Well, actually . . ." Cynthia said.

"How many times did they make a mistake of that magnitude?" Helena asked. "If they were making mistakes like that, they'd lose their license," she said. "I don't know what the answer is, but I don't think it's that."

"Well, it has to be," Cynthia said. "And maybe it was an honest mistake—"

"I don't think you should call Grant a mistake," Helena said gently.

Cynthia colored. "No," she said. "I didn't mean he was a mistake. I meant he was . . . oh, God. I didn't say he was mistake, did I?"

"You didn't mean it like that," I assured her. "We both knew what you meant."

"Of course," Helena said. "I knew what you meant. I just hope that Grant didn't overhear."

I glanced into the playroom, but Grant seemed completely absorbed in what he was doing.

"I hope they call back soon," Cynthia said. "We've been on pins and needles about this for so long."

"They will," Helena replied. "I'm sure if they think there's even a chance, they'll call back."

"I hope so," I said. "It would bother me to my

very soul if I had a customer make a complaint of that magnitude and I didn't do anything about it."

"But that's because you're a good person, Michael," Cynthia said.

I raised my eyebrow. "You don't think the doctor was a good person?" I asked Cynthia.

"I'm sure he was," Helena said. "All healthcare professionals take a Hippocratic oath to not do harm. I'm sure he didn't do this."

"How can you be so sure?" Cynthia almost looked like she was accusing Helena.

I stepped in before the two of them started to argue. "She's just trying to play devil's advocate," I said. "Aren't you, Helena?"

"Absolutely," Helena said. "And I also want you both to know that no matter what's wrong with Grant, I think he's a wonderful and sweet little child."

"So do we," I assured Helena.

"Good," she said. "I'm sorry. I didn't mean to cause any problems."

"You didn't," Cynthia said and glanced at me. "I'll be upstairs."

As soon as she was gone, I breathed a long sigh.

"I'm sorry," I said to Helena. "She's just really stressed by the whole situation."

"It's fine," Helena said. "I'm sure she'll see reason soon."

"You don't think she's seeing reason?" I asked.

She shook her head. "No," she said. "I really don't. I don't mean to be rude or disrespectful. It's just that accusing a doctor of such a mistake is a big thing."

"I agree," I said. "But I don't know what the answer is."

"You know," she said, "there are a lot of drugs out there for schizophrenia for adults."

"I know," I said, confused.

"A lot people can hide it very well," she said. "Especially if they take their medication and they don't see people very often."

I tried to put the pieces of her sentence together.

"So . . ."

"And it's an embarrassing disease," she said. "Even though there should be no shame in it. So I think that if I were you, I'd be more thinking down the route that there is someone in your family who is hiding it."

"But we asked for medical purposes," I said. "Because our child is sick. Surely, no one would hide that."

"You'd think that," she said sadly. "But I can think of a few times over my career when I've seen someone hiding it. They are very good at the normal act most of the time."

"I didn't think that it would be possible," I said.

"Oh, it is," she said, and her eyes drifted back to me with a half-smile. "And most people can do it if they really try."

"Well, that's frightening," I said. "I hope they're getting help. I mean, you're the one working with them. Do you know how supportive the healthcare system is? Once Grant is an adult, what is our future?"

"I think that he will be well cared for and looked after," she said. "I wouldn't worry too much about that. You never know how much your circumstances could change."

"Of course," I said. "But if all goes well, things don't change. Just in the sense that we're still a family, still living in this house, you know, all of that."

"Well, of course," she said. "It's rare to find someone who is so devoted to their family."

I felt a spot of guilt because I wasn't always devoted to my family. I didn't know if she knew that, and I decided not to share that.

"Of course," I said. "There's nothing better."

"I agree," she said with a smile. "The boys are so lucky to have you in their lives."

"The . . . boys?" I asked. "Your boys?"

"Yes," she said. "Because they don't have another male in their lives. They need a good strong father figure. I hope you don't mind."

"Oh," I said. "I mean, I don't think I mind too much. It's just . . . yeah. I know what you mean."

"And I know what you mean," she said with a twinkle in her eye. "You and I understand each other, Michael."

"I know," I said. "The truth is, the second you walked in the door, you had the job. I just felt something click."

"Sometimes, it's good like that," she said with a smile. "And sometimes, it's not. I've had bad employers before."

"Oh?" I said. "I guess we didn't check your references, so we don't know what happened before."

"Oh, I wouldn't worry about before," she said. "What matters is right now, with your family."

"Of course," I said. "And things really are going well with Grant?"

"They are," she said. "He settles down to sleep

right away and there are no issues. I'm sure you've noticed that he's not screaming at night?"

"I have noticed that," I said. "And it's lovely."

"Well, thank you." She blushed. "I hope everything is going to be okay between you and Cynthia."

"You mean tonight?" I said. "It was nothing. A minor disagreement."

"You should go and talk to her," Helena said. "I'll go and get dinner ready."

"Thank you," I said. "You know, when we hired you, we never asked whether you could cook. But this has worked out perfectly. Has anyone ever told you that you're an overachiever, Helena?"

She smirked at that.

"Well, I mean it in a good way," I said. "And I think that you're really going to go far in your career."

"Thank you," she said. "But I'd be happy to settle down one day too."

"Well, of course," I said. "Isn't that the dream?"

"That's the dream," she said with a smile "Go on."

I was in a much better mood as I climbed the stairs to my room to go talk to Cynthia. I was sure she wasn't too angry, and if she was, I could patch it up.

"Hey," I said as Cynthia was sitting on the bed.

"I just got a really weird call," she said. She didn't seem angry, but she did seem frightened.

"Oh?" I asked her.

"Yeah, it was the police," she said. "They wanted to know if we knew Amanda Dragu?"

"Amanda Dragu?" I said. "The nanny we interviewed and wanted to hire but then she ghosted us?"

"The very same," she said. "It was just a voicemail, but they said to call them back right away."

"That's strange," I said. "I wonder if she's in some kind of legal trouble."

"I don't know," she said and put the phone to her ear. "Guess I'm going to find out."

I sat down beside her and gave her a little kiss while she called. She batted me away, but I knew that she loved it. I hoped it was nothing serious, but whatever they were calling us about, I would be there for Cynthia. Everything was going to be fine.

"Hello?" she said when they finally answered. "My name is Cynthia Thompson. I believe someone left me a message about Amanda Dragu?"

Chapter 27

CYNTHIA

I wasn't prepared for what they told me on the phone. I wasn't prepared for the fact that I was going to be told something so graphic and so disgusting that I felt like I was going to throw up.

"Unfortunately, she's been found dead," the police officer said on the other end of the phone. "We're informing you because her family said that she was excited to work for you and she wanted very much to become a part of your household."

I choked and put my hand to my mouth.

"She's dead?" I asked. "How? Where?"

"We can't release too many details," the officer said. "But I'm sure you'll see it on the news, so I'll tell you what it's about to say. She was pulled out of a landfill. She was shot in the back of the head at close range."

I squeaked and put my hand to my mouth. I didn't want to know the details, but at the same time, I needed to know what happened to her. "Who did this to her?" I asked.

"We don't know at this time," he said.

I managed to ask a terrifying question. "Are we suspects?"

The police officer reacted in surprise. "Uh, no," he said. "I don't think so. I was just informing you."

"Well, thank you," I said, even though my voice was shaking. "Thank you."

"Please call us if you have any questions or concerns," he said and hung up the phone.

Michael was looking at me like I'd grown a third head, and I could barely form the words to tell him what happened.

When I did, he looked absolutely horrified.

"Who would do that to her?" he asked. "She was such a sweet girl."

"Yes," I said. "I don't know, maybe she was involved in terrible things . . . but I don't know. I doubt it. She was perfect, our first choice."

"I know," he said and sank on the edge of the bed. "That's terrible."

"Should we tell Grant?" I asked, but he shook his head.

"No," he said. "I doubt he'll remember her. And if he asks . . . then we can tell him, maybe when he's older."

"Yeah," I said. "I mean, he is pretty happy with Helena, despite . . . everything."

"Despite everything?" Michael said in surprise. "I think it's because of everything."

"Whatever," I said and tried to smile at him. "That was sad, but I think we just have to keep going."

"Exactly," he replied. "Carry on and all that. Let me know if you want to talk about it."

"No, I'm fine," I said.

At least, I thought I was fine. But later that night, when everything was put away and the three of us adults were just discussing the schedule for the coming week, I couldn't help but feel a little sad.

"Is everything okay?" Helena asked me.

I took a deep breath. "Everything's okay," I replied. "Just we got some news that someone we knew passed away . . . and it was a bit shocking."

"Oh?" she said. "I'm so sorry. Was it unexpected?"

"Yes," I said. "It was actually . . ." I looked to

Michael, unsure if I should tell her, but he nodded. "We had planned to hire someone before you, actually. This was before we even found you or interviewed you. The person we found was perfect, but then . . . when we went to hire her, no one could find her. And now we've just gotten news that . . ." I felt choked up again.

"It appears that someone killed her," Michael said.

Helena turned pale. "No," she said. "Why would anyone kill a nanny?"

"I don't know," I answered. "I don't know. She seemed like such a good person, and I don't think she was involved in anything bad. But . . ."

"You never really know someone, do you?" Helena asked.

"I guess not," I replied and then took a deep breath. "I just . . . that's two people who have died in connection to Grant being with us."

"Two?" Helena asked. "Oh, yeah, your surrogate mother also passed away."

"Yes," I said.

Michael put his hands on my shoulders, and I leaned into him.

"I know it's been seven years, and I know I only knew her for a short time . . . but I miss her."

Helena gave me a gentle smile and sat down beside me.

"What was she like?" she asked.

"Olive . . . was just so kind and lovely," I said. "She was a wonderful person who always had a kind word for everyone. She was someone I wouldn't hesitate to welcome into my family in a heartbeat."

"To welcome into your family?" Helena asked.

"Well, yeah," I said. "She . . . I guess she was part of the family, wasn't she, Michael?"

"She was," he said.

Helena looked a little bit pale. "Will you excuse me?" she asked and then left the kitchen.

I turned to Michael. "That was odd," I said.

He shook his head. "I think that she's a little bit freaked out," he said. "Because I mean, she is connected to Grant's life, and you've just told her that two people have died who are connected to him."

"Right," I said. "I never thought of that. In any case, it doesn't matter. It's not about Grant. It's just a terrible, terrible coincidence."

"Yeah," he replied. "I know. But it still would be scary to learn that."

"I suppose," I said and put my head in my

hands. "I don't know what to think, frankly, after all of this."

"Yeah, I know. It's been a rough time," he said. "But remember, you said that we were going to try and think about happy things instead?"

"I remember," I said and leaned into him again. "I just . . ."

"I know," he said. "Why don't we go to bed, and in the morning, things will seem better?"

"I hope so," I answered. I didn't think that things could possibly get better, but I was willing to try.

We eventually went to bed, but I lay awake all night. I kept picturing Olive and then Amanda. I saw their faces, and then I shivered to think what they might look like right now. I shivered to think that both of them were nothing more than corpses now. They had been so kind to us, and now they were gone.

The only reason I didn't have any nightmares was because I didn't really sleep. I couldn't get their faces out of my mind. I was terrified and I didn't know if I would ever sleep again. What if Helena was right about being afraid? What if something had happened to them and we were next?

I told myself that was absolutely ridiculous.

Who was going to come after us? Michael didn't have any enemies and neither did I. And it wasn't like Grant wandered around with eeriness either, so I didn't really know what to make of it.

Eventually, I managed to drag myself out of bed. I went downstairs, and Helena was of course already there. I was starting to think that she never slept and she never took time for herself.

"Hello," I said. "How did you sleep?"

"I slept okay," she said. "How about you?"

"Not very well," I admitted. "I kept thinking about what happened."

"Ah," she said. "Yes, that would be bothersome, wouldn't it?"

"I just can't stop thinking about what happened to those poor women," I said. "And I'm sorry, I don't want to freak you out or anything."

"No, I know what you mean," she said. "It must be terrible. I don't think that anyone is going to come after me, don't worry. And if they did, keeping Grant safe would be my top priority."

"That's so kind of you," I said. "I don't fear for Grant's safety. I think it's just a coincidence . . . a very unfortunate one."

"Yes," she agreed. "And it sounded like the

universe was very picky about who took care of Grant."

"Yes," I said. "It does seem like that. And that's so incredibly cruel."

"I agree," she replied. "I wouldn't worry anymore, though. I think that everything will work out in the end."

"Well, it didn't work out for Amanda and Olive," I said a bit too bitterly.

Helena smiled at me, but she didn't say anything. I went to get a cup of coffee and sat at the kitchen table. She seemed surprise that I was still there, because normally, I would storm off after a conversation like that. However, something about the fact that Amanda was gone made me want to talk to Helena more. It was like I understood that life was short, and I didn't want to waste talking to her now.

I did like Helena. I thought she was a little strange and I resented that she was talking to my husband a lot, but I did like her. And I liked the fact that she was so dedicated to Grant, even if I thought it was a little too dedicated.

"So, what are your plans for today?" she asked me. "Will you go out?"

"I think I'll stay in," I said. "So whatever you have planned for the kids, count me in."

"Oh," she said. "I don't actually have any plans with them, aside from the normal day stuff."

"That's okay," I said. "I don't mind just sitting with them while they do their homework or something. How was last night with Grant?"

"He was fine," she said. "I really do think he's sleeping better now that I'm sleeping with him."

"Oh," I said. "I thought he wasn't doing much better when I was sleeping in his room."

"Sometimes, it just takes a magic touch," she replied.

"I like to think I have the magic touch," I said, "being his mother and all."

"Of course you do," she said and then placed a plate of eggs in front of me.

I was surprised because I thought that she was going to eat the eggs she was making herself. "Oh," I said. "I'm not . . ."

"It's fine, you eat whatever you want," she replied. "I made it for you because I knew that you were having a rough night."

"Well . . . thank you," I said. I couldn't exactly say no to that, especially given that she was trying to be nice. I dug into the eggs and found that I was quite hungry. Helena was a good cook and I asked her where she had learned.

"Oh." She shrugged. "Just normal mother stuff."

"You could have been a professional chef," I said. "If that interested you."

"Thank you," she said. "But I think I'm going to stick with childcare."

I smiled. "Well, you're good at that too," I replied as I finished the eggs. "Thank you, those were great."

"Of course," Helena said and took my plate away.

My phone went off, and I looked down to see that it was Cally, reacting to what I had told her about Amanda. I picked it up and texted her back.

"Thanks, Helena," I said to her as I left the kitchen.

This is crazy! Cally said. *Are you okay?*

I'm okay, I texted back. *Just . . . shocked.*

Yeah, she said. *Be careful, girl. The world is a scary place.*

I know. But I don't know what to do differently. Never let Grant go outside. Never let anyone get near us?

Your nanny isn't acting like a murderous weirdo, is she? Cally asked.

I rolled my eyes.

No, I said. Just her normal brand of weirdness.

Be careful, Cally said. *I don't want you ending up on the evening news.*

Ha, I said. *Sleep deprived housewife takes down Nanny in a fit of confusion.*

LOL, she texted back.

We talked for a bit more, and the longer we talked, the better I felt. Everything was going to be okay. I knew that. And Cally was there to support me. I knew that. As long as Cally was there, I had a feeling I was going to be just fine.

Chapter 28

MICHAEL

It was rare that I was actually alone with Grant and Anna. Normally, Helena's kids were around, or Helena herself. However, this evening, Helena was downstairs with the boys and so I had the opportunity to sit with Anna and Grant while they played. Anna was starting to get a bit old for toys, which made me sad. It seemed like just yesterday, she was born, and now, she was starting to look into makeup rather than dolls. Of course, I wasn't going to stop her from growing up, but at the same time, I hoped that she had an interest in dolls a little while longer. Currently, she was playing with her brother, which made me happy. The two of them were playing some imagining games with her dolls and his trucks, and there was a lot of laughter. I didn't want to interrupt, but now seemed like the perfect time to have a conversation.

"Hey, kids," I said. "Why don't we stop playing for just a minute? I want to ask you something."

"Are we in trouble?" Anna looked up at me.

My brow furrowed. "No, you're not in trouble," I said. "Why would you be in trouble?"

"Just because you never want to ask us something," Anna said as she put the doll down.

Grant responded in a similar manner. "Are we in trouble, Daddy?" he asked.

"No," I repeated "Neither of you is in trouble. I just wanted to talk about how you were getting along with Terrance and Roman, now that they've been here for a while."

"I like them," Grant said. "They're like my brothers."

I chuckled at that. "It certainly seems like they trust you like a brother," I said. "How does it feel?"

"I love it," Grant said. "They're never leaving, right?"

"Well, they aren't leaving for a while," I said, "so I'm glad you're happy."

"Yes," Grant said. "I love them."

"How about you, Anna?" I asked. "How are things going?"

"Good," she said. "I'm friends with Terrance now."

"That's good," I said. "So, you decided to be friends?"

"He was being really mean to me," she said. "But eventually, he decided to not listen to his mom."

"To not listen to his mom?" I asked in surprise. "What do you mean?"

"Well, his mom told him to not be friends with me," she said. "But he decided that he wasn't going to listen to her anymore."

"Oh," I said. "So she really said that?"

"Yes," Anna said. "And she said something else that was weird."

"Oh?" I asked. "What's that?"

"Terrance told me that she said you were going to be his new dad," she said. "And that you two were getting married."

"What?" I asked. "What are you talking about? She said that?"

"Yes," Anna said.

I couldn't figure out whether this was just kids playing or whether she had really said that. I couldn't believe that Helena would say something like that unless there was really something that I didn't know about Helena. I didn't think she would say that, but I was sure there was some things about her that I didn't know. However, Helena was taking care of my kids and I trusted her.

I was trying to put the words together to ask more questions, but we were interrupted. All of a sudden, we heard a crash from the kitchen.

The last person I knew who was in the kitchen was Cynthia, so I jumped up. The kids followed.

"Cynthia?" I asked.

She was lying on the floor, and she looked completely out of it and like she couldn't breathe.

"*Cynthia!*"

I got on the floor beside her, and she flickered in and out of consciousness. I reached for my cell phone and called 9-1-1 right away. The kids were shrieking, and I was trying to focus on the voice on the phone.

"Hello, 9-1-1, what is your emergency?" said the voice on the other end.

"Hi, my wife just collapsed in the kitchen," I said as I held Cynthia's hand. "We need an ambulance, right away."

"Is she conscious?" they asked.

"Barely," I replied.

"Then she's breathing?"

"Barely," I responded. "Please, send an ambulance."

"Okay, give me your address, sir, and we'll be right there."

I gave the address and then put the phone down, on speakerphone. There was still a lot of noise as the kids kept shrieking and trying to get Cynthia to wake up.

"Anna," I said. "Anna, listen to me. Are you listening?"

"Yes," she said, but her eyes were wide, and she looked terrified.

"I need you to go to the front door," I said. "Open it for the ambulance. Then, I need you to go downstairs and find Helena and tell her to come up right away."

"But I want to stay with Mommy," she said.

"I know you do," I said. "But Mommy needs you to be strong right now."

Anna eventually listened to what I was saying, and then she went to open the door. She was clearly terrified. I was so proud of her, and I heard her run downstairs quickly.

Helena came upstairs then, and she looked surprised.

"What happened?" she asked.

"I don't know," I said. "She just collapsed. I'm not really sure what's happening. Can you take Grant out of here? I'm going to go to the hospital with Cynthia."

"Okay," she said and took Grant by the hand. She did not seem scared at all, and I thought that it was admirable that she could stay calm in the face of an emergency.

Eventually, the paramedics burst into the door, and they came right to us.

"Does she have any medical conditions?" they asked me.

I shook my head. "No," I said.

"What about any medications?" they asked.

Again, I shook my head. "There's nothing," I said. "And this has never happened before."

"Okay," one said and then turned his attention to Cynthia.

Everything happened so fast in the next few minutes. They took her vitals, hooked her up to some monitors, and then managed to get her onto a stretcher in one quick move.

"We're going to take her to the hospital. Are you coming along with us?"

"Yep," I said. "Let me just get my jacket and keys. Do you know what's wrong with her? Do you know if she's going to be okay?"

"No, but we'll find out at the hospital," he said. "Come on, we don't have a lot of time to waste."

I didn't know anything about medical things, but I had a feeling that this was really bad. I decided to drive my own car on the off chance that everything was going to be fine and Cynthia was going to be sent home in a few hours. Somehow, though, I really didn't see that happening.

Once they got her to the hospital, it seemed like it was a flurry of activity. They rushed around, taking her vitals, getting her set up in a room, and then rushing her out of the room again. I watched, terrified, as they put a tube down her throat and then pumped her stomach. I begged them to tell me what was happening, but it wasn't until hours later, when she was stable, that I finally got some answers.

"It looks like your wife took an overdose of painkillers," the doctor said. "She's going to be okay for now, but this is obviously something we're going to have to deal with in the next few days, mentally."

"An overdose of painkillers?" I said in shock. "No. She wouldn't. Cynthia would never—"

"Mr. Thompson," said the doctor. "Let me tell you, I see people of all walks of life come in here. And many of them don't look like the type to take an overdose. Sometimes, when life is very stressful, they see that there is no other choice."

"But Cynthia doesn't take painkillers," I said. "Cynthia doesn't . . ." I couldn't believe this. I shook my head and tried to regain my emotions. "Can I see her?"

"Of course," he said and led me to her room.

Cynthia was sitting up in her hospital bed, and she looked small and fragile She had a few IVs going into her hand and an oxygen tube under her nose. When she saw me, she reached for me, trying not to cry.

"Michael," she said. Her voice was hoarse, no doubt from the tube. "Michael!"

I reached my arms around her and gave her a long hug.

"Hey, babe," I said. I realized there were tears coming to my own eyes as well. "I'm so glad you are fine"

"I . . ." she struggled to form words. "They said I took an overdose of painkillers. I didn't do that, Michael. I would never do that."

I sat on the edge of the bed and held her hand.

"Well . . . then how did it happen?" I asked. "You know yourself that medical tests are usually pretty accurate. So . . ."

"I don't know," she said. She seemed a bit dazed. "I don't know. All I know is that my last glass of milk tasted really off. I left it on the counter and then I remember getting really dizzy."

My stomach dropped into my shoes.

"You think there was something in the milk?"

"I don't know." She looked terrified. "After what happened to Amanda and Olive . . ."

I took out my phone and was already dialing the police. Cynthia watched me in half-dazed fear as I gave the details to the police.

"What if they don't believe me?" she asked. "After all, there must be a million housewives in here all the time who take overdoses. What if they think I'm lying?"

"They won't," I said. "If you really didn't do it, then everything is going to be okay. We're going to get to the bottom of this."

"It's just because of what happened with Amanda," she said. "And what happened with Olive. What if somebody really is out to get us?"

"We'll get to the bottom of it," I assured her. "For now, the only thing that you should be worrying about is resting."

"Thank you," she said and reached out for me again. "I just want to go home."

"I know," I said. "But you have to be here until you're okay again. Maybe in a few days."

"Michael, I don't want you to bring the kids here," she said. "I don't want them to see me like this."

I kissed her forehead.

"Everything is fine," I tried to assure her. "Tomorrow, you'll be back to your old self, and the kids will be happy to see you whenever you're ready."

As she drifted off to sleep, I texted Helena, who responded right away.

There was a glass of milk on the counter, I said. *Cynthia thinks there was something wrong it with. The police are coming.*

Oh, no, she replied. *I already cleaned it up! I didn't know! And it was the last of the milk too.*

I swore out loud at that.

Okay, well just . . . leave everything, I said. *I think someone is trying to hurt Cynthia.*

Who would do that? she asked.

I don't know, I said. *But whoever it is, we're going to get to the bottom of it.*

Sounds good, she replied. *This is so scary. Are you okay?*

I'm fine, I said. *I'll be back soon.*

I didn't know anyone who would hurt Cynthia, but she was right. With Olive and Amanda seemingly murdered, there was something really strange going on. We had to find out what before anyone else got hurt. Otherwise, we could all end up the same way.

Chapter 29

MICHAEL

I DIDN'T KNOW WHAT TO BELIEVE, BUT IT SEEMED like every time I thought I'd figured something out, it was met with a dead end. The police were able to come and test the milk left in the carton, but there was nothing suspicious there. They told me right away that they didn't believe me and that Cynthia should get help. That made me upset, but then a nagging thought pulled at me. Maybe she had done it? Maybe she was lying? Maybe she was a lot more depressed than I thought?

I was sitting in the kitchen, and Helena was sitting with me. We were both shell shocked and we didn't know what to say.

"So the police don't believe me," I said. "So . . . I don't know what else to do."

"Are you sure that she . . . didn't take it?" she asked me.

"I'm sure," I said, but Helena's face changed. I realized that she might know something that I didn't, and I looked up at her. "What?"

"Nothing," she said, but I knew I had to push.

"Helena, you need to tell me if you know something," I said. "You're here with her all day. If there is something that you know . . ."

"It's just that Cynthia has been very depressed lately," she said.

"Did you see her taking pills?"

"No," Helena said. "But she said that she was sad and she didn't know what to do. She often said that she was lost."

"What?" I asked. "I never heard her say something like that."

"Really?" Helena asked. "You never heard her say anything about being sad or lost?"

I searched the far corners of my mind. "I mean, it's possible," I said. "I don't want to say no . . . but—"

"Exactly," she said. "Michael, I don't want to point fingers, but I really think she did it."

I took a deep breath and then went to the fridge. I pulled out a beer and cracked it open. I normally didn't drink on the weekdays, but this seemed like a good reason to drink.

"So . . ." I said. "You think my wife tried to kill herself in the kitchen, with her kids around? And doesn't it take a while for painkillers to knock someone out? Why would she do that?"

"I don't know," she said. "That just seems like the most logical option, considering the fact that the police found nothing. You can't really think that someone is after you, do you, Michael? After all, you and Cynthia are the nicest people I know. No one would hurt you."

I took a gulp of beer.

"I don't know," I said. "I really don't know."

"Well," she said, "I suppose we're going to find out. If the police find out anything, they're going to let us know."

"Right," I said. "Well . . . I don't think she did it."

"I suppose we'll have to agree to disagree," she said. "And I suppose we'll have to hold those opinions for quite a while, until the police tell us otherwise."

"Yep," I said. "I'm going to go to bed. I've asked Anna to stay with Grant tonight."

"What?" Helena asked. "Why?"

"Because," I said. "I just think it's better right now."

Helena looked at me in shock.

"You can't possibly think that I—"

"Helena," I said and held up my hand. "I don't know what's happening right now, so what I want is to just drink my beer and go to bed."

"Sure," she said.

She seemed to know that it was time to back up, and she let me go up to my room without any other issues. It was late and Anna was already asleep in Grant's room. I hated that Anna had to act like an adult, but I didn't mind having a night off once in a while. I just didn't know what to do.

I had only intended to drink one beer, or maybe two, but soon, it turned into several. I had also found a bottle of Jack Daniels in my den and started into that.

It had been a long time since I had been even tipsy, and even longer since I had been drunk. I soon found myself in the half floating state that I used to get into in college. I was hammered, and I tried to make sure that I stayed quiet and stayed in my room.

I missed Cynthia. I missed sex. I missed being free to have sex whenever I wanted.

I thought I was hallucinating when Helena turned up at the doorway in her lacy nightie again. She looked even more beautiful than the last time, and my cock sprang to life while looking at her.

"Does your son need aspirin again?" I managed. "Does he need something?"

"No," Helena said, and she leaned in my doorway.

There was a long pause, and then I tried to figure out exactly what was going on.

"Do *you* need some aspirin?" I asked. I was sure that I was slurring my words, but she didn't seem to have any trouble understanding me.

Helena approached me with a small smile on her face and shut the door behind her. "There is something I need," she said.

I stayed on the bed, confused. "Oh?" I asked.

She raised her eyebrow. "Yes," she said and walked forward.

She looked so gorgeous, and I could feel my cock getting harder with each step she took. I had thought about her so many times in the past. I had considered what I would do to her if she ever turned up like this. Last time, it had been tough enough to turn her away. This time, I didn't know if I had the power to do so.

"What's that?" I asked.

"Well, Michael, you must be so lonely without Cynthia here," she cooed. "You must really wonder whether she's coming back."

"I . . ." I swallowed hard. "I'm okay. She's coming back."

"But *is* she coming back?" Helena asked. "You know, it's very hard, sometimes, for people to come back once they've done that once."

"She didn't do it," I said.

She looked right into my eyes. "Didn't she?"

I wanted her. God, I wanted her. There was nothing I wanted more than to grab her and take her there on my bed. I wanted to touch her and kiss her and bang her.

But I didn't. I couldn't do that to Cynthia. I couldn't do that to my kids. I couldn't do that to the family I had worked so hard to build.

"Helena, get out," I said.

She reacted in surprise. "What?" she asked.

"You heard me," I said. "Get out. Get out now."

"I . . ." She leaned back. "Are you sure? I made all this effort for you, Michael. It's all for you."

"Get out," I repeated.

Her face turned red. She retreated out the door

and down the hallway. I could tell that she was incredibly angry, but I didn't care. There was so much that didn't make sense right now.

Why had she insisted that Cynthia had tried to kill herself? Why wasn't she listening when I said that I didn't want her to touch me?

Why had Anna said that Terrance reported weird things? What was happening?

I knew I wasn't in any shape to comfort anyone, so I decided to just let it go for now. In the morning, everything would be clearer. In the morning, I would at least be sober.

However, I was barely sober in the morning, which surprised me. I really didn't think I'd had that much to drink, but I guess I was a lightweight these days. I took my time getting up. I had already decided that I wasn't going to go into work that day. No one needed to know why. It was the first time that I had kept something like this from the company, and it didn't make me comfortable. We all were a family there too. We normally supported each other. Today, however, was different.

What if Cynthia had died? That thought had floated across my mind many times. If she had died, I think I would have killed myself. I loved her so much and I couldn't live without her.

She didn't really try to kill herself, did she? She wouldn't really leave me.

The truth was, this morning, I wasn't sure.

I went down into the kitchen, and to my surprise, Helena was actually nowhere to be found. I was prepared to have an awkward conversation with her because she may think that I didn't remember last night. However, I did remember last night, and I really thought what she did was inappropriate. We were stuck in our house, and we needed to actually be away from each other. I couldn't believe that she had done that. Had I led her on? Had I accidentally given her some indication that I wanted what she had done? Had I perhaps flirted with her accidentally?

I thought of all the times that we had inter- acted, and I realized, to my sinking stomach, that we had flirted in the past. It hadn't been intentional, but it had happened.

Maybe this was my fault. Maybe I had done this.

"Daddy?" Anna asked. "Is Mommy okay?"

I hadn't even heard her get up. Her little voice sent pain up and down my spine.

"She's fine," I said. "But she has to spend a few more days in the hospital."

"Why?" she asked. "Is she going to come home? Was she sick?"

"Yes," I said. "She is very sick, but she's going to be okay."

"Good," she said and clung to my side.

"Was that scary?" I asked her. "Do you want to talk about it?"

"No," she said. "I'm okay. I know that you and the ambulance people are going to take care of Mommy."

"That's right," I said. "So there's nothing to worry about."

"But, Daddy," she said. "Do you think that she made herself sick?"

"What are you talking about?" I asked. "Who said that?"

"Helena said that maybe she did it to herself," Anna said.

I shook my head. "That's not true," I said. "She didn't do it to herself."

"Oh," she said. "So why did Helena say that?"

"I don't know," I said. "But you don't need to worry. Everything is going to be okay."

"I know it is," she said.

"How was Grant last night?" I asked.

"He was fine," Anna said. "He slept the whole time."

"That's good," I said. "I'm so proud of you."

"Oh, I don't mind," she said. "It reminds me of when we were little, and Grant and I used to talk all night long."

"Well, hopefully, you don't talk all night long now?" I asked.

She shook her head. "No," she said. "Only sometimes."

I gave her a kiss on the head.

"You're awesome, little girl," I said. "Now, because Helena isn't up yet, would you like some breakfast?"

"Yes please," she said.

I went to the cupboard. It had been a long time since I got her breakfast, but I wanted to get her something that would make her happy. I found her favorite cereal and poured it into a bowl and then handed it over to her.

"Thank you!" Anna said.

I grinned. "Of course," I replied. "Now, let's see what else we can find for Grant."

I didn't know where Helena was, but I suspected that she was embarrassed and not showing her face after yesterday. Frankly, I didn't really want her to show her face, so I was glad that she was staying away. We needed to sit down and really talk about what happened before we were both in trouble with everything that was happening. If Cynthia ever found out about this, I knew it wouldn't end well.

Chapter 30

CYNTHIA

"I DIDN'T DO IT," I REPEATED FOR THE THIRD time that hour. I knew how it looked. I knew the doctors were suspicious. "Look, I was a nurse before I started staying home with my kids. I was a nurse, and if I wanted to kill myself, I'd know exactly what to take. And I wouldn't do it this way."

"You wouldn't do it this way?" the doctor asked. "So, how would you do it?"

"Oh, my God," I replied. "Oh, my God, I wouldn't do it at all. I'm just saying I would know exactly what to take."

"So you would——"

"No," I cried. "Look, you have to believe me."

The doctor made a couple more notes and then looked back up at me.

"Okay, Cynthia, I'm going to have you see a psychiatrist," he said. "Just to get his opinion on everything."

"No," I said. "No, I didn't—"

"And if he says that you can go, then everything will be fine. Does that work for you?"

"Yes," I said, at last. I didn't know what else to say, so I just agreed to it. The doctor wasn't going to release me until I talked to the psychiatrist, so I was going to have to agree. "Fine."

"Good," he said with a smile. "I'm glad that you agree. I'll send him in."

I didn't want to talk to a psychiatrist. I had nothing against them, of course, and I knew that some people needed them. My son had severe mental health issues. I obviously believed that mental health was real. But I didn't think I needed that.

When the psychiatrist walked in, I felt like I was preparing for war. I took a deep breath and sat up in bed.

"Cynthia," he said. "My name is Dr. Reed. It's really nice to meet you."

"It's nice to meet you too," I said. "I'm hoping this will be a quick chat."

"Of course," he said.

He looked ridiculously young, and I briefly wondered how long he had been practicing He sat down in the chair opposite my bed and I tried to smile.

"So tell me, Cynthia, what brought you in here?"

"I suffered an overdose of painkillers," I said. "But I did not purposely take them."

"You didn't take them?" he said in surprise. "Really?"

"I didn't," I said and then paused, thinking back to what I'd been doing. "Maybe I took one or two, earlier in the day. But certainly not enough for an overdose."

"Well, the amount of painkillers found in your system didn't show just one or two," he said. "It was move like a full handful. So tell me, if you didn't do it on purpose, how did it get into your system?"

"My nanny," I blurted out. I didn't know that I actually believed that until I said it, but now that I said it, it hit me like a tidal wave. "My nanny poisoned me." As I said it again, I knew it was true. It had to be Helena.

"Really," he said. "So why don't you tell me more about that? What is your nanny's name?"

"Helena," I said. "And she has always been a little bit weird."

"Oh?" he asked.

"We hired her to take care of our seven-year-old son, Grant."

"Who's we?" he asked.

"Oh, my husband, Michael, and me," I said. "Grant has childhood schizophrenia, and we needed extra help. Someone who really specialized in it to help me."

"What do you do?"

"I'm a full-time mother," I said. "But it's a lot, with Grant and our daughter, Anna. Anna has no medical issues, thankfully, but having two children, especially one with mental illness, can be a bit hard."

"So you're a full-time mom, but you have a nanny?" he asked.

I felt so incredibly judged. "Yes," I said. I was trying to own it, but I felt like a failure. "I do."

"Okay, so you hired this nanny, Helena, after you gave birth to your son?"

"Well, no," I said. "I didn't give birth to Grant. After my daughter Anna was born, I almost died. We wanted another child, so we used a surrogate for Grant."

"Is he your biological son?" the doctor asked.

"Yes . . ." I said. "Or at least he's supposed to be," I said. "But we suspect he may not be. Childhood schizophrenia is very uncommon and mostly runs in families. So when Grant was diagnosed with it, my husband and I were very confused, because we didn't have anyone in either of our families who has it. So that was . . . strange. After a lot of research, we think someone switched the egg or sperm during the procedure."

"Really?" he asked. "How do you think that might have happened?"

"I don't know," I said. "I don't know who would do that on purpose. His surrogate mother was the sweetest, nicest person ever, so I don't think it had anything to do with her. I'm really confused on how it could happen."

"Where is she now?"

"She's dead," I said. "About a month after Grant was born, they pulled her car out of the river. They never found her body . . . but . . . yeah."

"Did she have schizophrenia?" he asked.

"I don't think so. It wasn't in the records we reviewed before choosing her," I said. "She was such a sweet person."

"I see," he said. "So she's dead . . ."

"And then there's Amanda," I said, my mind turning to her. "She was the nanny we planned to hire before Helena. We were really excited to have her work with Grant, but when we went to officially hire her, we couldn't find her. And then the police called a few days ago . . . and said they found a body in the landfill, and it was her, and that she was shot in the back of the head."

"Wow," he said. "So, someone killed her?"

I nodded.

"And someone killed Olive?" he said.

"Yes, I believe that's what happened," I said.

"So, then . . ." He paused. "You think that someone is trying to murder you?"

"I don't know," I answered. "I don't know anymore. But don't you think it's too much of a coincidence? To go from Olivia dying, to Amanda being killed, and then my being poisoned?"

"Mrs. Thompson." He paused. "You said that your son suffers from paranoid schizophrenia?"

"Yes," I said hesitantly.

"Well, frankly, I think you're sounding a bit paranoid yourself," he said. "I'm a bit worried that what you're currently suffering is a delusion."

"You think I'm delusional?" I said, completely

exasperated. "If I wanted to overdose, I would have done it correctly! None of this is my fault."

"I'm going to put you on a thirty-six-hour hold," he said.

"No," I begged. "No, you can't! I've already been away from my children for a few days, and I don't think I can do it again. I can't do it another day."

"Well, this is for your own safety and the safety of your children," he said.

"They're not safe in the clutches of that nanny!" I cried "Please, please do not do this to me."

"Look, I will reevaluate you in thirty-six hours, and if all is well, then you can head home. Maybe you've just had a string of bad luck. Maybe you've heard some rumors and it's really bothered you. I don't know. But I think that you'll benefit from some rest here for a while."

"I don't want to rest," I said. "Please. Please."

"I'll reinstate your phone privileges," he said. "So you can at least talk to your husband and kids. Would that work?"

I wanted to punch the man in the face. I wanted to take him and throw him from a top-floor window. He was a terrible doctor, and what was worse, he thought I was crazy. But my years as a nurse had taught me that there was nothing I could do about the situation. There was nothing I could do in terms of trying to figure out my mental state because they wouldn't let me. My best bet was just to remain calm and try to make things as smooth as possible so that I could get out of there as soon as possible.

I wanted to call Michael, but I waited a few hours, until the kids were in bed and I knew he wouldn't be around Helena. I watched the hands of the clock change until I knew we would be alone, and then I called him.

"Hi," Michael said when he answered. His voice was sweet, and he had clearly missed me.

"Hi," I said. "They won't let me out. They don't believe me. They think I'm crazy."

"Oh," he said. "Oh, no. So, when can you get out?"

"I don't know," I said. "They said they would reevaluate after a thirty-six-hour hold. I can't believe that they don't believe me."

"I mean . . ." he paused. "If I wasn't in this whole mess, I don't know if I would believe it."

"But you believe me, right?"

He sighed. "I don't know what to believe," he

answered. "Of course, I want to believe you . . . but—"

"No," I said. "Michael, you have to believe me."

"Look, Cynthia, things are very complicated right now," he said.

"What do you mean, things are complicated?" I asked. "I'm the one in the hospital."

"I know," he said. "I think we should wait till you are well and get home and then we can talk."

"You can't just cut me off," I said.

"I'm not trying to cut you off," he said. "I just want you to completely focus on your recovery."

"How are the kids doing?" I asked.

"They're okay," he replied. "They miss you. You should have called earlier."

"I wanted to wait until they were in bed because I wanted to talk to you," I said. "I wanted you to know that I didn't do it. I didn't do this to myself."

"Cynthia," he said. "It's okay. Everything is okay. You're sounding a bit . . . stressed out."

"Well, wouldn't you be stressed if you were held against your will?" I asked.

He sighed. "What can I do to help you?" he asked. "I want you to feel supported."

"Just . . . come and get me out of here," I said. "You can sign me out and that's it."

"I think you might need some help, though," he said. "You haven't been sleeping well for so long. At least look at it as a vacation."

"It's not a vacation!" I said. "Michael, please."

"Darling, you need to know that I'm trying to do the best thing for you and for the kids," he said. "And it's so hard to do everything. Please understand."

I sighed. I knew that there was a lot of pressure on him, but I was the one who was stuck in the hospital. "Fine," I said at last. "But I'm telling you that I'm not crazy."

"I know, darling," he said. "I know. I know you."

"Thank you," I said and went to lie back against my pillow. "Thank you."

"You should go to bed," he said. "It's late."

"What about you?" I asked. "It's late and you have to go to work tomorrow."

'Yeah," he said. "Yeah, I should get back to the office."

"You haven't been to work?" I asked. That was a real comment on how he was doing because he was a workaholic. He would go to work no matter what.

"Just for a few days," he said. "While everything is . . . you know, up in the air."

"Wow," I said. "I don't think I've ever seen you not go to work."

"Well, we all need a break once in a while," he said with a small laugh. "I miss you so much."

"I miss you too," I said. "I love you and I'll see you soon."

"I love you too. See you soon," he replied, and we eventually hung up the phone.

I lay back on my pillow and closed my eyes. I wished that I were home right now and that I could play with the children. I knew I just had to wait it out, and I'd be out of here before I knew it.

I just hoped that Helena would behave herself until then. I was afraid that Helena and Michael being together in a house that long was a problem, and I was afraid that Helena might hurt the children. I needed to get home soon.

I heard the IV beep and took a deep breath. Just one more night and one more day. I could do this.

Chapter 31

MICHAEL

I was just as suspicious of Helena as Cynthia was. I really did think there was something up. But if one was going to judge her just by having breakfast in the kitchen with her, then they would think that I was crazy. She was acting like a perfectly normal person who had nothing to hide, and she was smiling and laughing.

The truth was, I was completely overwhelmed by everything that was happening and I was also soul-crushingly lonely. I needed to have breakfast with the kids and Helena happened to be there.

"Do you want some orange juice?" Helena asked. "Fresh squeezed? Anna?"

"Uh . . . maybe," Anna said, looking toward me.

She seemed to need approval for everything, and I felt guilty about it. I don't know what we had done to make Anna so unsure of food, but she was really scared of eating these days. I wondered if it had anything to do with her mother being in the hospital. I didn't know that she knew anything about the situation, but she was so in tune with her mother that she probably knew something was up.

The twins were sitting at the breakfast table with us, and they kept glancing at each of us and then glancing at their mother. Eventually, Roman brought up something very confusing.

"Mother," he said. "When are you going to tell Michael?"

"What?" I asked. "Tell me what?"

"Yeah," said Terrance. "When are you going to tell him?"

"I have no idea what you're talking about," Helena said.

"Yes, you do," Terrance replied. "You told us last night that you were going to tell him soon."

"Tell me what?" I asked. I was trying to act like everything was normal, but I honestly had a shiver running down my spine.

"Orange juice is ready." Helena changed the

subject and handed us all a glass. She gave Anna hers last and then stood there. "Drink up, Anna."

Anna looked between Helena and me and then took a sip. Her face changed, and she put it down.

"No, thank you," she said. "It's bitter."

"Excuse me?" Helena raised an eyebrow. "I worked hard to make that for you! How could you say that?"

Anna looked frightened, and I was about to say something, but I wasn't sure what. Of course, Helena had worked hard and made it after Anna had accepted the offer. But at the same time, Anna didn't have to drink something she didn't like.

"I love orange juice!" Grant cried and reached for it. He started to take a sip, and Helena reached out and violently knocked it out of his hand.

For a moment, nobody moved. It was as if everything had happened in slow motion. The orange juice had splattered everywhere, and the glass was shattered and broken across the floor.

"What the heck?" I asked, confused.

"I, uh . . . I saw some mold in it," Helena said.

My eyes narrowed. "You saw mold in it?" I asked. "When Grant drank it, but not when you gave it to Anna?"

"Yes," she said. "Sorry, I should have been more careful."

Alarm bells were ringing in my head, especially after the strange conversation with the twins.

"I apologize," Helena said. "Let me clean it up."

"I'll get it," I said. "Please get Anna a new glass."

I went to pick up the pieces, but I couldn't shake the feeling that something was terribly wrong. When no one was looking, I slipped the largest piece of glass into my pocket. I had to be very careful to not cut myself and to make sure that no one caught me.

"Sorry, I'm sure that's better," Helena said as she gave Anna a new glass.

"I want water," Anna said.

Helena said, "You can't have water for breakfast."

"She can have it if she wants," I said.

"Okay." Helena seemed to know not to push me any further. She wiped up the orange juice and I leaned down to kiss both of the kids.

"You guys have a good day, okay?" I said to Anna and Grant. "I'm going to head out for the day."

"Daddy?" Grant asked. "Is Mommy going to come home soon?"

"Not yet," I said. "But hopefully soon."

"Is she really sick?" Anna asked.

"She's getting better," I said. "And I'll see if you can talk to her tonight."

"Yay," Grant said.

I noticed the twins giving Helena a look. She was giving them a look right back, and I had no idea what was going on.

Once I left the house, I decided to take the glass to the police station. I figured that they would want to test it and see what was happening. But when I brought it to them, they looked at me like I was crazy.

"We don't test things just because," the officer said.

"This is not just because," I said. "I think my wife was poisoned by the nanny."

"And this glass was given to your daughter?"

"Yes," I said.

"Is she showing signs of poisoning?"

"No," I said. "But—"

"Mr. Thompson," the officer said. "We cannot do things based on people's hunches. We investigated after your wife was hospitalized, but we found nothing. So therefore, we have closed the case."

"This is new evidence," I said.

He shook his head. "I'm sorry, sir," he said.

I sighed. "Fine, whatever," I said. "I'll get it tested by myself."

"I'm sure you can do that," he said. "There are lots of places that you can pay to do that."

"Great," I said. "Thank you so much for your help."

I was so sarcastic about it, but he didn't seem to notice. I took the glass and was careful not to cut myself as I placed it back in the bag.

I'm sure I could get it tested, but I had no idea where. I sat in my car and Googled a few places, and eventually, I called one. I didn't care how much it cost. I just wanted it done.

"Hi," I said to the first place that answered. "I think my nanny is trying to poison my wife and my daughter. I have a cup she used. Could you test it for poison?"

The woman on the other end of the phone choked. "Uh . . . what kind of poison?" she said.

"I don't know," I replied. "That's your job."

"Sir, we need a police report in order to do the

testing," she said. "Otherwise, our evidence could be used for unlawful accusations."

"That doesn't make any sense," I said. "Why would you need a police report?"

"I just told you," she said. "I'm sorry. We can't help you."

"That's fine, I'll call someone else," I said and hung up the phone. I went through several labs and eventually found one that seemed interested.

"Yes, we can do that," the man at the other end of the phone said. "When can you bring it in?"

"I'll bring it in right away," I said. "Give me your address."

I felt like a private detective as I drove my car toward this lab. I was starting to think it was a mistake when I turned into the parking lot. The parking lot was sketchy, and the building was even sketchier. I wasn't even sure I was in the right spot until I pushed through the doors and recognized the voice that had been on the phone.

"Are you Michael?" he asked.

"Yes," I said. "Was it you who I talked to on the phone?"

"Yes," he said. "My name is Aidan. Nice to meet you. Sounds like you have some juicy history."

"Not really," I said. "I don't know if this is all just a . . . delusion. But I have to know."

"And the police won't do anything?"

"Nope," I said. "Because they didn't find anything the first time."

"Yeah, that's the way it is," he replied. "They don't care half the time. If your investigation is going to be a lot of work for them, they get rid of it and leave you to your own devices."

"Yep, that's exactly it," I said. "And it's horrible because my wife is in the hospital because of this. So it would really help if you could give us some answers."

"It'll be fifteen hundred dollars for the first set of tests," he said. "And then another thousand if we need to do a second round to dig deeper."

I didn't even question the amount he told me. I just handed over my credit card.

"Oh, we don't take credit cards," he said. "Cash only."

"Oh," I said. "I don't have that much cash on me."

"Bank around the corner," he said.

I nodded. I knew at this point that I was involved in something very sketchy, but I wasn't going to say anything.

"Sure," I said and headed to the bank. I got all the money out, trying not to think of what Cynthia's hospital stay was going to cost us. I went back to him and was grateful that I didn't get robbed on the way back. "Here you go. How long will it take?"

"About a week," he said.

"Can you make it faster?" I asked.

"For another grand," he replied.

I raised my eyebrows. "Well, how about I give you another grand if you get it done in three days?" I asked.

He met my eyes. "What is it that you do?" he asked.

"I run a multimillion-dollar architect firm," I replied. "You can Google my name. I'm good for the money."

He paused and then nodded. "Sure," he said. "I'll get it done."

"Thank you, sir," I said, and we shook hands. I headed out of the shop and took a moment in the car before calling the hospital. I was hoping to speak to Cynthia, but they said that she was busy. I wondered if she was in therapy or if she was taking a walk or if she had made a break for it. Part of me smiled, thinking of how she was in college. Cynthia in college was a whole different person, so full of force and so full of strength.

She was still strong, and she was still resilient. But I felt like life had really beaten her down after having Anna and then dealing with Grant's illness.

I headed to the office, but I found myself completely distracted. Every few seconds, I was checking my phone. I wasn't sure whether I was waiting for the results or wondering if the kids' school was going to call me and tell me something was wrong.

She couldn't be hurting my kids. What would be the motivation? Why would she hurt Cynthia? What was the reasoning? Maybe she didn't do any of it. Maybe she would never hurt a fly and we had completely misjudged her.

I thought of her in my room the other night, though, and I knew she wasn't as innocent as she seemed. She knew exactly what she was doing when she came into my room. Who knew what else she was doing?

I was willing to pay that man another million if he could get the results done right away. If there was nothing on it, then I would admit that I had completely misjudged Helena and that we needed to look down a different path. But if he did find something, I would make sure that she never saw my wife or children again.

I love you, I texted Cynthia, hoping that she could check her phone soon. I wanted her to know that I was thinking of her and that I missed her. She was the love of my life, and I felt guilty that I had ever chosen anything but her. She was my everything and I was certain I would never stray again.

I briefly wondered if I had driven her to do this. I hoped not. I hoped that this was just a bad dream, and soon, we would go back to normal.

Chapter 32

MICHAEL

I COULDN'T SHAKE THE THOUGHTS FROM MY MIND that we were in a bad situation. I couldn't believe that Helena would have poisoned my kids. Why would she save Grant, then? Why would she take the job? What was happening?

I was starting to realize that maybe, just maybe, Grant's genetic issues were my fault and I was the one who was talking like I was paranoid. I couldn't believe that I was in this situation.

It had, of course, been suggested that someone in our family had the issues and were just hiding it. These days, my mind drifted back to every family encounter I had ever had. That cousin that I had only met twice? Were they a little off? The uncle who always sat quietly in a corner? Was he over-medicated instead of just quiet?

I'd have liked to think that we were an open enough family to talk about these thing and support each other if something like a diagnosis of schizophrenia were to pop up. But then, you never knew how you were going to react until it was right there in your face.

On the way home today, I decided to call the kids. I wanted to know that they were okay and there weren't any problems.

I also wanted to know that they weren't dead from some sort of poison.

"Hello?" I thanked my lucky stars that Anna answered the phone.

"Hi, Anna," I said. "It's Daddy. How are you?"

"I'm good," she said. "School was fun."

"That's good," I said. "Is Helena there?"

"She's downstairs," Anna said. "Do you want me to get her?"

"No," I said. "Is Grant there, though?"

"Yes," she said. "Do you want me to get him?"

"Can you go up to Grant's bedroom and put the phone on speakerphone?" I asked. "I want to talk to him and you at the same time."

"Okay," she said. "Are we in trouble?"

"No, honey, you aren't in trouble," I said. "Can you just go and do it? And make sure the monitor in Grant's room is unplugged."

I figured she thought that was weird, but she did as I asked. Soon enough, both of them were on speakerphone. I thought about pulling over to talk to them because my mind was all over the place.

"How was school, Grant?" I asked.

"It was good," he said. "When is Mommy coming home?"

"Soon," I said. "I just wanted to talk to both of you about Helena."

"I love Helena," Grant blurted out.

"Yeah, but . . ." Anna interrupted him. "She's a bit weird, isn't she?"

"Yeah," Grant said. "She is. But some people are just weird."

"She's really weird," Anna said.

Grant sighed. "Well, sometimes, she says weird things," he said.

Anna coughed. "Sometimes?" she asked.

"What weird things?" I asked them. I knew it took a lot for Grant to consider someone weird because he liked most people and accepted all of their quirks.

"Well . . ." Grant paused, and I could tell he

was wrestling with himself. "Sometimes, she asks me to call her Mommy. And when I don't, she yells at me."

I felt my heart sink. "She does?" I asked, concerned.

"Yeah," he said. "Or she says that the twins are my brothers. It's so weird. I like them and they're my friends, but they aren't my brothers, not like for real."

I felt like I'd been slapped. It occurred to me how much the twins looked like Grant in that moment. They could easily be his brothers. What if they actually were his brothers?

This was a rarity that I really didn't want to explore.

"Oh," I said. "Well, that is weird."

"They look like you," Anna said, confirming my fears.

"Just a little," I said, not wanting them to follow down the path my mind was going on. I was super worried, but I decided that I was going to get home and investigate further. I couldn't rush the lab results any more than I already had, but I certainly needed to figure out what was going on before things got even more confused. "I just wanted to make sure you guys are okay."

"Yes, we're fine," Anna said. "Should we not be?"

"No, you should be fine," I said. "Just stay and play in Grant's room."

"Okay," Anna said. "Helena is downstairs taking care of Terrance, anyway."

"Is he sick?"

"She said he was," Anna said. "Are you coming home soon?"

"Yes," I said. "I'll be home in like twenty minutes. See you soon."

"Bye," Anna said and hung up the phone.

Now that I had that conversation with them, I was even more confused and even more upset.

I was no longer of the mindset that Cynthia had tried to kill herself. This was extremely upsetting, and I needed to do something. I didn't have any proof, but my gut told me that I needed to get Helena out of there as soon as I found even a pebble of proof.

When I got home, the first thing I did was go into the fridge. I had my phone out and I also took a tiny sip of the orange juice and the milk, and each of them tasted fine. To my suspicious mind, that meant that the whole bottle hadn't been poisoned. It meant that just the individual glasses had been poisoned, which made me incredibly worried.

But why save Grant? *Unless Grant is her son,* I realized.

But that couldn't be the case. Unless she had been in league with Olive all this time, there was no way Helena could be his mother. There were too many coincidences. How could she possibly do that? How could she possibly be there when it was seven years ago and we didn't even know her then? If I told this to anyone, they would tell us we were crazy and we didn't know anything. They would say that we were nuts and needed to just relax and move on with our lives.

But something was very, very wrong in my house. I quickly texted in an order for all new groceries. I wanted to replace it all, just in case.

When the groceries were finally delivered, I threw out everything in the fridge and replaced them. I'd made sure to buy the same brands so that Helena didn't suspect a thing.

I didn't know why I was so worried about Helena suspecting anything. I was worried that she might catch me in the act, but she stayed downstairs the entire time.

I was also worried that she might do something

horrible if she caught me. This wasn't right. I shouldn't be concerned with whether or not my nanny approved of my actions.

"I'm hungry," Anna said as she clung to me just as I finished throwing everything out.

"I'm hungry too," I said. "Do you guys want to go out and get some pizza?"

"Yes!" Anna cried and Grant looked excited. "Should we go and get Helena?"

"No," I said. "I think it will be just us. Why don't you guys go get your coats, and we'll just go?"

I wanted to get them out of the house and get them away from Helena as soon as possible. I knew, traditionally, that we took everyone out, but I didn't want to risk it with everything going on. I didn't even tell her that we were going. I just bundled the kids up and headed out of the house.

"Which pizza place did you want to go to?" I asked the kids, as soon as we got in the car.

"I want Pizza Express," Grant said.

"I want Pizza, Pizza," Anna said. I had to make a choice, but I wanted both of them to be happy. Pizza, Pizza was first, so I decided to stop there and get Anna what she wanted, and then went on to Pizza Express. Both kids were satisfied, and I was happy to just eat food that I didn't think was poisoned.

"Daddy?" Grant asked. "Helena isn't my mommy, is she?"

"No, son," I said really quickly. "But you know that you were born differently from Anna. And we've told you about Olive."

"Yes," he said. "Olive sounded so nice."

"She was really nice," I replied. "And I think you would have liked her."

"How come you didn't do that with me?" Anna asked.

"Because when you were born, Mommy wasn't sick," I said. "And she could carry you just fine. But after you were born, we decided it was safer for Mommy to have Olive carry Grant."

"Oh," Grant said. "Are any of my friends like me?"

"I don't think so," I said with a smile. "You're one of a kind."

"Is that a bad thing?" he asked me.

"No," I said with a smile. "It's not a bad thing to be one of a kind."

"Oh," he said and then looked down at his pizza. "But Mommy is coming home soon, right?"

"She is," I promised him. "She was just very sick."

"Is it my fault?" Grant asked. "Helena said that Mommy wasn't supposed to be very sick."

"What was she supposed to be?" I asked.

"I don't know." Grant shrugged.

I had a horrible feeling that what she was supposed to be was dead.

"It's okay," I said. "Just finish your pizza."

"Daddy?" Anna asked. "Do you think that you might have another kid someday?"

"Uh, I don't think so," I replied. "Why?"

"Helena thinks you might," Anna replied.

"Oh, good," I said, almost sarcastically.

I really didn't want to get into that, so I just finished my own pizza as an indication to them that we should really just get out of there. The kids seemed happy that they were out of the house and just with me, and they asked if we could go to the arcade. The arcade was incredibly overstimulating, and I was worried that Grant might have a meltdown. However, I wanted to keep them out of the house and happy as long as possible, so I agreed.

"Not for very long, though."

"Please, please, please," Grant said, and I smiled. "Can we stay for one hour?"

"How about I'll buy fifty tokens?" I said. "And you can play for as long as that lasts?"

"Yes," Grant said with a grin.

I ended up caving and buying more than fifty tokens. We kept playing until the kids were yawning, and then I loaded them back into the car and took them back home.

I got a message on my phone from Cynthia as soon as we were home that said she was going to be released tomorrow. That made me breathe a sigh of relief. I couldn't wait until she was home and life could return back to normal.

At least, as much back to normal as possible, considering the fact that our nanny was crazy.

That night, which I hoped was my last night at home alone, I Googled Helena's name again, trying desperately to find anything about her. When I came up with nothing, I Googled Olive's name as well, just hoping that maybe something would pop up. To my dismay, there was nothing. Neither Olive nor Helena existed, as far as the internet was concerned.

That made me so worried. I was worried that both of them had used fake names. I hated to say something bad about Olive, but it had been seven years and we still didn't know what had happened to her!

My paranoid mind formed some sort of conspiracy theory that she had somehow managed to team up with Helena and switch eggs or something. I knew that was crazy, but I couldn't deny the similarities between her and Grant. I couldn't deny the fact that the twins looked just like Grant.

I didn't know what to think at the end of the night. I couldn't stop thinking about Cynthia, alone in her hospital room, surrounded by people who thought she was crazy. I made a vow that as soon as the lab results came back, I was going to do something one way or another. Either Helena was going to explain herself, or the lab results were going to do it for me. Either way, this would be over soon.

I put my laptop away and sank down onto my pillow and tried to sleep. My mind was whirling, and I couldn't stop coming up with crazy theories. I eventually drifted off to sleep, but I dreamed of waking up and finding Helena in my bed, saying that she was Cynthia. Once, it would have been a good thing, but now, it was a nightmare.

Chapter 33

CYNTHIA

I COULDN'T WAIT TO GET OUT OF THERE. Everything Michael had brought me was packed, and I was ready to go. I couldn't wait to leave and never come back. No one here believed me, but I was released with a clean bill of health and no signs of schizophrenia. I was sure the terrible psychiatrist thought I was suffering from something, but because he was bad at his job, he couldn't come up with a concrete diagnosis. So instead, he handed me my discharge papers and told me to take care of myself.

I still felt weak and sick, and I was ordered to rest for a few weeks, but I wasn't sure that was possible. If anything happened to my kids, I was pretty sure I really would throw myself off the bridge downtown or actually take an overdose of pills. Today, however, all I wanted to do was get out of there. Michael was on his way, and I was counting down the seconds until he came into the room.

Looking in the mirror, I certainly wasn't proud of my appearance. I looked haggard and tired, and my roots were starting to grow in. I used to think that I didn't look my age, but these days, I thought I looked much older than just past forty. Parenthood and a child with a mental illness would certainly do that to you.

When Michael came in the door, I practically threw myself on him and hugged him tightly.

"Hi!" I said. "I missed you so much."

"I missed you too," he said. "How are you feeling? Are you ready to go?"

"So ready to go," I answered. "Also, I'm starving."

"Well, that's a good sign," he said as he picked up my bag.

"Where are the kids?"

"They're at home," he said. "But they have my cell number, and I told them to call if anything happened. And I told them not to eat anything."

"Good call," I said. My heart rate was pounding in my throat and I felt like I was going to explode. I needed to see my kids, and I needed to know that everything was okay in my house. "Michael? You look nervous. Is something wrong?"

"No," he said as we got out of the hospital and into the parking lot. "Just . . . there are some things that I need to talk to you about."

I felt my heart sink. *This is it*, I thought. *This is where he tells me he wants to leave me. This is where he tells me he wants to be with someone else.*

"Some things like what?" I asked as he helped me into the car and started the engine.

"Just, uh . . ." He looked over to me, and I could see him steeling himself. "I wanted to say that I was sorry for doubting you. I'm sorry that I ever thought that you were trying to kill yourself."

"Oh," I said. "Well, that's very kind of you. Thank you for saying that."

"A lot of things have happened since you've been gone," he said as he drove. "Helena has been acting really freaking weird."

"Weird how?" I asked.

"Just . . . skittish. And avoiding me. Although she has good reason."

"Does she?" I asked. "Have you called her out on anything? Have you yelled at her?"

"Well . . ." he paused. "The other night—the first night you were hospitalized—I was in the bedroom . . . and I was pretty drunk, I admit. I was trying to numb everything I was feeling. She came up in this lacy nightgown and she tried to seduce me."

"What?" I asked in shock. "And what happened?"

"Nothing," he swore to me. "I told her to get out and I was pretty clear about it. She ran back downstairs, and she's been pretty much avoiding me ever since. We pretend to be normal for the kids, but that's it."

"Really, nothing happened?"

He nodded. "I swear," he said. "Nothing happened. I would tell you if it did. I love you, and I wouldn't bring you home to that kind of mess."

"Okay," I replied. I wanted desperately to believe him with all my heart, but I couldn't quite do it. "Is there anything else?"

"There was the orange juice incident," he said. "Helena insisted that Anna drink some orange juice that she didn't want. She said it was bitter. Grant went to drink it, and Helena freaked out and knocked it out of his hand. She said that there was mold in it that she'd just noticed, but I wasn't too sure about that."

I felt my stomach sink. "Really?" I asked.

"Yeah," he said. "I couldn't believe it. She violently knocked it out of his hand too. The glass shattered everywhere."

"Destroying the evidence," I said.

He half smiled. "Don't worry," he replied. "I'm getting a sample analyzed."

"Sample of what?" I asked, confused.

"I took some of the glass to an independent lab," he said. "Just to get it analyzed and see if there was anything on it."

"And?" I asked.

"I don't have the results yet," he said. "But I'm sure I will get them soon."

"Well, I'm hoping that you get them soon," I said. "It will answer a lot of questions."

"Well," he said, "Even if it doesn't answer a lot of questions . . . to be honest, I have some questions of my own that need to be asked. Helena has been asking weird things of the kids."

"Like what?" I asked, confused.

"Like, she told Terrance that I was going to be their new dad," he said. "And she told Grant to call her Mommy."

I almost choked. "No, she didn't," I said in disbelief. "Please tell me that she didn't."

"Yeah." He winced. "And she told Terrance to not be friends with Anna."

"I heard that one," I replied. "But I just couldn't believe it. Tell me it's not true."

"Yeah, unfortunately, it's true." He shook his head. "I don't know what to make of any of this."

"I do," I said. "I want to call the police and have her arrested."

"But on what charge?" he asked. "Being a little weird? We can't do that, Cynthia. She could sue us."

"But she's done some really weird things," I said. "Like really weird things. Surely, we could get rid of her on those grounds."

"Possibly," he replied. "But I want to go about this carefully, so that there are no issues."

"And what if she hurts the kids before then?" I asked. "You can't just assume that she won't, Michael. She already hurt me."

"I know." He gripped the steering wheel. "I know. I've also thought of something else."

"I'm afraid to know," I said.

"I think that the twins look a lot like Grant," he said. "And so does she, because she's told Grant they are his brothers."

Of all the chilling things that he could have told me, this seemed like the worst one.

"No," I said. "This can't be possible. How could it be possible?"

"I know it's crazy," he said. "But you can't deny the resemblance in any of them. And the fact that she's told him to call her Mommy really has me freaked out."

"But it was seven years ago," I cried. "And Olive was the one who carried him."

"He certainly doesn't look like Olive," Michael said. "But maybe Helena and Olive were in league together?"

"I mean, maybe," I said. "Maybe this runs a lot deeper than we thought."

"I've also tossed around the idea that we're both being paranoid," he said to me. "And I hate it."

"It's hard not to be, given all that's happened," I answered. "I think what we need to accept is that there is something very strange going on in our house, and we need to do something about it."

"So, what?" he asked. "We just tell Helena that we no longer need her services?"

"We could," I said. "But then, what if she's actually done something criminal?"

"Well, that's the problem," he said. "She could have, and we'd be releasing her into the wild, to another family, so to speak."

I covered my face with my hands. "I couldn't imagine this happening to another family," I replied. "I can't even imagine this happening to us."

"Do you know what I wish?" he asked. "I wish that we knew what happened with Olive. If we did, we'd have a better idea of what was going on."

"You mean, whether she died or whether she . . . was murdered?" I whispered. I could barely say the words. I couldn't imagine something happening to sweet Olive.

"Exactly," he said "If the police had ever found her . . ."

"I think it's a bit weird that they didn't keep looking," I said. "Like she was a missing person, but no one seemed to care."

"Unless they know something we don't," he said. "Which is also strange. Why wouldn't they tell us?"

"Maybe they don't think we need to know?" I

asked. "But . . . she gave birth to our son barely a month before. Why wouldn't they tell us?"

"We could make an inquiry?" he suggested. "See if they ever closed the case? I mean, they told us about Amanda, so you'd think they'd tell us about the rest."

"Yeah," I said. "Yeah, let's do that. Do you remember who to call?"

"I'm sure I could figure it out," he answered. "I can look into it when we get home."

"What's the plan when we get home?" I asked. "Do you think that we should confront her then and there?"

"I don't know," he said. "She wasn't around when I got up this morning, but I'm trying to avoid her. I know she was awake and alive because I shouted at her down the stairs that I was leaving, and she was going to come up and stay with the kids."

"Well, that's good," I said. "I mean, I assume that she wouldn't do anything to Anna with Grant there? She doesn't want to kill us, does she?"

"I don't know," he admitted, which made me feel sick. "I don't know."

"Step on it," I said to him, even though he was going as fast as he could.

"I'm sorry," he said after a few minutes. "I feel like this is my fault."

"How is it your fault?" I asked, confused.

"Because I was the one who insisted on a nanny," he said. "I should have just left it."

"Don't say that," I said. "We did really need someone. We did this for Grant's sake."

"I know," he said. "But we could have just . . ."

"Michael, hindsight is twenty-twenty," I said. "We didn't know."

"No," he said. "We didn't know. But I will never do it again, if we survive this."

"I agree," I said and reached over to touch his leg. "From now on, it's just you, me, and the kids."

"Sounds like a plan," he said to me with a smile. "Should have been that way since the start."

"Well, we learned our lesson," I said as our house came into sight. I felt like I was suiting myself up to go into battle.

"Do you need help getting out the car?" he asked.

I nodded. "Sorry. I just feel shaky," I said, and he came around to help me.

"Don't apologize," he said as he kissed the top of my head. "You just survived hell."

"Why do I have a feeling that hell is going to

return?" I said as we headed up the driveway. My heart was pounding, and my mouth felt dry. I didn't know what I was going to find inside, but I hoped that it would be my children, smiling and laughing. I gripped Michael's hand, took a deep breath, and then pushed open the door.

Chapter 34

MICHAEL

WHEN WE GOT INSIDE, ABSOLUTE CHAOS ERUPTED, and I had no idea what was going on. There was a lot of screaming and yelling, and I couldn't figure out who exactly it was. It seemed everyone was in a panic.

"It's coming from the downstairs," Cynthia pointed out.

I hesitated for just a moment. "I want you to go upstairs."

Cynthia's eyes widened. "What?" she said. "No, I can't."

"Yes, you can," I said. "You're still not entirely well, and I don't want you stressing yourself out more than you have to. Go upstairs, and I'll come up as soon as possible."

"What if the kids aren't safe?" she asked, wide-eyed.

"The kids will be safe," I assured her. "Please don't worry. Go upstairs."

I'd never needed her to trust me more than in that moment. This was what I needed to do to keep everyone safe, including her.

It took a moment, but I managed to convince her to go upstairs at last. I waited until she was safely most of the way up the stairs before I went down to the basement quarters.

Helena was down in the basement apartment, and she was yelling and screaming at Terrance. Terrance was screaming back, but he wasn't making any sense.

"I told you!" she screamed. "I told you this would happen if you stopped taking your meds! I told you not to do that!"

I watched, in frozen horror, as I realized what was happening. Terrance was having some sort of schizophrenic episode. He was hallucinating something in front of him that he felt he needed to fight. His eyes were darting every which way and he looked absolutely terrified. He certainly wasn't lucid, and instead of helping him, Helena was yelling at him.

I felt terrible for him. I didn't have much spare energy left, but I felt like he just wanted help, and she wasn't helping him.

"What's happening?" I asked, trying to make my voice sound as innocent as possible.

"Help!" Helena turned to me with wide eyes. "Please, will you help me?"

"What do you need me to do?" I asked her.

"Grab him," she said. "Please try to calm him down."

I didn't know how that would help. It had never helped with Grant, but I decided to try. I reached forward and carefully tried to grab Terrance.

"Hey," I said. "Terrance. Hey. Terrance. Everything is okay. Terrance."

"Why do they want me to jump?" he asked me frantically. "Why do they want me to do this?"

"I don't know, buddy," I said. "I don't know, but I don't think that you need to listen to them."

"I need to jump," he said. "Or I need to fight them."

"They'll go away," I said. "They'll go away."

"They won't," he said. "They've never gone away before. They never go away. They're always there."

"Always?" I asked. "I don't think they're always there. Can you think of a time they're not?"

"No," he said. "Maybe once."

"Once?" I said. "When were they not there?"

"At the zoo," he said. "At the zoo, they weren't there because the animals scared them off."

"Well, that's good," I said. "That means there are other times they could go away. Did they go away because you were focused on the animals?"

"*I hate them!*" he screamed again, and his focus went away.

I realized that I had lost him, and I turned to Helena. She reached out for his wrists, to try and take hold of him.

"Can you get his meds?" she asked. "They're in the bathroom cabinet. Can you get them, please?"

"Sure," I said, like everything was fine.

I made sure she had a good grip on him and then headed off to the bathroom. It had been a long time since I had been in the guest bathroom, but I didn't think she would have completely taken it over. There were pill bottles everywhere, and empty wrappers everywhere, too. I opened the bathroom cabinet, and I found the two bottles that were prescribed to Terrance. I recognized that this was the same type of meds that Grant took, but I didn't want to say anything to her. Just as I was about to close the cabinet, I noticed something else. There was a powerful tranquilizer right in the front that was prescribed to Helena. The bottle said fifty, but there were certainly not fifty of them in there. It looked almost empty and yet it was prescribed in the past month or so.

Something was very, very wrong. Without wanting to tip her off, I took one pill out of the bottle and slipped it into my pocket. Once it was securely in there, I took the meds back to Helena.

"Here," I said. "Is this what you were looking for?"

"Yes," she said and opened both bottles and poured out two pills from each. I recognized the pills as exactly what Grant took, and I knew that Terrance had the same illness.

It was a fight to get the pills in Terrance's mouth and then a fight to get him to swallow them. After a little while, they started to take effect.

"There you go," Helena said soothingly. "There you go, baby. Now, don't do that again, okay?"

He looked almost dazed, and he nodded while looking around.

Grant had once described it as coming back to Earth, and I saw that Terrance was going through the same thing. He finally smiled and Helena gave him a light pat on the cheek.

"Go and hang out with your brother," she said.

Terrance smiled and then skipped off to play. Once he was gone, Helena stood up and breathed a sigh of relief.

"Sorry," she said. "He's normally much better than that."

"Does he have juvenile schizophrenia?" I asked.

Helena looked pained. "He does," she said. "We just recently found out. It seems like quite a blow."

"But . . . you mentioned that it ran in your family?" I asked.

Again, she looked pained. "Well . . . it did," she said. "In my husband's family. But . . . these are not his biological kids."

"Oh," I replied. "Why not?"

"He, uh . . . he couldn't have children. So I went to a fertility specialist."

My heart sank even further.

"Who did you go to?" I asked.

"Dr. Andrews?" she said. "I'm not even sure he's still practicing anymore."

He was still practicing. That was the same fertility specialist that Cynthia and I had used. He was certainty still practicing, and he was supposed to call us back, but he never had.

Could this be some sort of sick joke? Could he have done the same thing to all of us? Switched the genetic material with someone with this disease, possibly just to make a quick buck?

I couldn't believe this. This couldn't be real. Yet, here it was, in my face.

"Oh," I said. "So, your husband . . . he's not around anymore, right? I assume he's not, given that he's not here right now."

"Yeah," she said. "He's not."

She didn't seem to want to offer any more details, so I didn't ask. I did, however, look over to where the boys were playing. They were just sitting there, watching TV, and they seemed completely normal now.

"Have you ever . . . you know, gotten them tests? DNA and all?"

"Nope," she said. "I mean, they're my children. They're in my care. That's what matters."

"I agree," I said. "And they're clearly your kids, given their coloring."

Helena smiled at me, but it was pained. I think she knew I was onto her, but I wanted to see how far I could push things.

"So . . . how are you doing?" I asked. "Coping with that diagnosis?"

"Well, if he had to have a diagnosis, I guess it's good that he got one I could handle."

"For sure," I said. "And Roman?"

"So far, so good," she said. "But sometimes, they say it shows up more when they hit puberty."

"Oh, my," I said. "That must be quite scary for you."

"It's okay," she replied. "I know what to do. And I know that there are medical advances every day."

"I know," I said. "We keep hoping for those."

"How is Cynthia?" she asked.

"She's okay," I said. "I've just brought her home and sent her upstairs."

"Oh," she said. "Still not feeling well?"

"No," I said. "She'll be okay, though."

"I could go and take care of her," she offered.

I shook my head, a bit too quickly. "No, thank you," I said. "She's fine. She'll be fine."

"Okay," she said. "It's on offer."

"Of course," I said. "So, uh . . . about the other night."

"Oh, Michael," she said, and she put on what I had come to learn was her fake smile. "I'm sorry about the other night. I shouldn't have come up. It's just . . . I thought you were interested."

"Did I give you some reason to believe that I was?" I asked her.

"Well . . . to be honest," she said, "you keep looking at me. And I've seen a few times that you are . . . more than interested, if you know what I mean. Like the night I came up to get aspirin."

"That was . . . that was from a dream," I said. "Nothing to do with you."

"It could make a girl feel like she is special," she said. "Or . . . feel like she needs to run away if she doesn't want that attention."

I gulped. I knew what road she was going down, and I didn't know whether she wanted my attention or she was just using it as a technique to bait me.

"Well, you shouldn't feel that way," I said. "I didn't mean to make you feel any sort of way, aside from that I was a good and fair employer."

"Someone could report you, you know," she said. "For that."

"Really?" I asked. "For what?"

"For making me feel harassed," she said. "And like I was just a piece of meat."

"If you felt that way, why did you come up to

me?" I asked. "You wouldn't have come up if you didn't think I wanted it."

"So now you are victim shaming?" she replied.

"No," I said, frustrated. "Because there is no victim here. There's literally just you trying to turn the situation into something it's not."

"That's not the way a court would see it," Helena said. "With a girl who looks like me, it's such a classic story."

I held her gaze with a glare. "You wouldn't dare," I said.

She shrugged. "I would do anything I could to protect my children," she said. "All the children."

"Okay," I said. "I think we've talked enough."

She turned sweet again. "Of course," she said. "You should go back upstairs to Cynthia."

"Yes," I said. "Yes, I should."

I turned my back on her, which felt like a bad idea, and then headed upstairs. My heart was pounding in my chest and my mouth felt dry.

I didn't know what to believe. There were so many red flags, and yet there was still a chance that she could be innocent. I wished that we had never hired her. I wished that we had never set eyes on her. I didn't care what her connection to Grant was.

I didn't want her around him anymore, if I could help it.

I went upstairs to see Cynthia. I paused outside the door and took a deep breath. I hated that she would have to shoulder this burden when she had just gotten out of the hospital. However, I wanted to make sure our children were safe, as quickly as possible. Cynthia would know what to do, and I would stand by her side, no matter what.

Chapter 35

CYNTHIA

"I'M TRYING TO PUT THIS TOGETHER," I SAID TO Michael as I sat there. I couldn't believe what he was telling me. "So . . . Terrance has juvenile schizophrenia as well. And Helena just found out?"

"Supposedly, she just found out," I said. "And she doesn't know about Roman yet."

"There is no way you *just* find that out," I said. "You have to know before that."

"I don't know," he said. "She said that it sometimes doesn't come up until puberty hits."

I winced.

"Look, I'm not an expert," I said. "And I think that is sometimes the case, but . . . not in an extreme case."

"Yeah," he said. "The other thing is . . . she accused me of harassing her."

"Do you know what she means?"

Michael swallowed hard.

"No," he replied. "No . . . I mean . . . you know there have been some issues. But I promise you that I haven't done anything wrong. And I promise you that there is no reason for her to even think that she has a case."

"But she came up here and tried to seduce you?" I asked.

"Yes, I turned her away," Michael said. "I swear."

I could see the honesty in his gaze, and I nodded. "I believe you," I said. "But that doesn't mean that everyone will."

"I know." He winced. "I know."

"So . . ." I tried to think, but he still had one more piece of news.

"I found this in her medicine cabinet," Michael said and held up a pill. I recognized it as the tranquilizer pills that we used to use at the hospital for very difficult patients. "And the bottle looked half empty."

"You think that is what she used?" I asked. "It would explain how I was feeling."

"I don't know," Michael said. "Maybe we could get it tested with the shard of glass?"

"Yes," I said. "And I think we should take the kids out of the house and go."

"I agree," he said. "Let me go and get the kids. Are you sure that you're well enough to go out?"

"Well, I certainly don't want to stay here," I said. "I'd much rather be out and getting answers."

"Yeah," he said. "I know what you mean. Just stay here until I get the kids ready."

"What are you going to tell the kids?" I asked.

"Nothing," he said and leaned to kiss me on the forehead.

I felt so loved and so surrounded by his support. I had no idea how everything was going to be okay, but I just knew that it was.

Michael went to tell the kids we were going out, and I managed to slowly get myself downstairs. I knew that he didn't want me to, but I couldn't spend another moment in that house.

"Where are we going?" Anna asked as Michael practically peeled out of the driveway. "I wanted to stay home and play."

"I know," Michael said. "But we have to run some errands, and Mommy and I thought it would be good for you to come with us."

"Why?" she asked. "We could have stayed with Helena."

"I don't think that's a good idea," I said. "Because Terrance is very sick and Helena needs to focus on him."

"I could have stayed with him," Grant said. "I could have stayed and cheered him up."

"Well, maybe when we get back," Michael lied to him.

I glanced at him, and we exchanged a look that was terrified. They certainly didn't prepare you for things like this to happen.

"Where is this lab?" I asked.

"It's, uh . . . it's in a bit of a weird area," he said. "It was hard to get someone to do it, so I had to go to the independent places."

"To the independent places?" I raised an eyebrow. "What exactly does that mean?"

"It means it's not the . . . most up to date," he said.

"How could a lab not be up to date?" I asked him, confused. But then, when I saw the area it was in, I completely understood, and it made me wince. "Oh."

"I think it's best if you all come in," Michael

said. "Just so you aren't . . . waiting in the car by yourself."

"Sure," I said. I was nervous about what I might find inside, and I took Anna and Grant by the hand.

"Hello," said a man when I walked in. "Your results are just about ready."

"I need you to test something else," Michael said and pulled out the pill. "And I need you to test it right now against whatever you find on the glass."

"I can't just get results instantly," the man said, but Michael pulled out his wallet.

"I will pay you literally whatever you want," he said. "Literally. I just need it tested right now."

"Okay." The man relented when he saw the amount of money that was being waved around.

Grant's eyes widened at the wad of bills. "Can we have ice cream after?"

"Sure," I said to Grant, although I didn't know when we'd get it.

"About half an hour?" the man behind the counter said. The lab didn't look state of the art and it looked like he was running it alone, so I had no idea how he was going to get the results back. But if the results on the glass matched the pill, then we'd be on the right path. Michael didn't give him any indication that he wanted it to match, which I was glad of. That was how we'd know whether it was a scam or not.

"Sure," Michael said and then turned to Grant. "You said you wanted ice cream?"

"I feel like we bribed our children with ice cream," I said to Michael as we drove to the nearest place.

"I know," he said. "And I would agree that we are basically doing that. But whatever."

Once we got the kids ice cream and headed back to the lab, the man handed us the paperwork.

"Here you go," he said. "Had to piss off a lot of people who are going to have late results now, but whatever."

"Thank you very much," Michael said and handed me the paperwork.

He assumed that I was the one who was going to understand, with a medical background. It didn't take a medical background, however, to understand the results in front of me. The two samples matched. Helena had tried to drug Anna with this tranquilizer. I had never praised the stars that she was a picky eater until now. I couldn't believe that Helena had done this.

She was a mother. She was a mother with children of her own living right there. How could she do that? How could she even try? I thought, once you became a mother, you couldn't possibly hurt a child.

"We can't go home," Michael said. "We can't go home until we have a concrete plan."

"I agree," I said to him as the children ran around in the parking lot, eating ice cream. "But what's the plan? If we call the police . . ."

"Helena is smart," he said. "She's probably already noticed that I found the bottle and gotten rid of it so that there's no evidence that it was her."

"Police have arrested people on less," I said.

Michael shook his head. "I want this to be an ironclad case," he said. "I don't want there to be any question as to what she did."

"Let me call the hospital," I said. "And see if I can get my paperwork with exactly what painkiller I supposedly overdosed on."

"It has to be the same thing," he said. "If she used something else, then that makes things seem a lot more complicated."

"I know," I said. "Let me see what I can do."

I didn't know how fast we could get the paperwork, but I did my very best to argue with the nurses and then the administration department. There were logical reasons they couldn't give it to me right away, but there seemed like a lot of illogical reasons. In the end, I thought that I got as close as I could to managing a rush job. Michael didn't look nearly as excited, but having worked in a hospital setting, I knew what I had managed was an accomplishment.

The worst part about doing this right in front of the kids was that both of them had proven to be quite good at sensing our moods. Michael and I had never been able to be those parents who could fight in hushed tones in the other room. The kids would somehow know we were fighting and one of them would pop their head in. In a way, they were quite good peacemakers because we couldn't fight in front of them. In another way, it was hard to get anything done.

In this instance, they kept glancing over at me. I was sure my heart rate was high and my nerves were showing. They kept looking over at me while they were playing, worriedly, like they were the parents and I was the child.

This wasn't the way it was supposed to be. I felt incredibly guilty that we had somehow put them in this situation. I felt like we had failed. We hadn't been cautious enough, and we had been too selfish.

Why couldn't we be happy with the child we had? Why couldn't I put more effort into looking after Grant? Why had I struggled so much?

Two beautiful women were dead because of our choices. I don't know that I could take any more.

"Well," he said when I finally hung up the phone. "Next step?"

"We need to go see Doctor Andrews," I said. "He has answers that we can't get anywhere else."

"We can go," he said. "But each of these steps, I'll admit, Cynthia, is making me more nervous for the kids' safety."

"I know," I said and took his hand. "We could just go home and fire Helena . . . but if I'm truthful with you, I don't think that will be the case."

"I don't think so either," he said and then looked at the kids playing. They were running and jumping, and they looked like perfect angels. "I can't believe we made them."

"I know," I said. We rarely had moments like this, and I took his hand to savor it. "Do you remember when we just started dating, and we used to dream about the kids we would have? A boy and a girl?"

"Oh, yeah," he said. "I remember talking about names. We used to fight about that, in the early days."

"Because we couldn't decide between Anne and Anna," I said with a grin. "And we were too busy arguing over that to realize that we were on the same path."

"We were, weren't we?" He grinned at me. "The entire time."

"Exactly," I said. "And now this is just another path. I think I know how to get the kids excited about going to see Doctor Andrews."

"Hey, kids," Michael said, practically reading my mind. "Come here. Mommy has a surprise for you."

"We're going to a very special place," I said and crouched down to talk to both of them. "You know how we went to see the hospital where Anna was born?"

"Yes, I remember," Anna said.

"Well, today, we are going to see the place where Mommy and Daddy met the woman who carried Grant."

"Olive?" Grant remembered her, which broke my heart a little bit.

"Yes," I said. "And here's how we're going to do it. We're going to go there, and I want you two to stay in the car. Mommy and Daddy are going to go in and make sure the same doctor is there who helped us. If he is, you can come in and meet him."

"Why can't we go in right away?" Anna asked. "We'll be very quiet."

"I know you will, sweetheart," I said. "But this is a place where people work. We don't want to disturb them if the person we're looking for isn't there."

"But we won't disturb them," Anna said.

"I know," I said. "Just in case."

It was the best way I could think of to explain to them why they had to stay in the car while we checked that everything was safe. I was a little nervous with the fact that we were bringing them at all, but there wasn't anywhere we could safety drop them. I realized how little of a support system we had without Helena. We had pushed away all of our resources to care for our kids, and we were on our own.

I knew everything was going to be fine, but I had no idea how.

"Are you ready?" Michael said.

I nodded. "Let's go," I said, and we headed toward the car. I was nervous, but I knew we needed those answers. With whatever Dr. Andrews could tell us and my blood test results, we should have enough to get rid of Helena once and for all.

Chapter 36

MICHAEL

When we got to the doctor's office, there were police cars everywhere. This was not good. I turned to Cynthia, who looked incredibly nervous.

"Maybe we should just go home," she said.

I reached over for her hand. I squeezed it and tried to give her a look of confidence. "It's going to be okay," I said to her. "If the police are here, it's safe."

"But why are the police here?" she asked. "Why are they here if everything is okay?"

"Well, if the doctor did those things, then it's not a surprise that he would be investigated," I replied. "But . . . how would they know?"

"Maybe Helena called and reported him?" she asked. "After your conversation?"

"No," I said. "I don't think she would do that. I think she knows that something is wrong, but she's the one who has done something wrong."

"No," Cynthia said. "Someone like that . . . I don't think she would know that she did something wrong."

"Are you talking about Helena?" Anna asked.

I had forgotten that they were there, and I turned around. "Hey, guys," I said. "Do you want to watch a movie? We have that headphone splitter, and you could use it while Mommy and I talk?"

"Okay," Grant said. "Want to watch *Frozen*?"

"Again?" Anna asked, but she went for the TV, so she didn't seem too put out by it. She seemed a bit annoyed as the movie started, but soon, both of them were absorbed in the movie with their headphones on.

"Now." I turned to Cynthia. "We should go in."

"I don't know if we should leave them by themselves," Cynthia said.

"Why?" I asked. "We leave Anna alone when we go for a walk around the block. She's responsible. In another year and a half, she'll be able to babysit."

"I know," she said. "But I . . ."

"Listen, what would make you feel better?" I asked. "Because we can't bring them in."

"Can I at least call Cally?" she asked. "And bring her up to speed? This isn't because I want to gossip. It's so someone knows where we are, just in case."

"What do you think is going to happen?" I asked. "Because you're safe."

"Maybe she can come here?" she asked. "Just to keep the kids safe?"

"You can call her," I said. "And then as soon as she is on her way, we can go."

She agreed and picked up the phone.

I waited while the phone rang, and then she put Cally on speaker phone so that we could both tell her the story.

I knew that she had known Cally for a while, and she was Cynthia's closest friend. I was worried that Cally was going to judge us or think we were crazy, but apparently, Cally thought what was happening made complete sense.

"I can't believe it got this far," she said. "I mean, I'm not blaming you guys or anything. I just . . . yeah. Wow."

"I know, right?" Cynthia said. "So, you don't think we're crazy?"

"No, I don't think you're crazy," Cynthia said. "I think it makes complete sense. Of course I can come and sit with the kids, but it's going to be a few minutes. I need to make sure the dogs are put away and all."

"That's fine," Cynthia said to me. "At least, I think it's fine. He closes at five."

"Did we mention the police are swarming the building?" I said.

I heard Cally choke on the other end of the line. "Why?" she asked.

"We don't know yet," Cynthia said. "There are a lot of medical offices in that building. But it's almost five, so we need to get in there before he closes."

"You will," Cally said. "I'll be there as soon as I can. But go in. You know you can count on me."

"I know," Cynthia said. "Why don't we wait five minutes, and then we'll go in?"

"Sounds like a plan," I said as Cynthia and Cally hung up.

"Well," Cynthia said. "Now if we get murdered or something, at least one person knows where we are."

"Are you kidding?" I asked. "Cynthia, we are not going to get murdered."

"I know," she said, but she didn't look like she believed me. "I know."

"What do you think is going to happen, with the police here?" I asked her.

"What if they are just like . . . a ruse?" she asked. "In order to lure us into a false sense of security?"

I gave her a look. "Are you kidding me?" I asked. "Come on. We are not going to be lured in by some fake police trap, Cynthia."

"Don't say that." She glared at me.

"What?"

"Don't say that I'm being paranoid," she said.

"I wasn't," I replied.

She glared even harder. "You were," she said. "You were going to say that I was acting paranoid."

"No," I said. "I was just going to say that you needed to trust me more."

"This isn't about trust, Michael," she said. "This is about the fact that we've had a bunch of crazy things happen to us already, so what's one more?"

"You really think Helena is capable of something like that?" I asked her.

"What if it wasn't Helena?" she asked. "What if it was someone else?"

"Who could it be?" I asked.

She shrugged her shoulders. "I don't know," she said. "Isn't this how they find out in horror movies that there has been someone watching from the sidelines all along?"

"Cynthia," I said. "*Now* you are being paranoid."

I knew it was a terrible thing to say, but it just fell out of my mouth.

"I would rather be paranoid," she said after a long silence. "I would rather be paranoid than experience all of this."

"You'd rather find out that paranoid schizophrenia runs in your family?" I asked. "And that we did this to Grant?"

"Grant will be fine," she replied. "It's us who won't be okay."

"Hey, hey." I grabbed her. "I love you. Remember that."

"I love you too," she said and then closed her eyes. "Okay. We should just do this."

"I agree," I said and then turned around to look at the kids. They were completely lost in the movie and I had to wave to get their attention.

"What, Daddy?" Anna asked, looking annoyed that I had to get her to take off her headphones.

"Mommy and I are going to go in," I said. "And

we won't be long. But we just want to make sure everything is okay."

"We can't come?" Grant asked.

I shook my head. "Not right this second," I said. "Remember what we said?"

"But what are we supposed to do?" Anna asked.

"Well, you seem pretty entertained right now," I replied. "So I want you to just stay here and don't open the car door for anyone."

"Except Aunt Cally," Cynthia said. "She is going to be coming to sit with you."

"When?" Anna asked.

"Soon," Cynthia replied. "Okay? So just sit here and keep watching the movie."

"Okay." Now Grant looked annoyed that we were interrupting his movie.

Cynthia and I blew both of them kisses, and then we got out of the car. I took her hand as we headed toward the building.

"Do you remember when we first came here?" I asked her. "We were so apprehensive. We weren't sure we even wanted to do it."

"I remember," she said. "I was scared, but all I could think of was Anna's sweet face and how I wanted another one. I couldn't wait to see you be a father again."

"Well, that's very sweet of you," I said. "I just wanted to find a way to have another child without putting you in danger again."

She looked at me sweetly. "You were thinking about that?" she asked. "I just thought you wanted another kid and that you went along with it because this was the way I said it had to be."

"No," I said. "I was okay with having another kid if it meant that you would be well."

I was sure that I had told her these things before, but she looked completely swept away by all of it.

"Oh," she said. "I had no idea."

"Anna would have been enough," I said. "And I would have loved and cherished her and been content. But I'm so glad that we have Grant."

"I am too," she said. "And I wouldn't change any of it."

The two of us wrapped our arms around each other and headed into the medical office.

Since we had last been there, they had completely renovated the place. Everything was upgraded, and I thought, bitterly, that it had been paid for by our fees.

"Wow," Cynthia said. "I would have been very intimidated if I came in here and saw this."

"Right?" I said, looking around. "We had just started the business, and I wouldn't be sure we could afford a place like this if our circumstances hadn't changed."

"You're so brave," Cynthia said to me, "taking that leap for our family."

"It was because of your support," I said. "You made me believe that I could do it, even when I wasn't sure. The first two years were easy, but maintaining it was the hard part. And it was all because of you."

She held my hand, and we went up in the elevator to where the clinic was.

To our dismay, that's where the police were. They were swarming the clinic, and I wasn't sure we would get in. However, it seemed like they were finishing up. I recognized the doctor's assistant. I thought she was also a nurse, or she was a secretary or something. Her name was Nancy Cheng, from what I remembered, and while she looked a little bit older, as we all did, she was pretty much the same.

"Nancy," I said, trying to pretend we were on closer terms than we were. "My name is Michael Thompson, and this is my wife, Cynthia. We were patients here a few years ago. We've been calling in for the past few months to get a few things cleared up."

"Oh." She looked terrified. "I'm sorry, we can't . . ."

"No, it's okay," I said. "I think we're here to talk about what the police were here about."

Her eyes widened.

"Really?" she asked. "You know what happened?"

"The doctor was involved in some egg switching?" I asked. "Is he here, or has he been arrested?"

Cynthia gasped at me for being so forward, but I didn't have time to waste.

"No," she said. "He's dead."

Both Cynthia and I choked in shock.

"I'm sorry?" I asked her. "He's dead?"

"Yes," she said sadly. "He was shot in the back of the head."

Cynthia and I turned to each other in shock.

"That's what the police were here about?" I asked.

Nancy nodded. "I can't believe it," she said. "He was such a good boss and a nice man. I can't believe it. I didn't think . . . that this would ever happen."

"I think you have to talk to us," I said. "There are a few things you should know."

Nancy looked nervous.

"About his being murdered?" she asked.

I nodded. I realized she was nervous, and I took a step back. "We didn't do it," I said really quickly. "But I think we know who did."

"I can talk to you for a little while," she said. "But I don't have much time."

"That's okay," I said. "A little while is all we need."

Cynthia stepped forward then and tried to put on a gentler tone than I had.

"Nancy," she said. "Do you feel safe right now?"

"I think so," Nancy said. "I remember you. Not from the phone, but when you were in here."

"Good," Cynthia said and smiled. "I remember you too. You were always so nice and kind to us."

"Oh," Nancy said. "People don't really say that about me."

"Well, that's what I think," Cynthia said. "Let's talk and see if we can figure all of this out."

Chapter 37

CYNTHIA

NANCY SEEMED TO SUCCUMB TO MY GENTLE TONE, and her voice faltered.

"I lied to you," she said. "About the doctor."

"He's not dead?" I asked.

Nancy frowned. "No, he is dead," she said. "But he wasn't a nice man. I felt trapped working here. He paid me such a high salary, so I could provide for my family . . . but he asked me to do some things. Some awful things."

"Like what?" I asked.

"Come with me," Nancy said and led us to the back room.

I was afraid of what we might find there, but we were alone. She started pulling down all sorts of records and I saw my name on one of them. She opened my file and pointed out some notes. "The reason he could pay me such a high salary, I suspect . . . is because he was constantly taking bribes from people. He would ask me to change records all the time that didn't make any sense."

"What kind of bribes?" I asked.

"He would alter or substitute genetic material," she said. "And the biological parents would never know."

I put my hand to my mouth in shock.

"Did he do this with me?" I asked.

Nancy nodded. "Yes," she said. "You weren't the first, but I remember you because you were so kind. If anyone didn't deserve that, you didn't. You were so nice to me, when so many of the people who walk into the clinic just bossed me around."

"Of course I was nice to you," I said, confused. "You were so young, and I remember thinking it was a great opportunity for you."

"I guess it wasn't," Nancy replied with a sigh. "And now I'm so tangled up in it, I don't know what to do."

"So . . . whose genetic material was it?" I asked. I was trying to push away the fact that Grant wasn't my son. Did it matter that he wasn't biologically mine? He was still my son, and I was going to love him and care for him all my life.

"Olive's," Nancy said. "Your surrogate mother. The doctor took a large sum of money from Olive, presumably most of the money you paid her, in order to inseminate her with Michael's sperm."

"So Grant is my biological son?" Michael asked.

Nancy referred to the notes. "Yes," she said. "She really wanted him to be your son."

"But why would she do this?" I asked. "Sweet Olive? I don't believe this."

"I wouldn't believe it either if I didn't see it with my own eyes," Nancy said. "Olive was sweet to you when you were here, but it was like she wore a mask. The second you left . . . she was a completely different person."

"Did childhood schizophrenia run in her family, by any chance?" I asked as the blood drained from my face.

"I can't say for certain," she replied. "But I can say it was like a switch that she would turn off and on."

"Wow." Michael turned to me. "Cynthia, are you okay?"

I nodded, although I must have looked as white

as a sheet. "Yes," I said. "It doesn't matter. It doesn't matter."

"Of course it matters," he said.

I looked up at him. "It's easier for you," I said. "He's your son. But—"

"No," he said. "It's a shock, and you have a right to be upset."

I gritted my teeth. "I'm trying not to be, because it doesn't matter," I said. "He will always be my son, even if my blood isn't running through his veins."

Michael gripped my hand and I turned back to Nancy.

"Do you know what happened to Olive?" I asked her.

"I don't," Nancy replied. "I heard she vanished."

"She's dead," I said. "At least, we think she's dead. Now I'm second-guessing everything. Had she been a surrogate here before?"

"I'm not sure," Nancy said. "I don't think so."

"Can you check the records?" I said. "There's a woman who works for us, Helena Griswold, who says that she also used your services. Her sons are twins, and they look just like my boy."

I had no idea how I was holding it together. I

felt like I was going to collapse, but I knew I needed to ask all the questions I could.

Nancy went through all the records, both on paper and in the computer, but she eventually came up emptyhanded.

"Sorry," she said. "I have no record of a Helena Griswold here."

"Could she have used a different name?" I asked.

Nancy shook her head. "Not unless she was very crafty," she said. "Some people want to use a fake name because they don't want their friends and family to know, but we insist on seeing all proper ID. You'll remember, we asked you for lots of paperwork."

"You don't think they are in league together, do you?" Michael said.

I shrugged my shoulders. At this point, I didn't know what to think. "I think that's everything we need," I said and reached out to touch Nancy's shoulder. It was easier to take care of someone else at the moment rather than comfort my own emotions. "Thank you so much."

"No, thank you," Nancy said. "Telling the police felt . . . mechanical, but telling you felt cathartic. I'm so sorry I didn't do anything to stop it."

"It's not your fault," I assured her. "Really."

"Thank you," she said.

I gave her a hug.

"We should go," Michael said. "Our children are in the car."

"Of course," Nancy said.

"Are you going to be okay?" I asked. "Can we give you a ride home?"

"No, thank you," she said. "But please . . . reach out if you need anything at all. I just want to help as many people as I can after I put them in this mess."

"Of course," I said, and then we headed out the door.

I turned to Michael with a look of shock as soon as we were walking back to the car.

"Can you believe that?" I asked.

He shook his head. "No," he said. "I'm starting to think that we're living in a bad fairy tale."

"Me too," I replied.

When we got to the car, I was relieved to see Cally there.

"What did you find?" she asked. She was standing just outside the car, with the door open, as she kept an eye on the children.

"Unfortunately, nothing to incriminate our nanny," I said and then broke. "Grant isn't my son."

I tried to keep my voice low, but it came out in a sob. Luckily, both of the children were still wearing headphones, so they didn't look up.

"What?" Cally asked.

The entire story came spilling out and she choked in surprise. "But . . . why?"

"I don't know," I said. "It doesn't make any sense. I can't believe that she would do this."

"I can't believe she would, either," Michael said. "Olive was the sweetest person alive."

"But remember what Nancy said?" I asked him. "That Olive was not actually that way? As soon as we left the room, it was like a switch was flipped?"

"Did she have schizophrenia?" Cally asked.

"Well . . . she must have," I surmised. "Because it's not in Michael's family and mine doesn't matter anymore."

"Mommy, I'm hungry," Grant called out.

I sighed. "We need to get the kids home," I said. "Cally, thank you so much for coming out."

"For sure," she said and gave me a hug. "Anything. Are you sure you want to go home, though? Are you sure you feel safe?"

"I . . . can't feel unsafe in my own home," I said.

431

"We need to figure out a plan, but if anything, it's Helena who needs to leave, not us."

"We still haven't figured out why Helena would hurt you and Anna," Michael pointed out. "Something is missing in this puzzle."

"I'm quite sure that you'll find it," Cally said. "Everything is way too weird for her to not be involved."

"Yeah," I said. "I know. It's just a missing link that will turn up. In the meantime, who knows what she's doing to our house?"

"Call me," Cally said as she gave me one last hug.

I promised I would, and we got in the car. "I think we should call the police," I said to Michael. We had both been silent most of the way, shell shocked, and these were the first real words I could pull together. "We have enough evidence."

"I agree," he said. "Something has to change."

We stopped and picked up some food for the kids and then headed home. The kids were exhausted, and although neither of them really napped anymore, they seemed quite content to lie down in Grant's room and drift off. We didn't even tell Helena we were home, although I was sure that she knew. As soon the kids were safe,

Michael picked up the cordless phone and dialed the police.

I sat on the edge of the bed, in a cold sweat, as he talked to them. At first, it sounded like they weren't going to send anyone at all. However, the more information he gave them, the more he convinced them to come.

"They will send a car as soon as someone is available," he said. "They said because no one was in immediate danger, they couldn't send someone over right away."

"But how do they know we aren't in immediate danger?" I asked. "I mean, we could be. We are. I mean . . ."

"Baby, hush," he said and wrapped me in his arms. "Everything is going to be okay, I promise."

I felt tears coming to my eyes.

"We should have done this before," I said. "We should have done this when we first suspected something."

"We did," he said. "Remember, I called them about the milk? They didn't believe me."

"We should have been more forceful," I said. "We're bad parents."

"Cynthia." He sat me down at the edge of the bed. "We're not bad parents. We're parents who

433

were in an incredibly difficult situation and we needed to work out what was best for everyone."

"But look what it's led to," I said. "Three people are dead. That can't be a coincidence!"

"No,' he said. "I don't think it is, either. But I'm hoping against hope that it is."

"I hope Olive is the innocent one in all of this," I said. "She really had me convinced. I couldn't imagine her doing anything wrong."

"Neither can I," he said. "Which is why I find this whole thing so alarming."

The two of us held each other for a while, and then we lay back. I remembered a time before we had children when we used to lie there for hours, dreaming the world away. We used to be enough for each other. When did that change?

Eventually, we heard a car pull up into our driveway. Michael got up to look out the window and confirmed that it was the police.

"I can do the talking, if you'd like," he said.

I nodded. "I think that would be better," I said. "I don't think I'm going to be very coherent."

"Do you want to stay up here?" he asked me.

I paused. Part of me wanted to, but the other part of me knew that I had to be there. I wanted to see this through to the end. "No," I said. "No, I'll come with you."

"Okay," he said. "Just . . . be prepared for wherever it might lead."

"As long as we're together," I said, "I can handle anything."

Just before we went outside, I stood outside the children's door to make sure they were okay. I didn't hear any sounds, so I assumed they were still asleep. I headed downstairs, trying to gather up all of my courage. Today was the day I made this right.

Chapter 38

MICHAEL

I DON'T KNOW WHAT WE SAID THAT MADE THIS more valid than last time, but when the police got here, they seemed very serious.

"Thank you for coming," I said like they were here for a snack. I don't know why I was so calm this time, but I suppose it was because I knew that we were doing the right thing at last. "She's right downstairs."

"Thank you," the officer said and followed me down into the nanny suite. Unfortunately, when we got down there, the suite was empty. "I thought you said she was here?"

"She was here!" I said, confused.

They looked around, but sure enough, Helena

was nowhere to be seen. The apartment was empty, all their things gone.

"Sorry. She was here. I have no idea how she would have known you folks were coming."

"The phone is tapped," one of them said to their partner, and both of them took a look at Helena's phone extension. Sure enough, there was a device on the connection, and I realized that she had been listening to every phone call that had been made.

"How long has that been there?" I asked in shock. "She heard me calling you, but . . ."

"This is an old device," the officer said. "To be honest, I haven't seen one of these in seven or eight years."

My stomach started to sink even further.

"Has she been living here for seven years?" he asked. His name tag read *Stoffer* and I felt like it was a name I had seen before. Had he worked on our case before, maybe?

"No," I said in shock. "No, she hasn't . . . but I would say that all of this started seven or eight years ago."

"All of this?" Stoffer asked. "Why don't you tell me about it?"

I winced.

"It's a long story," I said, and all the police officers took out their notebooks.

Cynthia had joined me by then, and she seemed ready to take the lead.

"So, eight years ago," she said, "we wanted to have another child, so we went to a fertility clinic. We met a beautiful young woman named Olive who was willing to carry our biological child—for a fee, of course. Olive was kind and caring and we both liked her. A month after our son was born, Olive's car was found in the lake and we presumed that she was dead. We got along for a while, but Grant started showing signs of childhood schizophrenia and we needed help. We have no idea how he got it, because it mostly runs in families, but we had no idea how he contracted it since neither Michael's nor my family had it. Originally, we had planned to hire a nanny named Amanda . . . but she vanished before we could hire her officially, and so we hired Helena."

"Ever since we hired Helena, things have been weird," I said. "She and her boys could be twins to my son. She started asking him to call her Mommy and saying that I was going to be their Daddy. She told her boys to be friends with Grant but not to my daughter, Anna. And then Cynthia collapsed and was near death. She was hospitalized, and they pumped her stomach. It had been a painkiller overdose . . . except she didn't give herself the overdose of painkillers. That's when we called you the first time."

"Yes, we have a record of that. There was nothing to indicate that someone had attempted to poison her, from what I can recall," Officer Stoffer said.

"Because she cleaned up the scene before you all got here!" Cynthia added.

"Okay, what else leads you to believe this Helena is responsible?"

"Are you aware that I tried to bring in more evidence?"

"I don't have that in the file. What evidence?" Officer Stoffer asked.

"While Cynthia was in the hospital, Helena offered to make my daughter some fresh-squeezed orange juice. Her sons were at the table with us, which was unusual. They usually kept to their suite. However, that morning, they were eating with us. They were acting oddly, so it was already a weird morning. Helena handed out the glasses of juice and stood by Anna and demanded that she drink it. Anna took a sip, but it didn't taste right, and she set the glass down. Grant had just come into the room and said he'd drink it, but Helena violently slapped the glass from his hand. She claimed that she saw mold in it, but I didn't believe her. I brought in a large piece of the glass to give to you all as evidence, but you wouldn't listen."

Officer Stoffer nodded. "I imagine you took it upon yourself to get it tested?"

"I did. And while I waited for the results, I was able to bring Cynthia home. However, that day, there was a great deal of screaming coming from Helena's suite. I went down to find her son Terrance in a full-blown hallucination. It seems he's also got childhood schizophrenia. Helena asked me to retrieve his meds for her from her bathroom. When I went looking, I discovered a pill bottle of tranquillizers. It was a new bottle, issued this month, and yet more than half the bottle was missing. I took one of the pills and had it tested against the glass. It was a match."

All of the police officers were staring at me like I was crazy.

"Never mind that Amanda was found dead, shot in the head and dumped in a landfill," Cynthia said. "And now the fertility doctor, Doctor Andrews, who Helena claimed she went to, to have her twins, is also dead. Also shot in the head. And we checked the records with his nurse. She was never a patient there."

"Holy cow," Officer Stoffer said. "I think we have a lot to look into."

"Uh, yes," I replied. "I'd say so."

"So let's go over it one more time," he said.

It took over an hour to get the details and time-line explained. The police wanted to know every single detail of everything. We even told them about the nanny cam and monitors that were hacked. Eventually, they managed to get what they needed.

"Well, Mr. Thompson," the officer said. "I think that you have quite the case here."

"Yeah, no kidding," I said. I looked around to take a break from the investigation and noticed that there were several things missing. Cynthia had decorated the house, and there were several family heirlooms that were gone. "She's taken some things."

"Oh, my God, I didn't even notice!" Cynthia looked up to see that things were missing, and she jumped up, making note of everything. I couldn't believe we hadn't noticed it when we first came down.

The police made a report of that too, and their

notebooks soon became full of scribbles, just with our case.

"I think if I were you," Officer Stoffer said, "I would change the locks."

"Yeah, I'll do that right away," I said. "Anything else? What are you going to do?"

"We're going to put an APB out so that everyone can be on the lookout for her," he said. "Don't worry. Even if the rest of this theory is rough, we can nab her on theft until we can figure it out. I don't know what we can do today, but if we find her, we'll let you know."

"You have to believe me," I said. "I mean, the same pills that nearly killed my wife were in her cabinet."

"Do you have that evidence?" he asked.

Cynthia pulled out her phone.

"Yes," she said. "My test results are right here. Look, they match the lab results that Michael got on Anna's orange juice glass and the pill. I'll send you copies."

The officers took notes of that too and then said that they would be in touch. I wasn't sure why, but I didn't believe them. At this point, I wasn't sure who I believed. I didn't trust that anyone was who they said they were. Once they were gone, Cynthia turned to me in shock.

"Is this real life?" she asked me.

I was already Googling locksmiths, but I looked up to meet her eyes. "It's okay," I said. "Now that the police are involved, we're going to make it right. They'll find Helena and everything will be okay."

"But we shouldn't have to change our locks," she protested. "We shouldn't have to do any of this because this is our house. I can't believe that she did this to us."

"I know," I said. "But now, we should do it to make sure the kids are safe."

"God, the kids," she said. "I can handle her hurting me, but I can't handle her hurting the kids. She tried to hurt Anna. How much of a horrible person do you have to be to hurt kids?"

"I'm just glad we're all still standing here," I said as I hugged her tight. "Okay, I'm going to call the locksmith and pay whatever it takes to get him to change every lock in the house."

"Should I go check on the kids?" she asked.

"No, I'm sure they're fine," I said. "Just stay down here a little while longer while I call the locksmith. I want you feel comfortable in what I decide."

She smiled. "Thank you," she said. "For including me."

"Of course," I said. "I'm going to make sure that everything is what you want from here on out. You and the kids are my first priority."

She looked at me with a look that she hadn't given me since we were married. I dialed the locksmith and explained that we had an emergency situation. I told him that we wanted the most secure solution no matter the expense, and he seemed inclined to agree. He promised to be over within the hour, which made us both feel a lot better.

"They're going to catch her, and everything is going to be okay," I promised her. "Come on, let's go check on the kids."

Cynthia gave me a kiss and then hand in hand, we headed up the stairs. This wasn't going to be easy, but hopefully, it would be over soon.

Chapter 39

CYNTHIA

To my absolute relief, the kids were fine. They were both awake, but I think they sensed that there was something wrong because they were playing quietly in the room and hadn't come to find us. I sat down on Grant's bed and Michael sat on the guest bed. Both of us looked at each other, and I felt it was my place to start.

"Kids," I said. "Mommy and Daddy need to talk to you. Do you think you can put those toys away for a while?"

"Are we in trouble?" Anna asked.

I shook my head. "No, of course not," I said. "Why do you ask that?"

"Because we've been having a lot of talks lately," she said. "And I keep thinking we're going to get in trouble."

"I don't think you've done anything to get in trouble, have you?" I asked her, and Anna shook her head. "Then you aren't in trouble. But we need to talk to you about Helena."

"Where is Helena?" Grant asked as he put his truck away. "I miss her."

"Well," I said and held out my arms for him. "Helena had to go away, and she isn't coming back."

Grant looked absolutely shell-shocked.

"Why?" he cried. "I love her."

If I was worried about breaking his heart, I also had to acknowledge that he was breaking mine. I knew he liked Helena, but the insecure part of me worried that he liked her more than he liked me.

"I know you do, but Helena had to go away because she was trying to hurt Mommy and Anna. And possibly Daddy."

Grant's mouth fell open. "What?" he asked. "How?"

"She was putting bad stuff in our drinks," I said. "It made us very sick. So she had to go away."

"But . . ." Grant said. "But . . ."

"Why would she do that?" Anna asked.

I looked at Michael again.

"Did she want to take your place, Mommy?" Grant asked before Michael could speak up.

"Yes," Michael said. "Yes, that was what she wanted. She didn't want Mommy or Anna here."

Grant seemed to think about this for a long time before he spoke again.

"Is it like the mommy cuckoo leaving her egg in another bird's nest?" he asked.

I was slightly confused until I thought back to the book that Helena had read him on their very first day together.

"Yes," I said. "Yes, it's exactly like that."

"Oh," Grant said and then hugged me.

I could tell he was very upset, but he was also wrestling with himself. These were big adult emotions, and he should not have to deal with them so young.

"I'm sorry," I said to him. "It was for the best. For all of us."

"I know," he answered, and my heart broke because my little boy was growing up. Anna, who seemed a little more aware of the situation, started asking a few more questions.

"Mommy, did she put something in my orange

juice?" she asked. "The same thing that was in your milk?"

"Yes," I said. "Yes, she did."

"But she hurt you so bad," Anna cried.

I could tell she was afraid. "She did," I said. "But you don't need to worry because she is not going to hurt anyone like that again."

"How do you know?" Anna asked. "Did the police get her?"

"Not yet," Michael said. "Not yet, but they will."

"What about Terrance and Roman?" Grant asked.

Michael and I hadn't exactly discussed what would happen to the boys.

"I don't know," Michael admitted. "But hopefully, they'll have a safe place to go to."

"Could they come here?" Grant asked. "Could they be friends with me?"

"Uh, maybe," Michael said. "But I think Helena might have mentioned that they have other family."

"Really?" Grant said. "I thought they didn't have any other family at all. That's what Terrance said."

"Maybe they weren't aware of their other family," I said. "But I'm quite sure that they will be taken care of."

"Well, I think that's sad," Anna said. "Everyone should have family."

"Yes," I said. "But sometimes, you have to find a new family."

"That's not fair," Anna said. "It's not Terrance or Roman's fault that their mother wasn't very nice."

"I know," I said. "I know. Are there any things you wanted to tell Mommy or Daddy about the things Helena did that you didn't already tell us?"

"No," Anna said, but she looked unsure.

"Anna?" I asked her, and she took a deep breath.

"Well, there was one thing," she said.

I reached out to touch her shoulder. "You can tell me anything."

"Helena said that I wasn't her daughter," she replied, "so she didn't have to be nice to me."

"Well . . . that's true," I said. "You aren't her daughter. But that doesn't mean she doesn't have to be nice to you."

I didn't want to tell Grant that he wasn't my biological son. I felt like that was too heavy for one night, and a glance over at Michael showed that he agreed.

"I know," Anna said. "It's like bullies at school."

"Exactly," I said. "Everyone should just be nice to everyone."

"So she will never come back and take care of me?" Grant asked. "Who's going to be taking care of me?"

"I will take care of you," I said.

"Are we going to get another nanny?" Anna asked. "I don't think that I want another one."

"I don't think I do, either," I said. "And I don't think we need one. I'm sorry that I didn't take good care of both of you while Helena was here. I should have taken better care of you and noticed what she was doing."

"Mommy," she said, "it's not your fault."

"Thank you," I said. Anna, as always, was a lovely person, and she knew just how to make me feel better.

Once the kids stopped hugging me and started feeling a little bit safer, Michael heard the locksmith knocking on the door.

"I'll get it," he said. "You guys stay up here, okay?"

"Aren't we allowed to ever go outside again?" Anna asked.

Michael and I chuckled, although it was an uncomfortable chuckle.

"You are," Michael said. "Just not right now. We're going to get new keys for the house so Helena can't use her keys to get in."

"I'm afraid," Anna said.

I reached to kiss the top of her head. "I'm not," I said. "Daddy is going to take good care of us, and we're all going to be okay."

"Mommy, I'm hungry," Grant said.

I breathed a sigh of relief. If he was hungry, everything was going to go back to normal shortly.

"We can go downstairs soon," I said. "And then we can eat whatever you want."

"Do you think that I'll ever meet someone like me again?" he asked.

"You mean with schizophrenia?" I asked. "Maybe."

"But I never met anyone before," he said. "Terrance and Roman were like my brothers."

"You'll meet others," I promised. "Maybe I can look to see if I can find any children like you near us, in a play group or something."

"Okay," he replied. "No girls allowed, though."

"Hey!" Anna cried.

I chuckled. "We'll see," I said as I heard the locksmith downstairs. "I wanted to let you both know that Mommy loves you very much, no matter what happens."

"What is going to happen?" Anna asked.

"Nothing," I promised. "I just don't feel like I've told you that for a long while."

"I love you too," Grant said and hugged me.

Anna seemed a little more apprehensive, but she eventually hugged me as well. I had never felt more comfortable and safer in my life. My children were surrounding me, and everything was going to be okay.

I heard Michael's comforting voice downstairs and the sound of tools being clinked around. He was having all new locks and a security system installed. Soon, Helena would have no means to get into the house, and we'd be safe. Her things were gone, from what I could see, and so as long as she was locked out, I felt confident that she probably wouldn't come back. She knew we were on to her, and she knew that we could take her down now. Her power was gone. We would move forward, and everything was going to be okay.

Chapter 40

MICHAEL

I was normally a very patient person. I knew that good things came to those who waited. But the longer I waited for the police to catch Helena, the more I felt like they weren't going to. I felt like she would not be so stupid as to be caught by the police when she had been tipped off by bugging our phone.

"We need to do something," I said to Cynthia the next day. We had a remarkably normal night, and nothing odd was happening today, although we both felt on edge.

"Like what?" Cynthia asked. "We can't give them any more evidence, Michael. We've already talked to them half a dozen times."

"I know," I said. "But we need to do something

455

more than that. Listen, I did some preliminary searches for Olive and Helena's data. You are much better than me at searching for everything. I was always bad with even Googling pizza places."

"I don't know how I can help," she said doubtfully. "I mean, records like that would be pretty easy to find, with social media these days."

"Olive had a family," I pointed out to her. "She mentioned a family, remember? And other children? If she was dead, or even presumed dead, there would have to be some sort of funeral announcement."

"Maybe," Cynthia said and pulled my laptop closer to her. She looked like she hadn't slept a wink, and I didn't blame her. My mind had been whirling most of the night as well. "Let me see what I can do."

I watched her fingers fly and sat back, thinking that we made an amazing team. She searched several different record sources and combed through Facebook, but eventually, she sat back, disappointed.

"Nothing," she said.

"There was has to be something," I said. "It's like she didn't exist."

"Maybe she didn't," Cynthia said.

I felt chills go down my spine. "Well, then, who gave birth to our son?" I asked her. "What about the police report? That would be public record by now. Was there a body with the car, after all?"

Cynthia went back to work, but it didn't seem to matter what she searched. Olive was clearly an alias, and she had lied to us.

"I just . . . can't believe it," Cynthia said. "She was so sweet and so kind. How could this be?"

"I guess people can put on all sorts of masks," I said. "Remember what Nancy said?"

"God, this is horrible," Cynthia replied. "All I can think about is the innocent people who have died because of this."

"Search for Helena," I said. "I'm sure you'll be able to find something. You may be able to hide yourself, but she's got children involved. She couldn't have hidden them."

"I have an idea," Cynthia said. "Maybe the local vital records office has something?"

"Was she from here?" I asked.

Cynthia shrugged. "Worth a shot," she said and picked up the phone. I thought at this point that anything was worth a try, and I listened while Cynthia made the phone call. She had a way of charming people into doing just about anything, and after a few moments, she managed to get some poor clerk to start chasing down old records.

In the end, the wait was worth it. She managed to get a few things that I would have never thought we would find. I also realized, when I looked at them, that they were things I never really wanted to see.

"So . . ." Cynthia said. "These are birth announcements for the twins, so they are real, at least."

"I would hope so," I said as more records came through her email. I recognized one of the names from a name that Helena had mentioned. "That's the twins' father. He's dead?"

"Looks like it," Cynthia said, half in shock. "I didn't think that he was dead, did you?"

"No," I replied. "I thought that he'd be . . . you know . . . I thought he left her. She didn't say he had passed on."

"I wonder what killed him," Cynthia mused as she looked through the other records. There was one that caused us to both gasp.

"Oh, my," I said. "Oh, no. Is that . . . ?"

"It is," she said. "But it's not the same Olive."

There was another funeral announcement for an Olive who was Helena's firstborn daughter. That baby wouldn't have been old enough to be the Olive that we knew, even if she had lived.

I shivered.

"This just gets creepier and creepier," I said. "I can't believe that someone would do this."

"So . . . who was Olive?" Cynthia asked. "Was she . . . Helena?"

"That's not impossible," I said. "But I think it's very clear that Olive is connected to Helena. That's an unusual name. It's not a coincidence."

"I just feel so bad," Cynthia said. "What did we expose our children to? What have we done?"

"Cynthia, darling, we didn't do anything wrong," I tried to assure her, even though I knew that she didn't believe me. "We didn't know."

"But we are their parents," she cried. "We should have known something! We should have known that they were in danger. Isn't there supposed to be some sort of natural instinct?"

"Not always," I said. "I guess it doesn't always kick in."

"Oh, God." She put her head down on her hands for a moment. "I'm not sure if I can read any more, to be honest. I don't know if I can take what we find."

"Do you want me to take over?" I asked, and

she nodded. "Okay. You go and lie down. It'll be okay."

"Thank you," she said. "Apparently, ODing on painkillers takes a lot more out of you than you think."

"Especially when you weren't the one who did it," I said dryly. "You know, I wonder . . ." I looked at her as the thought hit me. "I wonder if she'd been dosing you with those tranquilizers the whole time. It would explain how tired you were."

"Oh, God, I don't even want to think about that." She came over and hugged me. "I'm gonna go lie down."

As soon as Cynthia was upstairs, I dove right back into the records. I couldn't find out how Helena's husband had died, and I couldn't find out how the baby girl had died, aside from the fact that she had died young. This was honestly the most frightening thing I had ever come across.

Like Cynthia, I felt guilty for what we had exposed our children to. I was so grateful to hear their sounds of laughter in the other room. It wasn't just because I was glad Helena hadn't killed them but because I was glad that they were here at all. When you're a parent, reading about the death of a baby, even one with such a crazy mother, made you pretty upset.

I eventually went back to the records of Olive that we had. I wasn't sure why I was doing it. It was partly because of nostalgia and partly because I didn't know what else to do. I remembered when we first met her. It was Cynthia who had warmed to her first and Cynthia who had convinced me that this was the woman who was going to carry our child. That seemed so long ago now.

I remembered how devastated I was when Olive had died. She had been my confidant, my friend, and the person who had carried my child, all at once. It was a complicated relationship, and I mourned her.

But what if she wasn't really dead?

The more I stared at the photos, the more a sinking reality came to hit me in the face.

I took the laptop upstairs and tried not to drop it. My hands were shaking, but I had to show Cynthia what I knew.

If I was right, then everything was about to change. If I was wrong, then we were no farther along than before.

"Cynthia," I said as I went into the bedroom. "I think I found Olive."

"What?" She sat straight up. "What?"

"She's been here all along," I said and sat the laptop down.

When she saw what I saw on the screen, her face turned pale.

"No," she said and met my eyes.

"I'm afraid so," I said. "I'm sorry."

Cynthia didn't say anything. She simply put her head down and started to cry. I put my hand on her back and closed my eyes. I wanted to cry too, but I needed to be strong for my wife. This was the worst thing we could have found.

Chapter 41

CYNTHIA

I COULD SEE AS SOON AS MICHAEL PUT THE computer down. I saw the overlay of the picture that he did with Helena and Olive, and I knew it was true.

Olive had been here the whole time. She was Helena. It had taken a little bit of plastic surgery, hair dye, contacts, and a few other tricks of the trade, but now that I saw it, I could never unsee it. She was Helena.

I didn't know what to feel. On one hand, I was incredibly thrilled because it meant that Olive was here and we wouldn't have to mourn her any longer.

On the other hand, I didn't know what was going on. I couldn't understand my life anymore. I couldn't understand why Helena did this. I couldn't understand *how* she did this.

"At least," Michael said, "we know why she felt so familiar to us."

"Yeah, but . . ." I managed through my tears. "Not this way. Our Olive. Our friend, Michael!"

"I know," he said. "I don't know what to feel."

"Neither do I," I said. "So, she bribed the doctor . . . to have a baby by you. She was obsessed with you."

"Maybe she just wanted another baby?" Michael suggested. "And then it got out of control and she didn't know what to do? We did give her a lot of support during her surrogacy, both emotionally and physically. It must have been hard to leave when you could basically spend your life on easy street."

"But . . ." I shook my head. "Think about all the times she told Grant to call her Mommy or said that you would be the twins' new father. That can't be just because she wanted a baby."

"Yeah, that part was weird," he admitted.

"Or," I said, "the part where she tried to get rid of Anna and me because we didn't fit into the family plans. You can't deny that, Michael."

"Hmm." I could see the thoughts start to clear in his mind. "So . . ."

"So she did this, but why?" I asked. "Why would she do this? What was her motive?"

"I don't know," he said. "I don't mean to sound like I have a big ego . . . but couldn't I be enough to be her motive?"

"Maybe," I said. The tears had stopped flowing and my mind was calculating a few more things now. "Maybe, but I feel like . . . for a woman like that, that's not enough."

"Well . . ." Michael said. "Cynthia, we do have a lot of money."

"We have more money now than we did then," I said. "But I suppose it might have been enough. And nothing ever happened between you and Olive?"

"I swear," he said. "Nothing ever happened."

"Did you want it to?" I asked.

"Now is not the time to ask that type of question," he said, and my heart lurched.

"Michael, now is the perfect time to ask that type of question," I said. "The police need to know the truth if they are going to be able to process this. If you and Olive had a thing—"

"We didn't," he swore. "But yes, I wanted to. However, it wasn't in the way you may think."

"It wasn't in the way I think?" I quirked an eyebrow. "Tell me, Michael. What's an acceptable way for it to be, then?"

"You see, this is why I didn't want to tell you," he said defensively. "Because I didn't do anything wrong, and I knew that you would . . . have an issue with it."

"Have an issue with what?" I asked. I shouldn't yell, because the kids were in the other room, but I was already shaking.

"I felt a connection with her," he said. "A connection that I couldn't explain. We were friends, probably as much as you and I were friends. We were confidants. We told each other everything, but that was all. Nothing happened, I swear, and I'm not sure that it was ever going to happen."

"But if that was all," I said, "why didn't you tell me?"

"Because I didn't want to hurt you," he said. "And I knew something like that would bother you."

I sighed. "Well, it shouldn't have," I said. "I know what connection you're talking about because I felt the same way about her that you did. We were close friends. She carried my child. That has a special place in my heart, even knowing . . . knowing what happened here."

"I can't believe this is real," he said, staring at the screen.

I shook my head. "Neither can I," I said. "We have to call the police."

"Do you think they will believe us?" he asked me. "They barely believed us the first time around."

"Well, they will have to," I said. "Besides, when we show them the photos and lay out all the similarities, I'm certain they will see what we see. I mean, look at their heights and weights. Exactly the same. And there's a little freckle on her cheek that she never got rid of. God, why didn't we see this before?"

"Because we didn't want to," he said. "Olive was gone, and we weren't looking for her anymore."

I gazed at the photo as he picked up the phone to dial the police.

"What drove you to do this?" I asked the screen softly. Even though I was incredibly angry with her, I felt shock and pain and sadness all at once as well. "Why did you cause so much pain to me and my family?"

Of course, the screen couldn't answer me.

However, if I ever got a chance to see her face to face again, I knew I would have to get answers.

Michael was about to dial the police station when the phone rang. He looked down at it in shock and then raised his eyebrows.

"Speak of the devil," he said. "Officer Stoffer is calling us."

"Oh, no," I said with a groan. "What now?"

"Guess we will find out," he replied and picked up the phone.

Chapter 42

MICHAEL

"HELLO, MICHAEL THOMPSON SPEAKING," I SAID.

"Michael, this is Officer Stoffer. I'm afraid we have some news . . . and it's not the news that you were hoping for."

"Honestly, Officer," I said. "After today, I don't think there could be any news that surprises me."

"Well . . ." he said and then paused. "Are your wife and kids listening?"

"They are not," I replied.

"Good," he said. "Because the details are rather gruesome. Michael, we found Helena's car at the bottom of a canyon . . ."

"Oh, no." I felt my heart sink. "Not again."

"There were three scorched bodies inside," he said. "So I'm afraid she's gone."

"No," I said. "No, she's not."

"I know this may be hard to believe—" he said, but I interrupted him.

"It's not about being hard to believe," I replied. "Helena's done this before. She's faked her own death to cover her tracks. She fooled you people for years, and I'm sure that she is going to do it again."

"What?" Officer Stoffer asked. "We checked our records. She's never—"

"She's Olive," I said. "Cynthia and I combed through records of all the people connected to this. We found her husband, who is dead, and birth announcements for the twins. We also found a birth and death announcement for her firstborn daughter, Olive, who died very young. We overlaid the pictures of Helena and Olive and they are the same person. It's taken some plastic surgery, but they're the same."

"How is that possible?" Officer Stoffer asked. "Wouldn't you have recognized her?"

"It was very elaborate," I said. "And I wasn't looking for her. I mean, we thought Olive had died."

"Right," he said. "I mean, I suppose that could be the case . . . but the bodies—"

"I promise if you do DNA traces on those

bodies, you'll find they aren't who you're looking for," I said. "How long until you can get the results back?"

"The coroner's office is pretty backed up," he admitted. "Even if I got them shipped off today, they wouldn't be analyzed for days."

"Can I pay?" I asked. "For something faster?"

"Er . . ." He paused. "No. You can't."

"Well, let me know if I can," I said. "I'm not trying to bribe you, Officer. It's just that we don't feel safe in our own home."

"I understand," he replied. "Did you get the locks changed like I suggested?"

"Yes, sir," I replied. "Stronger than before, with a triple deadbolt. And a security system."

"Well," he said, "all you can do is wait. Either she's dead and that's her at the bottom of the canyon, or she's so far away from here that you don't have to worry about anything."

"I'm not sure what I prefer," I said. "But thank you for telling me."

"I'm not sure if I prefer you to be right or wrong," he said. "Either way, I'll keep you posted."

"Thank you," I said and hung up the phone.

I turned to Cynthia, who had clearly heard every word. She shook her head in shock.

"I can't believe this," she said. "I just can't believe any of this. If there are bodies at the canyon that are not Helena's and her boys', that means she has killed someone else. Three someone elses, to be exact."

"I hope that the twins are okay," I said. "They were screwed up by their mother, but they were pretty innocent in all of this."

"I know," Cynthia said. "Can we just agree that we're not going to tell the kids?"

"We certainly aren't going to tell the kids," I replied. "I don't even want to tell them that she could potentially be dead in case she resurrects herself."

"That would be just like her," Cynthia said. "I hope the police get to the bottom of this soon."

"Well, they said it would be a few days," I replied. "Which didn't make me happy. How long could it take to test bodies in the top criminal investigation in the city?"

Cynthia smirked at that. "You think we're the top?" she asked.

"I think we're something big," I replied. "Come on, you can't think there are more exciting cases going on, do you?"

"Do you think the police aren't telling us everything?" she asked.

I gaped at her. "What do you mean?"

"Well, scam artists doesn't usually focus on one city. Do you think that Helena has done this to other people?"

"Wow, I never thought of that," I replied. "I just assumed she was focusing her will on us."

"What scares me," Cynthia said, "is the fact that her husband is dead. But how is he dead?"

"You think she killed him?" I asked. "But why? I mean . . . I guess I don't have to ask why. She kills so many people on a whim."

"But that doesn't answer the question about her little girl," Cynthia said. "I feel so sorry for the poor baby."

"You don't think . . ." I paused and met Cynthia's eyes. "You don't think that she's sick and twisted enough to kill the baby too, do you?"

"I don't know," Cynthia replied. "I don't know. She would have . . . oh, God. I can't even picture it. There should be a mother's instinct stopping you from doing that."

"You'd think," I said. "But Helena is a very sick individual."

"I think she has schizophrenia," Cynthia said, which was a theory we hadn't explored yet.

"You think?" I said. "I mean, she doesn't have fits of rage like Grant or Terrance, but . . ."

"Adult schizophrenia can look much different," Cynthia explained. "And it's entirely possible that she's hiding it well or she's well medicated. Remember what she told us?"

"God." I shuddered. "I do. And it's terrible. She wouldn't . . . you don't think that she was forcing Terrance to take those meds, do you? He really had it?"

"What you're thinking about is Munchausen by proxy," Cynthia said. "And I think that's an entirely different thing. I think he really is sick. And I don't know if Roman is too, but that would make sense."

"It would also make sense how she came in and started dealing with Grant like an expert," I said. "She's been dealing with it all her life."

"And why she was vague about where she studied and got her degree," Cynthia said. "God, it was in our faces the whole time and we just ignored everything."

"It's okay," I said to her. "It's okay. We weren't looking. We wanted to give her the benefit of the doubt."

"I feel like I can never trust anyone again, now," Cynthia replied.

I reached out to hug her. "There are good people in the world," I said. "Like our kids."

Cynthia smiled at me. "Yeah, our kids are pretty great," she said. "And they deserve a reward for all the bullshit they have been through."

"I agree," I replied "What do you think? Zoo or ice cream?"

I saw her face change and I explained my reasoning for the zoo.

"I want a chance to start over. I think you were exhausted because she was dosing you with tran- quilizers. It's a miracle that you were able to stay awake at all," I said. "I want to forget about that day and make happy memories there, not sad ones. So if we went to the zoo with the kids and just became a normal family . . ."

"Thank you. I'd like that," Cynthia said. "I think we should take them to the zoo. As long as the kids agree."

"Sounds good," I said and kissed her on the forehead. "As long as you're feeling okay?"

"I feel fine," she assured me. "Maybe we could spoil them and take them to the zoo and then get ice cream?"

"Wow, now you're talking crazy," I teased her. "Come on. Let's go on a date, just the four of us."

I knew the kids were going to be over the moon when I told them. I just wanted to get out of here and have a chance for everything to return to normal again. The longer we were without contact with Helena, the more I started to feel like she was gone. Maybe we had scared her off, or maybe she really was dead. Either way, it didn't matter. We were safe, and we were going to start over and build a normal family life.

Grant's red hair as he turned to me when I approached the playroom, however, reminded me of the mark she would forever leave on our family.

Chapter 43

CYNTHIA

IT TURNED OUT THAT SUGGESTING THE ZOO right away was not the best choice we ever made. Grant was more upset than we thought about Helena leaving, and although Anna was being a doll and comforting him, it didn't seem to make a difference. I knew that Anna had a heart of gold, but I didn't realize quite how big it was until she came to me one day with a request.

"Mommy," she said. "Can I move into Grant's room to stay with him at night? He finds that easier."

"Oh," I said. I was cutting vegetables for their school lunches. It was a task I had stopped doing when Helena was here, and I didn't realize quite how much I enjoyed it. "Sure, if that's what you both want."

"It is what we both want," she said and hugged my waist. "Thank you, Mommy."

She tore off through the house, yelling to Grant that I had said yes. I heard their excited laughter and then their plans to move some of Anna's furniture from her room to his. I hoped that they wouldn't move anything too heavy or make too big of a mess. Secretly, I was glad when Anna had asked. Grant didn't do well sleeping alone, and I knew this would be a solution that would keep everyone happy. I knew I was going to start to get better sleep knowing Anna was keeping a watchful eye over her little brother.

"The police have done their final sweep," Michael said to me as he came upstairs. The police had entered through the downstairs door, so as to not scare the kids, and were looking for evidence one final time. They said that they had just about everything they needed, but they wouldn't tell us exactly what they had found. As soon as Michael came back upstairs to tell me, I put away what I was doing.

"I was hoping we could look as well," I said. "I'm sure she's left some stuff that wouldn't mean anything to them but would explain so much to us."

"They'll be done in just a few minutes," he said and then cocked an ear upstairs. "What is that noise?"

"Oh, that's just Anna and Grant rearranging the house," I said with a grin and filled him in on what Anna had asked.

"That's wonderful," he said. "I bet that makes you feel better too."

"It does," I said. "And I'm glad that she asked. I'm also glad to have the police out of my house, once and for all."

"Well, I hope it's going to be once and for all," Michael said as we got down to the basement quarters. The place looked like a bomb went off, and I couldn't believe that all of this stuff had been basically hidden away somewhere. I was annoyed that the police didn't find the need to notify us that any of it was down there.

I walked around, careful not to step on it. Some of it was forgotten makeup or clothes. However, instead of seeing Helena's items, I saw disguises. The red lipstick. The brow pencil. Who else had she used it on? What else had she done?

There was one thing I noticed that stood out to

me right away. I may not have been Grant's biological mother, but I knew what he looked like as a baby. His image was always going to be close to my heart. There were pictures of Grant, as a baby, scattered on the table.

"That's so creepy," I said. "She must have kept them."

"Yeah." Michael picked them up. "These were right after he was born, right? I think I took them, just after we got to the hospital."

"I mean . . . she gave birth to him. She has a right to a photo," I replied. "But not like this. Right now, I don't feel like she even had a right to lay eyes on Grant."

He gathered up the photos and put them in his pocket.

"Michael!" I said. "Those are evidence."

"The police are done," he said. "These are pictures of our son. They can debate all they want, but he's still our boy."

There was an item on the table I didn't recognize, and I picked it up. As soon as I picked it up, there was a weird noise coming from it.

"That's the noise," I said to Michael in shock. "That's the noise that was coming from the nanny cam."

"What?" he asked and took the recorder from my hands. It was still playing, and he held it close to his ear. "It's just gibberish."

"So apparently, she was just trying to scare me," I said. "That's such garbage."

"I know," he replied. "I'm sorry. I should have looked into it better. You just hear so many stories on the news about things being hacked and so you believe that instead of . . ."

"Olive was right in front of our faces the whole time," I pointed out. "And we didn't believe that. So I wouldn't worry about it."

I noticed a journal and I picked it up. It was a child's handwriting, and while it took me a minute to decipher it, I couldn't believe what I was reading when it finally made sense.

Or rather, I could believe what I was reading because of all that had gone on. An elephant could plow its way through here, and I wouldn't be surprised.

Dear Diary,

I hate my life today. It's so cold. There's no food. Mommy says that we are going to go to the food bank soon, but it's always closed. I hate that Mommy is all alone and that Daddy is dead and can't help her with money. She says that we are going to find a new Daddy soon who is rich.

I read it to Michael, whose eyes widened.

"Wow . . ." he said.

"Right?" I answered. "It's Terence's diary from a few years ago."

"She had this planned all along." He shook his head. "I can't believe it."

"It's okay," I said. "Neither can I."

"Cynthia." He looked me in the face. "Cynthia, I'm so sorry."

"For what?" I asked him.

"For being tempted by Helena and acting like it was no big deal. I can't believe I was caught in her act like everyone else."

"It's just . . ." I shrugged. I wanted to believe that Michael was truly sorry and that he would never do it again. I knew that something had changed between us, and I was hoping that this was the moment he never looked at another woman again. "I wish I was enough for you, Michael."

"You are enough for me," he said and came over to give me a hug. "And I was blind for not seeing that. I'm sorry."

"But . . ." I felt my lip trembling like a child. "But . . . I don't know that you won't do it again. I want to trust you . . . but I'm so afraid. I'm so hurt."

"I know," he said and held me close. "So let me

prove it to you. Let me show you I am worth trusting. Everything's going to be okay."

Every ounce of my body and soul wanted to believe him. Every fiber of my body wanted to say that everything was going to be okay, and we could move forward without fault. But I knew I would always be on edge whenever there was a pretty woman around. I wondered how much of that had to do with Michael and how much of that had to do with my own self -esteem.

"I love you," he said and kissed me gently. "I'll show you that I do."

I didn't say anything, but I closed my eyes and laid my head against his chest. I couldn't change the past, but I could try to start trusting him, here and now, and see what the future held. Maybe, just maybe, enough time would pass to heal the wounds in my heart, and I would feel whole again.

I did know one thing, though. I needed Michael by my side, and he was worth trying for.

"I love you too," I said softly.

Chapter 44

MICHAEL

A WEEK PASSED, AND IT SEEMED LIKE THERE WAS no progress. There was no completed autopsy, no further clues, nothing. But if I was looking on the bright side, I could say there was also no sign of Helena, which I thought was important. If she was trying to make a comeback, she would probably have done it by now. I didn't know how she was going to make a comeback, though, given that we would never take her back. Cynthia had recovered almost completely from her trip to the hospital, and Grant seemed to understand that Helena wasn't coming back. This time, when I suggested a trip to the zoo, it wasn't met with crying. Grant actually seemed excited about going, which made me excited as well.

"Can we get ice cream?" he asked, which made me feel like things were about to go back to normal.

"Sure," I said and spun around to look at Anna as I drove. "Do you want ice cream too?"

"Yes," Anna said, which surprised me. She had been doing a lot more things that Grant had wanted lately, which made me smile. She was going to grow up to be a lovely, well-adjusted person at this rate. I was hoping that both kids would forget about Helena and this whole mess. Frankly, I was hoping that Cynthia and I would forget about Helena and this whole mess.

When we got to the zoo, I made a beeline for the ice cream stand. I wanted to start the day off right. We picked up a map from the front and huddled around it as a family, trying to make a decision.

"Where should we go first?"

"The tigers!" Grant cried.

"The lions," Anna said, and I knew we were in trouble. Cynthia and I made eye contact and then decided.

"So I think," I said carefully, and Cynthia nodded. "I'll take you to the lions because it's farther away, and Grant, Mommy will take you to the tigers, because they are closer. We'll meet up at the end of the tiger enclosure, because that is where the lions start. Does that sound like a plan?"

"Yay!" Anna said as she licked her ice cream. Cynthia seemed okay with the idea, so we set off.

I didn't for a single second think it was a bad idea. I didn't for a single second think there would be a problem. I thought that the zoo would be safe, with all the people around. But I had let my guard down, and it was my own fault.

When Anna and I finished at the lions and got to the end of the tigers, there was no sign of Cynthia and Grant. I waited, thinking that maybe they were just slow. However, as the minutes ticked by, I was starting to get worried. I called Cynthia's phone as I walked Anna though the tiger enclosure backward, thinking she would pick up and tell me that Grant needed to go to the bathroom or something.

She didn't pick up, but on the third attempt, I heard her phone ring. She was right around the corner, just off the tiger cage.

I pulled Anna around the corner and came face to face with a terrible sight. There was Helena, with a gun in her hand, waving and shouting at people to get away. She had Grant in one hand, the gun in the other, and a terrifying look on her face. They were headed toward the parking lot. Cynthia was standing there, shocked and terrified. Everyone was staring, but no one was doing anything.

I put Anna's arm in Cynthia's hand and then raced after them. I caught up to Helena and Grant in the parking lot, and I shouted at her to stop.

For some reason, she actually did. I tried to keep in mind the fact that I was the one she wanted, and I could hopefully use that against her.

"Helena," I said. "I'm glad to see you aren't dead."

That confused her, and she stood there, with the gun still raised at me.

"Don't come any closer, Michael," she said. "I swear, I'll shoot you."

"I don't think you'll shoot me," I replied. "You want what I have too much."

"And what is it that you have?" she asked.

"Well, you should tell me," I said. "Seeing as you've been after me all this time."

"I'll give you a choice," she said with the gun still raised. "You either give me your fortune, or I'm taking my son."

"But he's not really your son, is he, Helena?" I asked. Grant was terrified and squirming, and I was worried that Helena was going to hurt him. "He's my son and he's Cynthia's son."

"No," she said. "Look at him. He's my son. He belongs with me."

"For the price of my money?" I said and shrugged casually. "I'll give it to you."

She looked shocked at that.

"You will?" she asked.

"I will," I said. "Because nothing is worth my son. My fortune, my house, it doesn't mean anything without my family."

I could tell that Helena wasn't expecting that answer. She wavered on the spot and her face changed.

It was enough for Grant to see his opportunity. He may be biologically her son, but he was my boy. As soon as she loosened her grip just a little bit, he bit her hard on the hand and kicked her. It was enough to make her release him, and he ran over to me.

Zoo security came tearing in at the moment, and Helena knew she was caught. She jumped in her car and fled, driving recklessly and almost hitting several people on the way out.

Frankly, I didn't really care about her driving like a lunatic. Cynthia and Anna came running, and the four of us hugged with such force that I was sure someone would break.

"You're okay?" Cynthia asked. "You're not hurt?"

"We're fine," I assured her. "Everything is fine."

"Oh, my God," she said. "Oh, my God. Michael, I'm so sorry. I don't know what happened. She just . . ."

I knew she was afraid that I would yell at her like last time. This time, however, I simply took her face in my hands and kissed her.

"It's okay," I said. "It's not your fault. We're fine now. And I think we should go home."

"I agree," she said, and then we heard a terrifying crash from down the road. There was the crunch of metal and then an explosion. Cynthia and I looked at each other, and I didn't know whether it was in hope or terror.

"Mommy, what was that?" Anna asked.

"It was just nature," Cynthia said, "taking its course."

We didn't find out the rest of the story until we got home. There was a story on the news that I made sure to wait until the kids were in bed to turn on.

"The body in the car has been identified as

Helena Griswold, a mother of twin boys who were found abandoned at the zoo."

"Oh, my God," Cynthia said as she watched the news. "Those poor boys, wandering around the zoo and having no idea that their mother is . . ."

"I know," I said to her. "But I'm sure they're in custody and someone is going to take very good care of them."

"I hope so," Cynthia said. "And I don't know if I believe she's really dead this time."

"Yeah . . ." I said hesitantly. "To be honest, neither do I. Even if I saw her body buried, I'm not sure I would believe it."

"I can't believe we narrowly escaped her," Cynthia said. "One slip and we would have been dead."

"She was unhinged. You can't blame yourself," I said. "And while I wish death on no one . . . I think it may have been the best thing for her."

"Do you think it was the illness?" Cynthia asked.

"No," I said. "You can't think that Grant's going to turn out like that. There's the illness and then there's just Helena."

"I know," she said as she stared at the news.

I eventually got up and turned off the TV. "Come on, my love," I said. "Let's go to bed."

She started at the TV for a second longer and then took my hand and followed me upstairs. Before we went to bed, we stopped in the kids' room to gaze at them for just a moment.

"They really are beautiful," Cynthia said.

"Our angels," I replied. "This is not the first time we'll have to keep them safe, darling. But I hope that it'll be the last time it ever involves guns, shootouts, and lunatics for nannies."

She lay her head on my shoulder and closed her eyes for a moment. I felt like I was in heaven there and then. The day was hard, and I couldn't wait to see what the next day brought. When the sun rose, we'd be ready for whatever came our way.

Chapter 45

CYNTHIA

It had been two months since Helena had died, and Michael and I had learned to heal and move on. We didn't miss Helena, of course, but the kids took some time getting back into their routine. I was happy to stay home with the kids now, more than ever. However, as I watched them play, there were two other kids that I couldn't shake from my mind.

"Michael," I said to him. "I think we need to go visit Terrance and Roman. I can't stop thinking about the fact that they're all alone, in a foster home, where no one knows them."

"I was just thinking that the other day," he replied. "After all, they are Grant's half-brothers. And they are not their mother."

"Oh." I breathed a sigh of relief. "I'm so glad you're onboard."

"Of course I'm onboard," he said and kissed me on the head. "Do you want to tell the kids, or shall I?"

"I'll tell them," I said. I was a little bit afraid of what they might say. I was worried that one would want to go and not the other, or that it would upset them. I chose my words carefully, and I was happy to be met with smiling faces.

"Yay!" Grant said. "I've been missing them."

"Even I miss them," Anna said with a smile. "And I didn't even really like them."

"Anna," I scolded, even though I was smiling. "That's not nice."

"Sorry," she said, but I had a feeling she couldn't wait to see them either.

Michael and I got ahold of where their foster home was, and we loaded up the kids.

To my happy surprise, it was in a nice, normal neighborhood. There was green grass on the front lawn and a porch with kids' toys everywhere. The twins must have heard our car coming, because both of them ran out of the house to greet us. They seemed like completely different people. They had wide smiles on their faces, and they looked healthy, full of color and even laughing. I didn't want to say that they were celebrating their mother's death, but they were flourishing without her.

"Hello," Terrance said and gave Anna a big hug right away.

That surprised me, but it also made me smile. Helena had really been such a horrible influence on them, and I was glad to see that their feud was ending.

"Hi!" Anna said, and the two started to chat like old friends.

Michael and I stood nearby for the first little bit, protective of our children as always, but it soon became apparent that it wasn't needed. The kids were playing great together, and the twins even apologized for being mean because their mother had told them to.

I stepped back to talk with the boys' foster mother, a kindhearted woman named Sylvia who seemed like she had done this before.

"Yes, they are lovely," she said. "It's just a bit different, with all their medication, but I'm managing just fine. I do wish . . ." She paused, and I picked up on some sadness in her voice.

"They didn't have so many meds?" I asked, but she shrugged at that.

"No," she said. "Nature gave them a challenge and science solved it. I just wish that they had some family to visit them. All of my other foster kids, they have family that they want to get back to. People come and visit them all the time. But these young boys, this is the first time they've had someone visit."

"Oh," I said and looked at Michael. "Well, I mean, technically, we are family. Grant is their half-brother."

"Yes, I can see the resemblance," Sylvia said with a smile. "And the children get along so well together. They will miss them when they're gone."

"Perhaps . . ." I knew I was going out on a limb, but I needed to try. "Perhaps we could arrange weekly visits for as long as they are here?"

Sylvia's face lit up. "Oh, that'd be wonderful!" she said. "Just wonderful! Yes, please!"

"We'll pencil it in," I said. "Michael works during the day, but there's always Saturdays and Sundays, or I could bring the kids after school."

"We should exchange numbers," Sylvia said. "And then I can text you when is good for us. I'm trying to take the boys to see a doctor regularly. It appeared that their mother ignored that."

"I wouldn't be surprised," I said. "She ignored a lot of things."

"Well, I'm glad that you have a good head on your shoulders, at least," she said to Michael and me. "They will have good experiences when you come, at least."

"Thank you," Michael said and took my hand. "We try our best. It isn't always perfect . . ."

"No, of course it isn't," Sylvia said with a chuckle. "But then, what is? It's not about how perfect you are. It's about how hard we try and how much we love them."

"You must have a very big heart," I said, "to take in children like this."

"No," Sylvia said. "I just . . . I couldn't have any children of my own, so this was the next best thing. I don't know if you've ever struggled with wanting children, but not having them . . ."

"Oh, yes," I said, gazing at Grant. "I know what you mean. I know exactly what you mean."

The kids were having such a good time, Michael and I let them play an hour longer than we had intended. I had never really seen the boys play with toys before. It was like they were getting back the child-hood that they had lost being under Helena's thumb.

Eventually, though, we couldn't delay any longer. We had reservations for dinner, so I told Grant and Anna to say goodbye and waited for them at the car. Sylvia waved us off and both kids were in great moods as we drove away.

"Mommy, that was so fun," Grant said. "Can we do that again sometime?"

"Actually," I said, "Daddy and I have arranged for us to come once a week. After all, Terrance and Roman are your brothers. You should see them once in a while."

"Yay!" Grant said. "But instead of going to see them here, do you think we could adopt them?"

I gave a little laugh.

"I think that is something we would need to talk about," I said and glanced at Michael. I wasn't actually seriously considering it. After all, the boys had been tied to a horrible experience we had, and I didn't think I wanted them under my roof anymore.

I did have to remind myself that they weren't Helena, and they weren't involved in anything she did. They had followed orders, yes, but you couldn't fault a child for not knowing any better.

I kept thinking of the house they lived in now and how happy they seemed. I knew the foster care system well enough to know that they could be moved out of that house and put into another one. They'd be moved around again and again until they were adopted or aged out.

That wasn't a life for a child, for any child. I knew, with the boys' age, that the chances of adopting them were slim.

"Michael," I said as we got ready for bed that night. "I know this is going to sound crazy, but—"

"You want to adopt the boys," he said.

I couldn't believe he could read my mind. "Yeah," I said. "I mean, maybe not right away, but . . . the longer they stay there, even in a loving home like Sylvia's, the worse it will get for them. And we have a big home, and plenty of space . . . and their own living blood relatives under one roof."

"Hmm," he said as we got into bed. "And do you think they'd do well here?"

"I think they'd do wonderful here with a steady schedule . . . and you as their father."

Michael, through it all, was the best father I had ever known.

"And you as their mother," he said as he cuddled me close. "Poor Helena. It took until she was six feet under, but it looks like she's getting what she wanted for her boys."

"In the morning, let's find out more," I said. "I don't think I'd mind expanding our family." I had meant by adoption, but apparently, that got Michael's engines raring to go.

"We could always try it the old-fashioned way," Michael suggested and kissed me.

I giggled a bit, but I urged him to keep going as the kisses deepened. Michael made me happy. He made me content and he made me feel in love. I was in my own room, my kids were safe, and I was being snuggled by my husband. If you told me a year ago where my life was going to be, I would have told you that you were crazy. Today, though, it was perfect.

———

IF YOU LIKED THIS BOOK, make sure to pick up my last book, What Happened Last Night! Keep reading for a preview!

If you have already read What Happened Last Night, then you will love my other book, Perfect Obsession. You can get it here!

Preview of What
Happened Last Night

Chapter 1

JAMIE

As the plane touched down on the tarmac, I couldn't help but feel the stress of being back in LA land promptly upon my shoulders. Eight weeks in Amsterdam had been an answer to a prayer, but, it was nearly time to get back to the grindstone. I already missed the cool, easy pace of life I'd had while I was there. However, family was here in LA, not to mention my job, but I didn't want to think about that.

Instead, I focused on my family. My mom had already called to say she'd be meeting me at the airport to drive me over to my abuela's house. I was looking forward to the feast I knew my abuela would be cooking in anticipation of my arrival, but that was as far forward as I dared to look for the moment.

I wasn't ready to start thinking about returning to work. And yet I was due to do just that tomorrow morning. I had worked for the LAPD for ten years, and I loved my job as a detective. Or at least I did until my last case. That shit still haunted me even after my two months of leave. Whenever I closed my eyes, I could still see what that monster did to that sweet little girl's body. Child murder was never pretty, but that case was by far the roughest case I had ever worked, and for a while there, I'd seriously considered walking away from the LAPD altogether.

That's why my boss insisted I take the leave. He didn't want me to leave permanently, and deep down, I guess I didn't want to go, either. Despite the nightmares, despite the shit I saw every day, I still loved my job. I wasn't ready to hand in my badge and flip burgers or something equally mundane. I wanted to make a difference.

I stepped inside the airport, grateful to be somewhere air-conditioned. I hurried to the baggage carousel and spent a harrowing fifteen minutes there, during which I managed to convince myself that my bag was lost. It wasn't, and relieved, I grabbed it and made my way through the crowds to the exit.

I was barely through customs when I heard my name being called, and I laughed out loud, shaking my head when I saw my welcoming party. I felt my cheeks getting hot as I blushed slightly at the fanfare. My mom was waiting for me as promised, but she had neglected to mention that Sasha, my sister, and her kids would also be there. The kids waved handmade signs with my name on them.

I took a moment to study my mom. It had been too long since I had seen her pretty eyes, so dark brown they were almost black. Her gray hair was neatly pulled back and twisted into a clip at the back of her head. Most women couldn't pull off gray hair. My mom wasn't one of them. It made her brown skin look more radiant, and rather than wanting to hide it, my mom wore it like a badge of honor.

Seeing my family there waiting to welcome me made me happy, yet at the same time, it sent a message, one I couldn't ignore. *You're home, Jamie. And that means you're even closer to being Detective Del Rey again. Is that really what you want?*

I was relieved when my mom threw herself at me, causing me to stagger slightly before I regained my footing. Her laughter and shouts of *welcome home* down my ear silenced my doubts. At least for now.

I hugged my mom tightly.

"I missed you, Jamie!"

"I missed you too, Mom."

I had missed her. I missed all of my family. We had always been close, although Sasha and I had our moments growing up. Ever since my dad died when I was five and Sasha was three and we moved in with my abuela, we had become a solid unit. We had very little money growing up. My mom worked three jobs to keep a roof over our heads and put food on the table, but it was a struggle. We didn't know it then, though. My mom made sure that Sasha and I were never short of anything we needed.

I disentangled myself from my mom and gave Sasha a quick hug. Looking at Sasha was like looking at a female version of myself. She had my olive skin and my thick, wavy black hair, although I had to admit that the waves looked much better on her.

"It's good to see you, Bro." She laughed as I hugged her.

"You too," I said, meaning it.

Finally, I crouched down so that Lucy and Mason, my niece and nephew, could hug me.

"Have you missed your favorite uncle?" I said.

Mason nodded solemnly, his big brown eyes locked on mine.

"Yes." Lucy nodded.

It came out as 'yeth' and I instantly saw why. Her two top front teeth were gone. I smiled to myself.

"You lost some teeth, huh?"

She nodded, beaming at me, her eyes shining with delight.

"The tooth fairy came, and she gave me two dollars for each tooth," she announced.

"Wow," I said. "She must have wanted your teeth pretty badly to leave you that much."

I stood up and ruffled Lucy's hair and then we headed out to Sasha's car, laughing and joking and catching up on everything I had missed at home. By the time the car pulled up outside of my abuela's house, I felt like I had never been away.

I stepped into the house and was instantly enveloped in the delicious smells wafting out of the kitchen. I could smell meat and spices and something sweet. It smelled like my childhood, and for a moment, I was back to being a kid again, running into the house to tell my abuela rambling stories about my adventures.

My abuela came out of the kitchen as she heard us come into the house. The whole block probably heard us coming into the house with my mom and Sasha talking at once and the kids laughing and shouting, feeding on our excitement.

My abuela smiled when she saw me, her face instantly softening. She wiped her hands on a stained apron and came to give me a fierce hug. She was a smaller, older version of my mom, but despite her age, she was still razor sharp and saw everything that went on in her family, no matter how much any of us tried to shield her from things.

She released me from her tight embrace and took a step back to look at me. She frowned at me and wagged her finger at me.

"You've been gone too long, boy."

"I know."

I'd needed the break, but now, being back at the heart of family, I saw that maybe I needed them more.

"You're a Del Rey, Jamie, but don't be fooled into thinking that means you're not still half Santos. And the Santos family don't run away from their problems. We face them, we fix them, and we move on."

"Mom..." my mom warned her, but my abuela ignored my mom and went on.

"You should have come to us, not flitted off to Europe. Do you hear me?"

I nodded. I heard her loud and clear. "I know, Abuela," I said. "But trust me. There's some things that you just don't share with your family. Some things are too ... disturbing to bring home with me."

"Nonsense. You can tell us anything," my abuela insisted.

I knew it was pointless to argue with her, but I also knew I was right on this one. There was no way I could tell her and the others how every time I closed my eyes through my last case, I saw that little girl's neck bent at an angle no neck should ever be. I couldn't tell her about the burn marks all over the girl's body. And I certainly couldn't tell her that the little girl had died in the most horrendous fashion. I knew they would listen to me and try to help me, but there were some things you just couldn't pass on to other people, no matter how much they might help you.

"Anyway, it's good to have you home." My abuela smiled.

She frowned for a moment, looking me up and down. She shook her head.

"You're too skinny, Jamie. Do they not have food in Amsterdam?" she demanded.

I laughed and we followed my abuela through to the dining room. She had made it her mission to fatten me up when I was about twelve, and she was still trying to do it now that I was almost thirty. It wasn't that I didn't eat enough. I ate enough for two people most days, and on days when I came here, I ate enough for three or four people. I was just naturally skinny. Sasha hated that she only had to look at a calorie and it attached itself to her waistline, and she regularly wound me up, telling me that when I hit forty, my metabolism would go to shit, and I'd be four hundred pounds within a month or two. She was always such a little ray of sunshine.

We took our seats around the table, and I couldn't help but gawk at the sheer amount of food that weighed down the table. My abuela had really outdone herself with the feast this time. My stomach growled as I looked at it all, and the whole family laughed.

"Welcome home, boy." My abuela laughed as I reached for an empanada.

We ate, drank, and talked. I told them all about my adventures in Amsterdam, about the people I had met out there and the things I had seen. They listened in rapt fascination and asked me a ton of questions. None of them had been to Europe, and they wanted to know everything that was different from our way of life, which was pretty much all of it. I tried to make it sound interesting, but I missed several of what were, in my opinion, the best parts, because they were the parts you just don't tell your family.

"Are you glad to be home?" my mom asked.

I nodded.

My abuela snorted. "Tell your face."

I looked at her, shocked to hear such an expression from her. My mom and Sasha laughed at my reaction.

"She heard it on the TV, and she uses it all the time now," Sasha explained.

"It just has a certain ring to it." My abuela grinned. "But seriously, Jamie, you don't look happy to be home."

"I'm happy to be back here with all of you," I

said, smiling around at everyone. "But honestly, I'm kind of dreading going back to work tomorrow."

"And that's why we face our problems rather than running away from them. You run away from your problems, they're always right there waiting for you. You fix them, and they go away," my abuela said a little smugly.

My mom threw her a warning look and put her hand over mine.

"You'll be fine, honey," she said, giving my hand a squeeze.

"I know," I replied. "I feel much better than I did before I went away. But whether or not I can put up with the ugly side of this job until retirement age and still be something close to sane is another matter."

"You're a Del Rey, Jamie—" my mom started.

"And half Santos," my abuela put in.

"That means you can do anything. You're strong enough and smart enough to do this," my mom said.

I felt myself nodding in agreement. Of course I could do this. All cops have that one case that haunts them, and they still get the job done. Maybe it's just that I had finally become one of them.

My mom gave my hand a last squeeze and then

sat back in her chair and looked at me, her eyes narrowed. "Now, when are you going to find a nice girl and settle down, Jamie? I want grandkids while I'm still young enough to enjoy them," she said.

I felt my cheeks turning hot as I blushed with embarrassment. I shook my head firmly. "We are not having this conversation," I said. I stood up and grinned at the kids. "Lucy, Mason, want to go play in the back garden with me?"

"Yay," they chorused, jumping up from the table and running for the door.

"Sorry, Mom. Favorite uncle duty calls." I grinned, hurrying away, leaving my mom grinning and shaking her head behind me.

"Don't think this means we're never going to talk about this," she shouted after me.

I pretended I couldn't hear her as I ran after Lucy and Mason and back into the warmth of the outdoors.

Chapter 2

CARLOTTA

I turned my back on William for a moment, going to the liquor cabinet. I needed a drink badly, but it wasn't just that. I needed a moment to think, a moment where I didn't have to look at William's face and see the betrayal there.

I poured out a large measure of scotch and started to put the lid back on the bottle, but then I thought better of it and added another large slug of scotch to the glass. I replaced the lid and moved to the window for a moment, nursing my glass.

I looked out over the Hollywood Hills, and for a moment, I felt lost looking at the familiar scenery. I asked myself, not for the first time, how I'd ended up here. How I ended up married to a man who cared only for himself. I mean, sure, he claimed to love me, but his actions told a very different story. How could it be possible that he loved me when he was constantly cheating on me with dolly bird interns? Airheaded little sluts who thought they could get ahead by sleeping with their boss. Gold digging little whores who slept with my husband to get the gifts he no doubt lavished on them.

William's cheating on me was nothing new. The first affair happened after he redesigned the docks. Or at least the first affair that I found out about happened after he redesigned the docks. I believed it was the first one, though, because subtlety was never William's strong suit, and I couldn't imagine a world where he managed to keep something like that under wraps from me.

The docks project was a big one, even for him, an accomplished architect. The buildings he designed were breathtaking. They were striking, functional, and all sharp angles, almost brutal to look at. But they were soulless, like him. He asked me to breathe life into them, and I painted a mural that ended up getting more attention than the buildings themselves. I'd thought we were a team, that my success was his success, but he didn't see it that way. He saw it as an insult to his work, and his ego couldn't take the hit. Instead of questioning why the mural was the life and soul of the design, or even taking the credit for choosing to add it, he decided that somehow, I had intentionally upstaged him and that I was to blame for his not getting the recognition he deserved.

I suppose it made sense, in a way. By blaming me, he didn't have to question his abilities, his designs. He could continue to think he was perfect and never made a single mistake and that I was some sort of weight around his neck, pulling him down, holding him back. Yes, it was much easier for him to assume I had sabotaged him than for him to try to see the truth of the situation.

I found out a week or so later that he was sleeping with one of his interns. He was hardly subtle about it. It was like he wanted me to find out. I thought he was doing it to hurt me, that in his mind, this was fair payback for his bruised ego. I should have spoken up then. I should have packed his bags for him and shown him the door.

But I didn't. I was afraid to lose him. I was afraid to try to make it in the world on my own, and so I played the role of the dutiful wife, pretending that I hadn't noticed the smell of perfume on his shirt when he returned from another night working late. That I didn't notice the constant phone calls and text messages, the weekends away, the way he was careful not to leave his cellphone unattended.

It all came to a head about two weeks ago when there was a knock at the door. I opened it and there was a girl standing there. A girl no older than nineteen, with red hair and blue eyes. There was a look in her eyes that I recognized. She looked lost, like she was drowning and desperately searching for an anchor. And I knew instantly who she was. William's newest toy. She made up some story about needing a file from William's office, but I knew William. If they had needed that file, he wouldn't have forgotten to take it with him. He always packed his files for work the night before and then double-checked them the next morning. It wouldn't have been forgotten.

She was sizing me up, looking me up and down, and I saw that lost look in her eyes fade away, replaced with a smug, amused look as she took in my paint-splattered overalls and my brown hair thrown back in a messy bun.

I wanted to shake her, to tell her William would never leave me for her. I was the wife he took to corporate events knowing I'd say all the right things, act the role perfectly. And when I was out of the overalls and in a ball gown, I looked the part. Not like this dolly bird who looked rough around the edges. She would never belong in William's world. I did.

He didn't want some loose cannon of a kid on his arm who would flirt with his bosses and show him up. I wanted to tell her the affair they were having wasn't even about her. It was about me. That William was only using her to punish me. I didn't say any of that. I bit my tongue, gave her the file, and watched her leave, her hips swaying as she walked. Even her hips looked smug.

I wanted to go back to my little world of denial, but I found that I couldn't. It was one thing turning a blind eye to what happened at the office or in some seedy motel on the outskirts of town, but having that little skank turn up at my doorstep, judge me, and find me lacking ... that pushed me over the edge into a rarely shown anger, and when William came home that evening, I confronted him.

We argued, but I could see that William was seeing me differently that night. Gone was his meek little wife, and in her place was a woman who was no longer willing to tolerate his disrespect. He agreed to end the affair, and the very next day, he did just that. I know he did because I got a scathing phone call from the girl, Candy, telling me what a bitch I was and how I had ruined her life.

I was angry with her for intruding on my life once more, but mostly, I was angry with William. Because I realized something on that phone call. Candy didn't know she was just another in a string of affairs. She had fallen for William's charm, just like I had all those years ago, only when he told her she was special, it had been a lie. She had really believed William would leave me and that they would live happily ever after. She wanted more than just the money and the lifestyle because if she'd played her cards right, she could have had all of that as mistress. She wanted him all to herself. She was still young and naïve enough to believe that if he was hers, he would never cheat on her. I had been that girl, the young, naïve one who thought he would never cheat, but I never could have convinced myself of that if our relationship had started out as an affair.

I heard William moving behind me, and I turned away from the window to see what he was doing. The air was thick, charged, another argument brewing, and for a moment, I thought he was coming toward me. I don't know whether I thought he was going to slap me or kiss me, but I thought he was going to do something to me. Instead, he went to the liquor cabinet and poured himself a drink. I looked down at my own glass, a little surprised to see it was empty, and I held it out.

William filled it for me, and for a second, our eyes met. I looked into his piercing blue eyes, searching for the truth about his feelings for me, but I saw only anger there. He sighed loudly as he moved back to his chair and slumped down in it.

"Why do you have to be like this, Carlotta?" he said.

"Like what?" I demanded.

How dare he try to get on his high horse because I had finally had enough of his ways? What the fuck did he expect me to be like after what he had done?

"Like this," he said, waving his hand in my direction. His hand wavered slightly, and I knew I wasn't the only one who was already well on my way to being drunk. "One minute you're yelling, the next minute you're silent. You told me to end the affair, and I did. What more do you want from me?"

I wanted the life he had promised me on our wedding day. The life where he loved and honored me. The life where he was meant to forsake all others. I wanted the fairy tale ending.

"I want you to stop your little skank whore from turning up here," I said, shocking myself slightly at the venom in my voice. "She was here again today. Parked at the end of the driveway, watching the house."

"I'll talk to her, all right?" he snapped.

"No, it's not all right," I said. "It's way past all right. She's unhinged, William."

"You're right about that. She's stalking me, trying to get me to take her back. I'll get a restraining order against her, and hopefully, that'll keep her away."

"Hmm," I grunted.

I downed my drink and went back to the cabinet to refill it. I handed William the bottle and he refilled his glass too.

"You don't believe me?" William said.

"No, I do," I said. "I just think it's too little, too late. You'll replace her with the next one, and I'll go back to being the one they all pity at parties. The one they laugh at behind her back. The one they're all secretly afraid they'll become."

"It's not like that, Carlotta," William said with a sigh.

"Isn't it? Because I've been on the other side of that scenario. Do you remember when we first got married and Justin from your office was having an affair? Whenever there was an office event, the other wives and I used to say how sorry for his wife we felt, how Justin was a bastard for doing that to her. And we meant it, but there was always a touch of smugness in our words because it was happening to her and not to us. And we used to wonder aloud whether she knew or not. Whether she turned a blind eye or whether she was genuinely clueless. And we all agreed that either way, she was an idiot. And now I'm the idiot. Thanks to you and your fragile little ego."

"You think that's what this is about?" William slurred.

"God, William, she's young enough to be our daughter. What else could it be about? Surely, you don't expect me to believe you actually felt something for her," I snapped, a bitter laugh escaping my throat.

"What if I did?" William threw back.

"Then you're more pathetic than I realized," I replied. "She likes the power of sleeping with the boss. She likes the money you no doubt shower her with. She likes what you represent, but she doesn't like you. As if someone like her would ever fall for someone like you."

William shook his head, at a loss for words for a moment. I looked at him critically. He was a good-looking man, there was no doubt about that. His piercing blue eyes were the color of the sky on a sunny day and they sparkled when he smiled. He had a neat black beard and black hair that was just starting to get flecks of gray in it at his temples. He was handsome, but to a nineteen-year-old, he would be someone you described as "not bad looking for his age." Except apparently, to Candy, but William didn't need to know that she did indeed want more than his money and his power. He had used Candy to hurt me because his ego had been bruised, and I had no qualms about doing the exact thing back to him.

"So what? Now you're pissed off because I don't have feelings for Candy?" William said. "I don't understand you at all, Carl."

"I'm pissed off because you cheated on me and made me a laughingstock at your company. What part of that is so damned hard for you to understand?" I shouted.

He stood up and went to the cabinet again. He picked up the bottle of scotch, and seeing it was empty, he opened the cabinet and pulled out another one. He filled his glass almost to the brim and I did the same.

When his glass was full, he turned to look at me. He swayed slightly on his feet and his eyes seemed not quite able to focus themselves. He was definitely past the point of drunk now and judging by the way my head felt a little fuzzy, I wasn't far behind him myself.

"You made me do it, Carlotta. You pushed me away, made me feel small. And you stopped trying. I mean, look at you," William slurred, indicating my paint-splattered overalls. "When we first got married, I thought I'd hit the jackpot. You were the most beautiful woman I'd ever seen. And now look at you. You look like a fucking tramp."

That did it. I felt something inside me snap, and I slapped William hard across the face. His head shot to the side as the clapping sound echoed around the room. He moved his head back to the center, bringing up a hand and touching it to the burning red handprint on his cheek. My palm was stinging from the slap.

I took a step backward, shrinking away from him, waiting for his fist to fly toward me.

"I—I'm sorry. I shouldn't have done that," I stuttered, feeling fear deep in my stomach.

William just stared at me and shook his head.

"No. You shouldn't have. But I'm not going to hit you, Carlotta. I'm not your damned father."

He stalked back to his chair, and I sat down on the couch, not looking at William for a moment. He was right. He wasn't my father. He cheated on me, belittled me at times, but he had never raised a hand to me. Not once. Not like my father who would punch me or hit me with the buckle end of his thick leather belt if I said so much as a word out of turn.

We sat in silence for a few minutes, drinking away our sorrows, our problems. I knew they would still be there tomorrow, still unsolved, eating away at me, at William, at our marriage. But for now, I was past caring. I just wanted to feel numb for a while, to not feel the hurting deep down inside myself.

I finished my drink and went for another one on unsteady legs. I stumbled slightly as I reached the cabinet and put out a hand to steady myself. William came over to stand beside me, and for a brief second, he put his hand gently over mine and I dared to let myself believe we would be okay. That we would get past all of this mess and be able to start over again.

He pulled his hand away, and with it, my hope. He poured us both another drink, and I went back to the couch, scotch sloshing over the side of my glass. I watched William weave his way back to his seat, and when he looked at me, his eyes were glazed. His eyelids looked heavy, and I knew anything I said would be a waste of my breath. He was on the verge of passing out, and he wouldn't remember any of this in the morning.

"Where do we go from here, Carlotta?" William said finally.

"I have no idea," I replied. "Honestly, I don't, but get that restraining order first thing tomorrow. That's the first step."

He nodded his head.

"I will. And tonight, we just drink and forget," he said.

I raised my glass.

"Cheers to that," I said in a voice devoid of any emotion.

Click here to keep reading What Happened Last Night.

About Cole Baxter

Cole Baxter loves writing psychological suspense thrillers. It's all about that last reveal that he loves shocking readers with.

He grew up in New York, where there crime was all around. He decided to turn that into something positive with his fiction.

His stories will have you reading through the night—they are very addictive!

Sign up for Cole's VIP Reader Club and find out about his latest releases, giveaways, and more. Click here!

For more information, be sure to check out the links below!
colebaxterauthor@gmail.com

Also by Cole Baxter

The Perfect Nanny

What Happened Last Night

Perfect Obsession

She's Missing

What She Forgot

Before She's Gone

Stolen Son

Made in the USA
Las Vegas, NV
09 April 2021